T0022069

MISTLETOE
MALICE

MISTLETOE MALICE

— ✕ —

Kathleen Farrell

faber

First published in 1951 by Rupert Hart-Davis
This edition published in 2023
by Faber & Faber Limited
The Bindery, 51 Hatton Garden
London EC1N 8HN

First published in the USA in 2023

Typeset by Typo•glyphix, Burton-on-Trent, DE14 3HE
Printed and bound in the UK by CPI Group (UK) Ltd, Croydon, CR0 4YY

All rights reserved
© The Estate of Kathleen Farrell, 1951
Afterword © Robert Cochrane

The right of Kathleen Farrell to be identified as author of this work
has been asserted in accordance with Section 77 of the Copyright,
Designs and Patents Act 1988

This book is sold subject to the condition that it shall not, by way of trade
or otherwise, be lent, resold, hired out or otherwise circulated without the
publisher's prior consent in any form of binding or cover other than that
in which it is published and without a similar condition including this
condition being imposed on the subsequent purchaser

A CIP record for this book
is available from the British Library

ISBN 978–0–571–37826–5

Printed and bound in the UK on FSC® certified paper in line with our continuing
commitment to ethical business practices, sustainability and the environment.
For further information see faber.co.uk/environmental-policy

2 4 6 8 10 9 7 5 3 1

CHAPTER ONE

The Day Before Christmas

RACHEL surveyed the room. She put a foot out to smooth the corner of a rug. Her movement was as quick as a girl's; only the cut of the black, heelless shoe with its buttoned strap showed her age. She looked discontentedly at the shoe. She felt hemmed in by the small tables, and yet there were the boxes of crystallised fruits, the silver ash-trays, the magnifying glass—where would these be if the tables were taken away? No, the tables must remain. On the whole, she thought, she had planned the arrangement very well.

Rachel's eyes, darkly bright, saw that her niece, Bess, was watching with the limply resigned expression of one who expects to be reminded of duties left undone, of preparations neglected. Rachel smiled and nodded: an aloof acknowledgment that for the present she had no fault to find. The precarious balance of their relationship must be maintained. Bess must always remember that although she was treated as an adopted daughter she was merely a niece by marriage. A relationship so remote, thought Rachel, that it is practically non-existent: a courtesy, nothing more.

Bess too looked at the room, seeing it not as a collection of treasured objects placed to the greatest advantage, but as a refuge from the icy air and the frothing sea. The room waited for those who were to come. Bess's fingers curled towards her palm with the tension of knowing that the visitors would soon arrive. She was momentarily dismayed by the prospect of newcomers, although they were her family; at least, they were Rachel's family, which, Bess supposed, was the same thing. To dispel the strained expectancy, Bess told herself how pleased she would be to see her cousin, Kate, who should be the first arrival. I shall be glad, thought Bess, when Kate is here. If only there were no beginnings. If one could be hurled into the centre of a happening without the preliminary glances at the clock or the greeting rasped from a dry and unprepared throat.

Bess listened. The frantic wind that whitened the waves, occasionally uprooting trees, sometimes overturning cars on the high, unprotected coast road, pushed heavily and noisily against the house. Another sound could be faintly heard. Footsteps on stone. Bess jumped up and opened the front door with the cautious, almost furtive, gesture of one who has had long experience of gales.

Kate, standing in the comparative shelter of the walled entrance, wondered why Bess peered out as if she waited for the hand on her shoulder, for the words of accusation.

Realising that this stranger was, after all, not a stranger, but Kate, Bess took her cousin's arm, drawing her into the room. There was neither passage nor hallway, so immediately one was in the middle of the household.

"Aunt Rachel! Aunt Rachel!" Bess called over her shoulder. "Here she is."

Rachel came forward from the recess by the fireplace. "Kate! How happy I am now you are here! Soon the family will be all together again. Closed in against the snow."

Kate put down her suitcase and kissed her aunt affectionately before replying. "Will there be snow?" She sniffed the air, noticing that even inside the house one could smell the sea.

"Of course it will snow, because it is Christmas. That is one good thing about not going out very often. The weather is as I want it."

"You go out a great deal," Bess spoke a trifle sharply.

Kate looked at her cousin, thinking that Bess appeared pinched and much older. Nobody would imagine, thought Kate, that we are almost the same age. Although perhaps we have both become indefinable. Now we are merely women over thirty, and that is all; perhaps a few years more or less hardly matter.

"I go out enough for me at my age," Rachel was saying. "But it's dull for you, no doubt, having to stay here to look after your old aunt." Rachel, short, plump and determined, faced Bess, a tall, uncertain figure with a slight stoop; a perpetual bending forward to disguise her height, which, as Rachel had often remarked, was somewhat unbecoming in a woman. "Dear girl." Rachel pecked the air as she spoke. "But, then, where else could you go?"

"Please, Aunt Rachel, don't begin all that over again."

Why, wondered Kate, when I am cold and hungry, must they choose this moment to disagree?

"Shall I make the tea?" asked Bess.

"Yes, dear. The tray is ready." Rachel's voice signified that the discussion was merely put aside for a more suitable moment. As soon as Bess had gone out of the room, Rachel

3

turned towards Kate. "Come over here, Kate, nearer me. Then you can feel the fire, and we can talk better. Put your hat and coat down anywhere, and don't bother about your bag. There's time enough for that later." Rachel pulled her chair towards Kate to say conspiratorially, "Marion will soon be here. I could easily imagine you and Bess as my children, but I don't feel like Marion's Mother. She seems so old, and she has such a dull life. I shall enjoy having you all here, though. Christmas wouldn't be Christmas without the family."

"Don't you feel lonely here in the winter, just the two of you?" How abominably draughty this house is, thought Kate, in spite of the thick curtains and the screens and the well-fitting windows. She was chilled not only by the wind, but by the slight sense of desolation which a change of surroundings brings.

"It's not very lively." Rachel remembered the afternoons darkening into evenings, and how she and Bess would sit for hours when all the words had been said and silence took over the house. "Sometimes I still miss London, but I daresay it would not suit me now. Of course I wasn't so grand then, but I was pretty, and that meant something— more than it does today. Money meant more, too, and no one took it from you, as they do now. You could buy things that were worth having. Ball-dresses and carriages; yes, and husbands for those who couldn't get them any other way. We were much happier then. People are so bad-tempered nowadays."

Kate smiled meaninglessly.

"What's the matter with you? Don't you agree with me?"

"Not entirely. You may have been happier then, but the majority of people were probably more miserable————"

"And what do I care about other people? I was happier." Rachel's chuckle softened her words. She wished Bess would hurry up with the tea. Kate was hardly a satisfactory listener, although, Rachel comforted herself, Kate will be better in an hour or two, when she has settled down. "There's no one I can talk to nowadays," Rachel continued. "Except when Adrian comes. I shall have so much to tell him."

"Perhaps he will be here by next Christmas." Kate's reply was a soothing sentence that did not expect belief.

"He is coming for this one first. He should be here tomorrow. I am an old woman, and cannot count on many more Decembers." Rachel looked serene and everlasting.

"Won't it make things difficult?" Kate asked in some bewilderment, startled by Rachel's words. "You know what happened. At least, no one does for certain. But we all think that Adrian knew what he was doing."

"Of course he did. He wanted more than all of you put together. Even if he did take what he wanted, why shouldn't he?"

Bess came into the room. Quietly she dispossessed herself of the large tea-tray, which she placed on a table by Rachel's side, saying: "What have I ever taken?"

"You'd have taken soon enough if you had to. Couldn't have stopped yourself. No blood in you." As Rachel spoke, her short, white fingers, ring-covered, moved gently, picking up the tea-pot, whipping a silver strainer off a cup,

5

handing sugar. "Never mind, Bess. We are here, just the two of us, for most of the year. I must talk sometimes, and you must listen."

"Adrian will come back"—Bess was both irritated and amused—"like a wrongly banished child. Why, he'll even make you forget that he had to be sent away."

"Not *sent* away. We thought it best that he should see other countries. But he was always so gay. He had too much life, that is all."

As they sat drinking tea, the air became warmer, the wind lessened, and the plush curtains that backed the front door were still. The warmth and the quiet room made Rachel's eyelids pleasantly heavy. She dozed even before she had finished her tea, but her face had an expression of watchfulness, as if even in sleep she was troubled by her ears' inattention.

Kate spoke softly. "I hope Rachel is not being too difficult? On high days and holidays she is a pet, but all the time is a different matter."

"In spite of that, we are fond of each other. There is no one else."

"You should have left her. You could have earned your own living. At least you could have kept yourself alive until you could do better than that. Perhaps you ought to have married."

"I wanted to. The men I met were either married already or would never marry. I am not a woman who makes a man change his mind. I myself cannot think of a single reason why anyone should want to marry me."

6

"You have one essential quality: you are a good house-keeper. Most men cannot order meals, arrange for the laundry to be collected, see that the silver is shining, and that the pewter is not shining."

"I can do that here. I should be nervous in someone else's house."

"If you married it would be your house, too."

"No, it would always belong to someone else."

"What kind of man would you like to marry? I know so little about you."

Beatrice agitatedly pushed hairpins farther into her hair as she said apologetically: "I like them all. I have always liked men."

Rachel opened her eyes, saying, as she picked up the over-ornamented tea-pot:

"You have liked the wrong ones, Bess—either married or ill. Just because a real man, a wonderful creature, looked at you, spoke to you, off you would run, spending money and time taking fruit to the hospital. Or you'd sit waiting for some wife to turn up, to shout about you, to cry, to demand her husband back—when you had not even got him!"

"Aunt Rachel would not mind the hospitals," Bess said, "or even the wives, if only I had trapped a man. If I had fastened one by a chain and brought him home. My fault is that no man comes near enough."

Rachel nodded. "That may be so. But you, Kate"—Rachel's eyes brightened—"you haven't done much better for yourself. Not that one would feel sorry for you."

"Tell me more about Adrian," Kate said quickly. "I thought that he would never come back to England."

"Why not? He is my son, after all, and what happened, or what everybody pretended had happened, is nothing to do with me. I don't believe it either. Besides, it was all so long ago."

"What does Adrian feel about meeting us?" Kate asked.

"He has seen hundreds of people since then and travelled thousands of miles. I should not think he's given it another thought. He has a good position, too. Earns a high salary. So you can leave all your doors unlocked this time, and rings and watches all over the place, and nobody will touch them."

Bess sighed: "Aunt Rachel, you are forgetting on purpose. You know very well that Adrian did not behave in such a straightforward way. We would willingly have given him what we could afford. But to take money for shares in a company and to swindle us as he did, that is another matter. Katherine and I, we don't mind. You can ask anybody you like to spend Christmas here, to stay for a week—or for ever. But there is Marion. She won't want to be faced with her dear brother Adrian."

Rachel smiled: "He was a good boy, always kind to me. Used to bring me presents. So loving, too. As for Marion and that white-faced husband of hers, they can just practise Christian forbearance, otherwise they must go away."

The house will not be itself, thought Bess. People bring their own lives. Rachel has only brought old age; but this house has had not only my youth, but each succeeding year. People discard their lives as carelessly as Kate has

8

thrown her coat over that chair. And in the same way as I shall move that coat, so, when everyone has gone, I shall spend hours, perhaps days, before I can efface the invisible traces of those who are strangers because they do not live here.

Later in the evening, when Kate had unpacked, when dinner was over, they sat, the three women, around the fire. The silence was that of contentment after food; of gratitude for the room that protected them from the winter air, protected them from the sad, insistent sea.

Footsteps, however familiar and expected, are invariably menacing: especially on a winter's night when one is almost convinced that nothing exists in the coldness outside the house.

Bess ran to open the door to prevent the strident peal of the bell, which would, she felt, have splintered the quiet air.

Rachel's daughter flung herself into the room, followed more soberly by her husband.

"Marion, dear—and Thomas, too!" Rachel sounded surprised.

Marion kissed her Mother. "I would hardly come here for Christmas and leave Thomas behind."

"No, dear, of course not. Now let us sit near the fire and be really comfortable. And you shall tell me all your news."

Marion's square face creased with annoyance: "How like you, Mother, to expect us to sit down without unpacking. Before we have washed. Almost before we are here."

Thomas, tall and uncertain, came forward to kiss his

mother-in-law, and laughed as if to say that he would deal with the bags, do what was needed, that no one must be disturbed.

As soon as Marion and her husband had gone upstairs to their bedroom, Rachel winked roguishly. She appeared, as she well knew, younger than her daughter:

"Just the same," Rachel said, "always tidy and reliable. Always washing her hands."

Kate nodded. She had not yet become sufficiently part of the household to take an interest in Marion.

Bess wondered abstractedly whether she had remembered to shut the window in Marion's room. Although Thomas was with her, it still remained Marion's room.

When, after half an hour, Marion came down the stairs, she looked brushed and shining, ready to make a speech or to decide dangerous issues. As if discounting her previous greeting, she came over to Kate, took her hand, saying: "How are you, my dear? Lovely to be back again. Quite a party. Bess all dressed up, too!"

Bess's body seemed to shrink away from the flimsy material, as if trying to deny the flesh, so that the frock hung limply from her thin shoulders.

"Silks and pretty colours don't matter to me. Tommy doesn't mind what I wear. I like to be comfortable." As Marion spoke she pushed her solid body into a squat fire-side chair.

Thomas stood by the foot of the staircase, one hand on the banisters, waiting for Marion to place him, or to send him on an errand.

"Come on, my boy. Draw up. We're just in time for coffee; aren't we, Mother?"

"How nice you are looking, Bess!" Thomas said as he jumped up to carry the coffee-tray which she had fetched from the kitchen. Seeing her flushed smile, Thomas touched her hand lightly to reassure her.

Rachel smiled slyly. "Be careful, Thomas. You'll break her heart. A soft heart it is, too. Why, Bess has often told me that you were the only man that she would have married. If Marion had not got there first."

"Aunt Rachel, please don't say such ridiculous things. Thomas will believe you."

"I thought you'd be here before now," Kate interrupted, hoping that Bess's angry refutation would go no farther.

"My fault," Marion said proudly. "I was kept at the office."

"What a busy wife you have!" Rachel mocked. "Quite a power in the firm. More like a man."

"More than most men are." Marion's tone was one of almost maternal fondness.

"The women of our family always speak their minds," Rachel said provokingly. "And we are none the worse for it."

"Oh, certainly not. Let the galled jade wince, our withers are unwrung."

"What an extraordinary thing to say, Thomas! I always said that you are the interesting one. You are the most deep. You could carry on a conversation with anybody that you could, and no one would be any the wiser."

Marion's laugh bellowed out: "There you go, Mother. Up and at 'em!"

Rachel was pleased with her success. "I speak my mind. Always have. Too late to alter that."

Bess ambled away to wash up the coffee-cups, refusing Thomas's offer of assistance. The four of them began to play a desultory game of whist. Rachel played with enthusiasm and such physical vigour that she bent the corners of the cards; yet again and again she lost. When she had to pay a few coppers to her opponents she could not have felt more unhappy if it were a sovereign that she pushed across the green baize. Rachel glared at Kate, who was her partner: it was all Kate's fault. Why couldn't she keep her mind on the game?

"I'll go to bed now," Rachel said peevishly. "You young ones stay and chatter. But don't overtire yourselves. Remember, breakfast at nine sharp."

Bess trailed after Rachel, carrying a spectacle case, a black lace shawl and a box of peppermint creams.

"Your Mother is as lively as ever," Thomas said gloomily.

"Thank God for it. Not like your Mother used to be, whining and complaining about the muddle her life was in. Life," said Marion loudly, "is what you make it."

"There are people like you and your Mother who do make their own lives. On they swarm, clearing a path, pushing and pulling." Thomas spoke excitedly. "You are all like that. Except Bess, perhaps—poor fool. And Kate, who just waits to see what will come next."

"Tommy dear, what a speech! Katie will think we are always quarrelling. You know that you prefer to have decisions made for you. You do not want to be bothered by little everyday affairs."

"Yes, of course. I enjoy coming to stay with your Mother, so that she and all the rest of your family have a chance of saying that you are the man of our household!"

"I can't understand you tonight. You are never like this at home. We are happy together in the evenings."

"That is because we are tired. To acknowledge unhappiness is to be rebellious. Tired people are not rebels."

"That is right," said Kate, hoping to stem the rising tide of anger, "for I remember once in Italy———"

Bess, who had quietly re-entered the room, interrupted: "Italy. That's where Adrian is coming from. I have had the fire on in his room for two days. He will feel the cold."

Marion's voice screamed out: "Adrian coming here? And all you can say is that he will be cold! That's your doing, Bess. You always were his favourite. He had no time for me, his sister. I was too sharp for him. You'd rather have him, I see that, to take you out on money he has stolen, to kiss your cheek, to hold your hand, than no man at all. It's disgusting!" Anger seemed not only to whiten, but also to flatten, her features.

From the babble of talk, of Bess's counter-accusations, Thomas's voice rose clearly: "Marion, you must be out of your mind. You do too much and tire yourself out so that you don't know what you are saying."

Bess turned her back on the others; her voice was harsh. "I had forgotten how cruel Marion is." Why, Bess wondered, did she attract cruelty?

Conscious of Thomas's fingers gripping her arm, and of his troubled face, Marion spoke with surprising calmness, pleased to show how quickly she could control herself. "Very well, Tommy; but it is unfair of you to turn against me when I speak the truth." Realising that some restitution must be made, Marion added, "You are never like this at home."

"There is no need to enlist your husband's support. You are sufficiently strong as it is."

Marion suddenly decided that she had caused enough confusion, and became competent and reliable once more: "Sorry, dear. Let us forget all this. Do remember that it is Christmas Eve." Having succeeded in presenting Bess as the attacker and herself as the peacemaker, Marion smiled forgivingly.

With arms linked, Bess stiff-backed, Marion bouncing, they climbed the stairs together, talking quickly and softly.

Thomas grinned at Kate as he said, "Amazing women! Now they will have a happy two hours in Bess's room discussing Adrian. Or perhaps us." He walked towards the window, drawing back a corner of the dark red curtain to show that the first soft, heavy coins of snow were clinging to the pane.

"Why did you marry Marion?" Kate asked curiously. She was pleased to realise that the sudden commotion had affected her hardly at all.

"I adored her. Sometimes I do still. Then she was like a jolly schoolgirl. A prefect, of course, telling everyone what to do. But she gave her orders with a lively grace. Now she merely gives orders. Unfortunately, I need somebody like that. Although she overdoes it. You were too young to remember Marion as she was at eighteen. We were photographed together. She is sitting on a garden chair, and I am leaning over her. It is obvious that I love her. Marion sees me like that now, and so I see myself that way, too. Do you think it is still the truth?"

Kate laughed. "As much the truth as any of us knows."

For a while they sat silently opposite each other, cigarettes in hands, watching the fire, listening for a recurrence of furious words from the rooms above, but there was no sound.

"You are a peculiar family," Thomas said. "Why do you spend each Christmas here?"

"My presence is expected. I need to come, too. I feel that one should be closed in, protected from outside influences—either good or bad. One is susceptible when anything is ending, whether it is a year or"—she paused slightly, then changed her mind—"anything else."

"Yet I imagine you could find other, gayer ways of spending Christmas?"

"Perhaps. But I shall always come here."

"This business of Adrian's return. Will it affect us? Shall we be upset, forced to take sides for or against?"

"That is inevitable. Adrian will love it, as long as we all concentrate on him, and do not indulge in minor feuds, forgetting the main argument."

"What do you yourself feel about him?" Thomas asked trustfully, ready, because he liked Kate, to take her verdict as his own.

"Absolutely nothing. Not as much as one would feel

for a stranger who came to the door, having mistaken the number of the house."

"Then he is not this deep villain?"

"He is vain, dishonest perhaps. Nothing more terrible than that."

"Dishonesty doesn't appal you?"

"No, of course not. We all tell little lies for our own purposes. But we are seldom called to account. Adrian was not so clever. He had to live the harder way. He had to tell obvious lies, to take money, to drape himself in false achievements."

Upstairs a door was opened, there was a sound of heavily pacing feet stamping along the corridor.

"Oh, Lord!" said Thomas, getting up from his chair, "that's Marion. The sweet midnight session is over. I can tell what Marion's walk means." He jerked his head towards the ceiling to indicate his wife and Bess. "My guess is that they have worked themselves up about something large and impersonal."

Kate smiled sympathetically, wondering why Thomas put up with such a fretful life. Perhaps all because, she thought as she switched off the lights and began to climb the stairs, he and Marion were once photographed together. Otherwise Thomas might have forgotten how he used to feel. There was a pleasant absurdity about this: a thought which could be enlarged and rearranged in an infinity of instances. A companionable problem to take to a lonely bedroom.

CHAPTER TWO

Christmas Day

EARLY the next morning the house was full of hurrying people and sounds of feet running along corridors, of paper crackling, as last-minute presents were wrapped up.

Kate, the last down to breakfast, was greeted by Rachel's smooth voice:

"Good morning, my dearest. You must have been very tired."

Kate looked towards Marion and Thomas, whose faces were bright and expressionless. Then she realised that her second cousin, Piers, had arrived and was smiling at her:

"Kate! I haven't seen you for so long. You look nice, but much older." He ate his porridge with concentration.

"Do I? That is hardly surprising. We had a hectic and quarrelsome evening when Aunt Rachel had gone to bed." We are all cousins, thought Kate. What a peculiar relationship! All of us, that is, except Rachel.

"Did you?" Piers asked delightedly. "How very funny!"

"Don't be silly, dear. Kate is teasing us. And happy Christmas, very happy Christmas to you all." Rachel was determined that nothing should interrupt her breakfast. If it had been the afternoon—that blank of time between luncheon and tea—she would have welcomed scandalous revelations. But until she had had her third cup of tea, the morning had not officially begun.

They smiled politely at each other. Marion and Thomas looked stolid, caring only for what they ate. Bess drank tea in agitated gulps.

"I think it is better if we give presents this evening, after dinner," said Rachel. "It will make the time pass."

"We should all be thinking of using our evenings and our days"—Marion glared accusingly round the table: she was an exceedingly quick eater—"filling every minute, because there won't be enough for any of us."

"Please do not force us to consider too unpleasantly, Marion. Not today. You were always a fussy, frightened creature, even as a child. Always preparing for the worst." Rachel spoke viciously.

"Talking of time"—Piers leaned forward to smile innocently at Kate. "How did you manage to lose that young man of yours, after all those years?"

Marion, who had great respect for facts and enjoyed collecting them, wiped her mouth with a table-napkin as a sign that she had turned her attention from breakfast and was ready to concentrate entirely upon Kate's reply.

As Kate did not speak immediately, Marion said, "We have never quite understood why you didn't marry Alec, after all."

"Such a shock, dear, wasn't it?" asked Rachel.

"Not exactly. I left him. At least, I think I did. So I was prepared."

"Now, Katie, that won't do. Here we are longing to be told the secrets of your heart, and you go on eating toast and marmalade. Drinking coffee, too. And jilting poor young men!"

Piers was enjoying himself.

"I am not very good at giving explanations so early in the day. There is nothing mysterious to tell you. Alec loved putting up shelves and mending broken window-sashes. When he had done all those there was little left of interest to him."

"How frivolous you are!" Rachel was deeply shocked because she had been cheated of her anticipations of frustrated desire.

"That is another reason, Aunt Rachel. Alec wasn't at all frivolous. He liked long walks and swimming in high seas. My preference, even in the summer, is to sneak up to bed with a hot-water bottle."

"Most amusing," Rachel said stiffly. Sadly she thought that Kate had robbed the word "bed" of any possibly salacious meaning. To be too old herself for such memories was wretched enough, but to be surrounded by young people who were either frigid or—she thought contemptuously of Bess—frightened to the point of impotent numbness, that was the fulfilment of the horrid prophecy of the world, at least her world, ending in ice. She said peevishly to Kate: "And was your room warm last night?"

"Thank you. Not very."

As Rachel had now finished her breakfast, she decided that it was her turn to enliven the morning hours:

"Piers is so awkward." She smiled affectionately at him. "Arriving before breakfast. Then to come in by the garden entrance. He seems taller than ever. He banged his head on the top of the doorway. He gave Bess such a fright."

"But, Rachel darling, you knew that I was coming. It couldn't have been such a surprise."

"Of course we knew. But we didn't expect you so early. Or to be so large. Besides"—Rachel glinted around her, then spoke directly to Bess—"he's a good-looking young man, isn't he? Too handsome to meet first thing in the morning. Unless one is very young—or very old, as I am." She sat back, pleased with her softly spoken malice. "What is the matter, Bess? Don't you feel well?" Rachel raised her hands in hurt astonishment, turning the padded palms upwards, curling her fingers to draw from each of them the assurance that her words could not have wounded the most sensitive creature. "To go off like that! Just listen to her running up the stairs. People nowadays are so difficult to understand. We were jollier in my day. Happy banter at meal-times was considered quite the thing."

"It's rather cruel of you, Aunt Rachel, to torment Bess in front of all of us. Now she will have a miserable Christmas."

"Just because you managed to get engaged to some man and then had the impudence to change your mind, you think you can run everything."

"Now, darling." Piers took every advantage. Although he was Rachel's nephew, he preferred to behave as her favoured admirer: a game which was a constant amusement to both. "You must not be matriarchal on such a morning. It's like a Christmas day in April. Sun on snow. Lovely. Let us walk off together down to the sea. Everyone will ask you who I am. What a wicked reputation you'll have!"

"I suppose you think that I am a foolish, fond old woman?"

As they walked together down the steps leading to the cliff road, their voices could be heard—Rachel's light, almost girlish questions and Piers's laughing replies.

Marion, bustling and practical, insisted on helping Mrs. Page, Rachel's daily woman, to wash up the breakfast dishes. Marion was heard explaining to a silently dubious Mrs. Page that roast turkey was quite uneatable unless accompanied by cranberry sauce.

"That will keep them busy for some hours," Kate said as she shut the door leading from the dining-room to the kitchen. "I'm glad, because I want to talk to you, Thomas."

"About Bess?"

"Yes. She is unhappy. Rachel should not badger her. Bess is becoming vaguer, blanker. She looks nondescript. She used to be quite pretty."

"So many women are quite pretty. That is not important. Besides, Bess asks to be dominated. She enjoys it, except when she is upset about something. Such as Piers coming here."

"Why does she hate him? He is irritating, perhaps, but charming to look at."

"My idea is—and for the Lord's sake keep this to yourself—that Bess has . . . well, not exactly fallen for him. But he bewitches her."

"That seems to be a reversal of the customary roles."

"Naturally, but you must admit that Piers would make a

likelier *belle dame sans merci* than Bess. Rachel is, I believe, pretty fed up about it. That may be why she invites Piers down as often as possible and dotes upon him so blatantly. Even at her age she is a more attractive proposition than Bess. More showy. Better company, too."

"This is all rather absurd, isn't it? Rachel wants to be liked by all men, especially young, good-looking ones. But the idea of Bess being infatuated by Piers! She is much older than he is. Anyway, she would not let herself get into such a wretched position."

"Bess doesn't let herself. Things happen to her. All her life she has been falling in love, and most unsuccessfully."

"Well, what's your remedy?"

"Oh, I've no advice to give. Except perhaps that she should walk the other way. I'd tell her that this is a looking-glass world. Whatever you want, don't go after it. Run away, and there it is, in front of you."

"Can you do that?"

"Too late for me. I have no particular end in view. By the way, what really happened between you and Alec?"

"It was not, of course, as simple as I made out."

"Did you have a last dramatically exhausting quarrel?"

"No, we just contradicted each other all day, and then all night."

Thomas grinned. "That's what Rachel wanted to find out. The night part, I mean."

"I am sure she knows. But a public announcement is always more satisfactory than private suspicions."

"Do you mind much?"

"Yes, in some ways. I miss Alec because he knows that I like to read for hours in bed. Because, in spite of his apparent heartiness, cold winds make him ill. Because he cares enormously for Ruskin as I care for Carlyle. Such details are important, and they take years to find out. I wouldn't want to begin all over again."

"We are all bound by such trivialities. You'll find others. You can't escape them."

"Of course we are bound." Her voice was slightly impatient. "Otherwise I should not be here. Bound by family affection and family fear."

Bess came down the stairs, walking swiftly, almost guiltily. She was dressed to go out. Her eyes had the brightness of recent tears. Her face was slightly flushed by an effort to remove traces of distress. Her scurrying walk was oddly attractive, making her a gently wary animal.

"Hallo, hallo," Thomas called out with purposeful obtuseness. "Going for a walk?" Then, seeing that she looked trapped, unwilling to speak or to be spoken to, he tried to make amends. "You look bright enough to outdo the snow. I mean the sun shining on the snow. Anyway, you do look very nice." His voice became weaker, striving for the effect which would not come.

Bess, forced as she was to listen, stood stiffly by the door, ready to run away before either of them could follow. Then she saw from Thomas's expression that this clumsy waylaying was kindly meant. She realised that Thomas was trying to tell her not to be hurt; that he liked her, that they all liked her; that in spite of the attacks made upon her, she was a cherished member of the household; that her going out was necessarily noticed because she was missed. She relaxed a little as she leaned back against the door, no longer standing sentinel. She smiled at them both, smiling casually from one to the other, to say that nothing was the matter, that all was as it should be, that she had no problem and neither was she a problem.

"Shall we come with you? We can have coffee in that jolly little place that is half falling over the cliff. I don't suppose lunch will be ready for hours yet." Seeing that Bess's face was merely blank, he tried again. "Perhaps we need something stronger than that today. Let's celebrate with cocktails in that revolting pub on the front which ought never to have been built."

"That's sweet of you, Thomas; but, if you'll forgive me, I'd rather go out by myself. I prefer to be on top of the cliffs rather than underneath them. Besides, I like walking towards the sun. But there are no cafés in that direction, and it would be dull for you and Kate. There aren't any pubs either." She spoke almost pleadingly.

"Perhaps you'll see Aunt Rachel—and Piers." Kate was anxious to drive the conversation towards a drastic admission. If, Kate reasoned, Bess admits that she is going out in the hope of seeing Piers, perhaps we can talk to her; tell her what a target such pursuit will be; tell her that she must put him out of her mind: that he is just an ordinary young man who happens to be very good-looking.

But Bess had already gone, and within a few minutes they saw her walking with long, jerky strides along the grassy cliff-edge, walking away from the house, against the wind.

"What on earth made you mention Piers?" Thomas asked.

"I wanted to shock her into telling us about him. So that we could show her how hopeless it is. Why, he wouldn't even look at Bess. I don't suppose he has ever noticed her, except as a vague adjunct to Aunt Rachel."

"Don't you believe it. The fact that Piers disregards her so ostentatiously shows that there is something between them."

"Something between whom?" Marion asked as she came in from the kitchen.

"Between us, of course," Thomas said as he took Kate's hand and kissed it with mocking ceremony.

Marion smiled indulgently, thinking, What a boy he still is. Always trying to make me jealous. She went over to her husband and patted him on the shoulder. "You can have your sentimental interludes with Katie. She doesn't count. Not in that way."

Kate laughed. "Am I so repulsive?"

"Oh, no, dear; you are nice to look at. You would be very personable if only you'd diet a little." Conscious of her squatly stout figure, Marion added: "No good for me. I am all muscle and bone."

"I'll think about it," said Kate. "But not before the new year."

"Kate's terrified you won't let her eat any mince-pies. Or that you'll set upon her and massage her into thin air."

Thin air, Marion thought. What expressions he uses, and Kate smiles admiringly at him, encouraging his nonsense.

"This won't do," Marion said abruptly. "We must go out and get our appetites up. Where's Bess? Snivelling in her room, I suppose?"

"As a matter of fact," said Thomas, "she has gone out for a nice brisk walk to blow the cobwebs away."

Marion stared distrustfully at him. "That doesn't sound like Bess." Was he making fun of her? Or of Bess? Or of the whole family?

"Whatever she has gone for," Kate said, "she is not here. We saw her going towards Seaford."

"Then there is no reason for us to go after her. I would prefer to stroll down to the village. Perhaps we shall meet Mother and Piers, and we can come back together."

Rachel had walked along the village street to the elm-bordered green, where, beyond the grass, ducks glided on a small, sandy-banked pond. The houses facing the pond had whitened stone façades; their long, slim windows shone like jet.

"This is your background, Rachel. You ought to live in one of these houses. You should know each duck by name," Piers said as they stood for a few minutes by the water's edge.

The thin, yellow bands of winter sunshine made Rachel blink and wrinkle her nose. She had not faced the sun for several months.

"Yes, I do feel myself in this part of the village. How seldom one is able to be seen against the fitting

26

background! If ever I wished to be young again it would be on a morning like this." She waited, half-expecting the customary courteous reply. "Well, why don't you say that I shall never be old? Or, at least, that age cannot wither me, and all that sort of mumbo-jumbo?"

"Not when we are alone, darling." Piers laughed down at the elderly, fierce little woman who managed to convey that she was still beautiful. "When we have an audience I'll offer you conventional phrases, so that you are considered a vain old woman and I an unprincipled rascal who takes advantage of your susceptibilities."

Rachel chuckled. "I know that, you scoundrel. I just wanted confirmation. I like to know that your abominable behaviour is deliberate."

"You had better be sure of that. Then you can assess my capacity for evil."

"It is easy to be a monster among rabbits. And that is what they are—except you and I. Rabbits with twitching pink noses and anxious eyes. And talking of rabbits, here comes Bess. She is looking for you, young man. No one wants to find me nowadays." Rachel decided to be magnanimous. She had her hand on the strings; the puppets could frolic awhile.

Bess looked pleased when she saw them, then she stopped uncertainly, as if she might bolt back in the direction she had come. She had run over the downs, playing a complicated game with herself, pretending that as she had scrambled down a steep bank that brought her to the top of the village any meeting with Piers would be accidental.

27

Rachel beckoned impatiently. "Come along, come along. Don't stand there staring at us. Unless you're getting short-sighted. Your eyes do look as though you had been awake all night."

"Perhaps I have," Bess said sullenly as she came towards them.

"Listen, my dears. I want a little rest before lunch. I shall walk back slowly, and you can follow later."

After leaving them together, Rachel wondered whether she had spoken too harshly to Bess. But she was such a milk-and-water child. Anyway, Rachel thought virtuously, I will not look back, and that is a concession.

Piers took Bess's arm. "You sulky creature. You have hardly spoken to me since I arrived." His voice was soft. "What have I done?"

"How dare you ask me that? You come down here to stay whenever you want to, either for a holiday, or just for no reason at all. And I am here whenever you come. You like that. And you like going away again and forgetting me, because you know that I shall still be here when-ever you choose to return. You use me as a comfortable waiting-room."

"My sweet Bess, my furious Beatrice! You look lovely when you are angry—quite young, and different."

In spite of the sourness of the compliment, her eyes became gentler; she was ready to translate his words into love for her.

Piers put his hands on her shoulders, swinging her around to face the sun. Then with one finger he flipped her hair, which hung loosely saying, "You are a fool, Bess! Put it up."

As her hands fumbled ineffectually in her haste to screw the brown hair into its customary knot, Piers snapped at her: "Not like that. On the top. That's better."

Bess had, as always when she was with Piers, been thrown into despair, into love and out again within the space of a few minutes. All she could feel was that she would like to sit down; her knees trembled.

"I shall walk down towards the sea and have some coffee in the café on the front. You can do as you please." Bess tried to sound as if she was indifferent as to whether Piers accompanied her or not.

"That is what I like to hear. I adore you when you detest me. Let us form a bond of hatred. So much stronger than love. More passionate, too. Shall I tell you something?"

"Not now"—Bess longed for the protection of walls and the proximity of other people: strangers, not Piers. "I have heard enough for the moment."

They walked without speaking until they reached the cliff's edge, where they leaned against the low, pebbled wall and looked down at the concrete steps leading to the beach.

"It is so horrible now. The front is quite spoilt. Do you remember the old slope that used to be here?"

"Yes, covered with slippery green fungus. That is just like you, Bess. You have caught the family's static attitude. You'd like everything to stay the same for ever, and you would continue to moulder in the midst of it."

He is right, she thought. I do want everything to continue as it is. Because I am frightened of what may come if this goes. Even this nebulous, unsatisfactory moment I dread losing. Even Piers as he is now, neither loving nor hating, just not caring. If I lose what little I have, what worse state may not take its place?

As the wind blew coldly from the sea, Piers shivered, exaggerating the reaction of his body.

Immediately Bess noticed and said, "Let's go in now."

As soon as they were sitting at one of the café tables, and coffee was brought to them, Piers said: "Aren't you curious? Don't you want to know what I have to tell you?"

Bess looked at his face, trying to decide whether he was being cruel or kind. Impossible to know: his expression was contradictory, as if a line had been drawn, cutting off the eyes from the mouth. The eyes were malicious, ready to torment her, while the lips promised gentle words.

"You have made up your mind to tell me. What is it?"

"When I last saw you, standing there on the platform . . ." Piers's voice was secretive, then, to tantalise her, he broke off. "You'd like some cream in your coffee, wouldn't you?" Without waiting for her reply, he stood up and walked over to the counter, standing there until he was handed a small jug, which he carried back to the table. Bess sat still, trying not to look impatient. A year ago she would have thought that such a sudden change of mood was youthful carelessness, that Piers did not realise how strained and nervous she became, waiting to hear his pronouncement of encouragement or damnation. Now she knew better.

Such a pause was calculated so that his climax should not be wasted on an unprepared audience. He left each sentence on an upward inflection.

"Thank you," Bess said obediently as Piers ladled a blob of thick, gluey substance into her cup. The stuff was not cream, and it was sweetened. She sipped distastefully.

"I suppose," she said, "you know that Adrian is coming today?" Perhaps that would make him forget what he was going to say? If it were pleasant, he would tell her later; if unpleasant, he might change his mind. At the moment of thinking this she knew that Piers was more likely to reverse the process.

"Yes. Rachel told me." Tenaciously he returned to his former sentence. "When I last saw you, going farther away from me, or so it seemed—as if I was in a stationary train and you were standing on a platform that moved backwards—I thought then that I loved you, that I loved you so much that I couldn't wait months before seeing you again. I wanted to write to ask you to leave Rachel. To suggest that I found you a job, so that we could always be near each other."

"What kind of job?" For once Bess had forgotten herself and was impersonally interested.

"Any kind of job," Piers said impatiently, wondering why Bess always would choose one trivial detail to fasten on, ignoring the important implication of his state of mind.

Suddenly Bess laughed. She had never found him funny before. No doubt he had been, but she had not dared to notice.

The idea was ludicrous. She could see herself packing her bag, leaving Aunt Rachel without explanation—for what could have been explained?—and rushing to the other side of England to take up some job for which she was quite unsuited. For what was she fitted to do, without experience, and without the ability to hide her lack? And for what? To live in one room in a boarding-house in an unfamiliar town, without even the sea to comfort her, so that she could have seen Piers occasionally when he felt like it? Could perhaps have darned his socks and washed his shirts? Could perhaps have stayed the night with him now and again, if his landlady was not too particular?

Before Bess laughed, Piers had felt loving towards her, remembering as he did the little unhappinesses which he had not admitted. How depressing the carriage had been on that day. The dusty cushions of the seat; the grimy windows; the communication cord that taunted him with having neither £5 nor sufficient reason for pulling it. These half-formed memories angered him. He scowled at her hand that held a cigarette, saw her flick off the ash with an air of determined bravado. Noticed the fingers, long and uncertain, trying, so he imagined, to look scarlet-tipped, like the fingers of a different woman, but remaining those of a girl who had outgrown girlhood in years, but whose hands still pleaded for understanding, for tender gestures, for time.

Bess looked up to see his mouth, thickened by temper. Helplessly she awaited the brutal words. Perhaps he had, for the first time, cause to attack her. She had taken his pride from him. That he should ever have needed her presence enough to consider sending for her, sending for her to come from one side of England to another, that should have made her give thanks to the gods. Last year it would, but this year, and so near to another year, was different. She had forced herself during the lonely early winter months to realise the uselessness of loving Piers. But she was still unsure of her ability to catch his anger in mid-flight, to minimise the hurt he could inflict upon her.

At that moment she saw three figures that hesitated outside the window, walked a few paces towards the sea and then turned back. Bess rapped excitedly on the window-pane so that Kate, Marion and Thomas looked around them and, seeing Bess's beckoning hand, walked towards the café entrance.

Piers's eyes flickered desolation and disaster to come: staring at her with a curse of a future when he had gone, never to return. In those few seconds Bess saw, as Piers intended, that there would come a time when she would regret most of all the laughter that had pushed him away from her. Piers's unwavering and prophetic gaze was inter-rupted by Thomas's voice:

"Hello, you two. Thought you'd be drinking something stronger than coffee on Christmas morning. Come along! Let's all go across to the pub."

"No, I'll stay here," Piers said in a voice harsh with the effort of restraining his anger both at Bess's behaviour and his foreshortened scene.

"Good God! what is the matter with you?" Marion asked loudly. She had an aversion to what she thought of as temperamentally unstable people, and Piers's reply sounded quite unbalanced. His reedy tone made her face redden and smart as if the words, although spoken to Thomas, had taken shape in the cold air and had flicked her cheeks.

"Oh, well, if you'd rather——" Kate said vaguely, feeling suddenly that she did not care either way, but hoping that all would be well; that Bess would cast off whatever it was that troubled her, that Piers would be unobtrusively charming; that she herself need not bother about any of them. The sunny morning had filled her with wonderful plans for the new year, for the new life. Surely each ending year should end, too, that year's muddle and indecision? Surely everything would become shiningly certain. The trees would part and her path would be there, white and sun-soaked, leading straight to some dazzling future at the path's end, a gleaming pinnacle. There was one flaw in the fairy tale. What would her peak of achievement be? The usual ending was all right for a beginning, but it would hardly suffice. Not that kind of happily-ever-after. There must be more than that. The legendary Prince might be allowed to arrive. She could see him cutting a way through the forest of her discontents. But when he drew nearer she could not see his face. He used to look like Alec; but not for long. Now he resembled first one, then another, or a mixture of many. At the moment he had no face at all, merely a grey blur. Even supposing that he came, what then? After walking proudly by his side, after presenting him first to her enemies, secondly to her friends, what then? No, that would not do. There must be something else. Moonily,

34

yet with a certain self-mockery, she thought of what life might be persuaded to mean. She would be content with one crumb of purpose. She started guiltily as she realised that Piers was speaking to her, laughing at her abstraction.

"I'm sorry," Kate said as they straggled out into the sunshine; "I was thinking." She felt happier now that Piers had evidently decided to accompany them without further commotion.

Piers, who was amused by Kate's remote, passionless air, transferred his attentions, to show Bess how enchanting he could be.

"What about, darling?" Deliberately he used the endearment which he usually reserved for Rachel.

"About me, of course. Most people do, although not always so noticeably. About life, and what purpose there is, if any."

Piers was delighted. At heart he was a serious-minded young man who, when neither working nor polishing up his charm, meditated for many hours about life. That was perhaps why he had neither personal conscience nor imagination to keep him in check. If he was madly in love with Bess one day, and the next day found her plain, middle-aged and tedious, this did not shock him. He studied his ins and outs of passion and mood with impersonal disregard. He was looking at himself; he was alive; therefore he was studying Life. The more he surprised himself by his un-expected revisions and reversions, the more interested he became in the complexities of existence. That Bess might have only the burden of misery without the alleviation of regarding her despair as a profitable mental exercise, had never occurred to him.

Thomas, who had all the time remained silent, glancing towards Bess with some pity, and at Piers with dislike, drew Marion and Bess back, so that Kate and Piers pushed aside the curtain leading to the saloon bar and entered together. Inside they stood in two separate groups.

"We'll let those two get on with it," Thomas said. "And remember, young man," he called across loudly to Piers, who was grandly ordering for Kate a champagne cocktail which she did not want, "no acrimonious talk when we get back. This is the day for peace on earth and goodwill towards men—and women." What had made him speak so pompously, as if he was a father publicly rebuking a swaggering son? Am I jealous of the boy? How absurd, almost obscene, that would be. He knew that they were staring at him in mild surprise; even Bess's colourless face had lost its expression of grieving, and she looked at him rather, he thought, as if he were a pet dog that had suddenly turned upon her. He wondered if she would put out a soft palm to touch his nose, anxious for reassurance that there was no warm, dry warning of possible distemper. I suppose— the thought was bitter—I can't say a word to that young whippersnapper. Otherwise I'll have Kate and Bess scratching my eyes out—oh, and Rachel, too. Mustn't forget her: she'd be the worst of the lot. That reminded him. He spoke again to Piers, but this time his voice was as usual:

"What happened to Rachel? I thought you came out together?"

"She went back to rest before lunch," Piers said in tones of sweet concord, showing how reasonable he could be, conscious of Kate's interested watchfulness.

"Didn't you go back with Mother?" Marion asked.

"No. She had gone before I realised it."

"That was my fault," said Bess. "I met them both by the pond. I ought to have gone back with her."

What a self-sacrificing fool! thought Piers, always rushing forward to shoulder any disapproval.

"Oh, I see," Marion said blankly. She looked from Piers to Bess, wondering why one answered for the other. The question was unimportant.

Piers ostentatiously turned his back on the others to concentrate on Kate. He was safe with her; she would not make him ridiculous with cloying protection.

"Have you made up your mind?" asked Piers.

"About what?"

"About life." He spoke teasingly. "I mean whatever aspect troubles you."

"It all troubles me," Kate said glumly.

Piers felt that this was too big a problem for him to tackle, preferring as he did the minutiæ of everyday doings and thoughts. He felt that Kate was adopting too objective, too masculine, a viewpoint. This thought did not solidify into coherence, but swam around in his head, making him irritable. Women ought to worry about love affairs, about clothes, about children, about retaining their husband's affection, and thousands of other suitable tediums; but for a woman, and a moderately young and attractive one, to retreat to a secret oblivion to try to fathom the meaning of the universe, that was emancipation running riot.

Kate, sensing that Piers's attitude towards her had changed, that he was no longer the smiling gallant, but a rather obtuse young man who regarded her as a trespasser in the manly world of pure logic, immediately became what she wanted to avoid: both personal and illogical.

"It's all very well for you," she said; "you can live easily, just because you are not a woman."

"Now, really, Kate, that is most unfair. I work harder than any of you."

"That is not at all what I mean. It is not work when you are trained for a specialised job which brings its own rewards. I do not mean money, but discovery, or at least the conviction that what you are doing must be done, and that if you were not doing it a substitute would have to be found—and not just anyone, but a trained intelligence." Kate spoke with the feverishness of one who knows she has chosen the wrong time, the wrong place and the wrong person.

"But women can get degrees now, and . . . and in fact are not hampered in any way. They may become just what they want to."

"Don't be silly. I can't. When I think of the dozens of futile, messy little jobs that I have had since I left school!"

"Surely that was not necessary? I mean, you have enough money of your own." Piers was bewildered by the conversation.

"Yes—at least, I had. It would not be enough now. Not for the kind of things that I want. And even when I could

38

live without earning money I did not choose to. Would you have said that to a man of my age?" Without allowing Piers to reply, she answered herself: "No, of course not. There are only two kinds of women that you know about—or think you do: the ones who are beautiful and those who are intelligent. The intelligent ones can fend for themselves, and the beauties are always looked after. But I am neither; I'm in between." As Kate spoke she worked herself into a fury at the injustice of it all, and at Piers's disinterestedness. Her eyes, large and of an indefinite changing colour, widened, her pale face flushed and her reddish-brown hair fell out of its slide and hung in a soft bundle that brushed her face.

Piers, who had been looking at her, rather than following her argument, thought that she was attractive in a peculiar, somewhat comfortless, way. What a spitfire, though; and so suddenly, without warning or provocation. He liked women to have ideas of their own, but not to go off at such a tangent. Perhaps Bess, usually compliant and yielding, was a jewel, after all? Bess, whom he could love and mock and put out of mind; Bess, who always took him back; Bess, who considered him before she thought of herself, not like this flashing, egocentric monster, who drank the champagne cocktails that he had paid for while she bawled at him.

"Apart from your obsession that the world is a hard place for women, what do you want for yourself?"

"I want something to believe in," said Kate emphatically, adding quickly, "and I don't mean someone. I want to believe that we, that the world, is working up to a grand climax, preferably of perfection; but even extinction would be better than nothing. That everything we think and do and are, every detail, is part of a plan. That all our lives are essential to the whole. So that if we don't get anywhere ourselves, individually, even if we don't know what it is all about, that there is something to know." Kate became conscious that she had had too much to drink, that she had talked wildly and loudly about matters that in her environment are left unsaid.

Marion, who had been eyeing Kate and Piers with some dismay, fearing that they were getting out of hand, walked over to them. "I didn't catch all that you were jabbering about. It seems to me that you both read too much. The more you know about books, the less you know about people. That's my opinion, and I am not far wrong."

"What's up, Bess?" Thomas asked softly.

"Nothing unusual. Just that each time Piers comes back it all starts over again. But I see that he is often ridiculous, yet that does not make much difference. Except that when he really goes I shall be able to remember how foolish he was."

"As long as you realise that he will inevitably go."

"Oh, yes; I don't feel that he is completely present. He is always thinking about rushing away, and that makes me feel that he is here by accident."

By the time they had walked up the steep hill, back to the house, the wind in their faces had blown away the exhilaration of the champagne and they felt soberly themselves.

Rachel, rested, freshly powdered and smelling of eau-de-Cologne, opened the door to them.

"Just in time, my dears. Luncheon will be ready in a minute. What a happy family party this is!" Then her plump face became petulant. "Not a word from Adrian."

As soon as they were seated around the table, Rachel proposed the toast, "To all of us. May we each get what we most desire." Her voice was mellow, but with an undertone of tears as she thought how little desire was left to her. "And may we be a larger family party next Christmas. I drink to the day when we shall see both Kate and Bess happily married. Piers, too, of course—but there is plenty of time for you, dear boy."

When luncheon was over there was a loud knocking. Rachel insisted on opening the door herself, because she wanted to be the first to welcome her son Adrian, so long and unhappily absent from her. They all followed, standing in a disapproving group. They had not really believed in the possibility of Adrian's arrival.

A small man hopped in. His body was thin-boned, bird-like, but the incongruity was his face, which was full-fleshed, sallow and heavy. His hands were white and thickly soft.

Adrian rushed at Rachel, gave her several loud kisses, and then hopped around to each in turn, kissing and shaking hands and crowing with laughter. Then he did it all over again.

"Shure me ould mither an' all you darlints. Shure 'tis plaised I am to be with ye again in the ould homestead," he crooned in a travesty of an Irish accent.

"My son! My son!" Rachel laughed and wiped her eyes, ignoring as best she could the Irish accent.

Adrian looked at the blank faces of the others and thought, What a lot of bloody snobs they are! Didn't want me back, I suppose?

"'Ullo, me old cock!" Adrian changed his tactics and his accent, and roared at Thomas, whom he had selected as likely to be easily baited. "So you've married the old bag of brains?" He pointed at Marion, who stood staring sternly at him. Then Adrian doubled up with laughter. He looked at Piers, "And 'oo may you be, young feller-me-lad? Perce, isn't it? And Bess, girl—well, I never! You look a bit peaky, duck. That's a nice little bit, a snappy bit of stuff." He winked at Kate.

They were united in their common plight.

"Naughty, naughty! Smacky, smacky!" Adrian playfully tapped his own hand. He was enjoying himself more than he had done for years.

"Come in properly, dear. That's right." Rachel's voice was weaker than usual, almost quavering. Then in an aside to Thomas, "Do you think he may be a little . . .? Perhaps some food? I mean on an empty stomach . . . even one drink, so I have heard?"

Thomas nodded. "Leave it to me."

Somehow they managed to get Adrian to sit down and to keep quiet long enough to eat. Bess took his hat and coat up to his room, while Thomas followed with Adrian's bag. On the way down Bess looked at herself in the mirror. Peaky? Yes, perhaps so.

They sat rigidly watching the horror eat. He threw food into his mouth and smacked his lips. "A little of wot yer fancies does yet good. Naw, p'raps thas was the matter wi' all o' you? Ho ho! ho ho! Thas a good one! thas a good one!" He opened his mouth widely to laugh, dropping pieces of food over himself and on the carpet. "You've 'ad more wot yer fancy than them. See it in yer floe." He leered at Kate.

"Maybe you've got something there," Kate said calmly as she lit another cigarette, leaning forward to blow smoke towards him.

He looked admiringly at her: "Perky bit of goods, ain't she? Bet 'er right 'and knows wot 'er left 'and's up to." His heavy jowls shook with mirth. "Unless she don't want it to. Eh, girl? Ho ho! ho ho!"

"Exactly," said Kate.

"And where have you come from, dear? Did you stay in London for the night?" Rachel asked, valiantly trying to trace the beginning of his disaster.

"Thas it. Fro' Lon'n. Come 'ere to be a fa-ha-mer's bo-hoy-hoy, too-hoo be-he a fa-ha-mer's bee-yoy," he sang happily. "Shure an' me darlints it's not too plaised at all at all ye are to see me?"

Rachel was overcome, not only by disappointment, but also by humiliation. He was her son, and as his father was dead the responsibility which should have been shared was hers alone. Marion was appalled at the entry of this vulgar little man, reeking of drink. Bess merely wondered how it could have happened, and felt sorry for Rachel. Piers, because he was the youngest, was terribly embarrassed by this freak which had been sent from hell to torment them. Only Kate and Thomas were not bowed down. They had more or less the same feelings about Adrian: that he would be very tiresome, especially if he continued to talk and sing in bastard accents. But was the Cockney speech such mockery? Kate wondered. Perhaps he really spoke like that, exaggerated today by gin and bravado.

It was Thomas who persuaded Adrian to go to bed to rest, and who left the Alka Seltzer at hand; and it was Thomas whose good-tempered reasoning impressed Adrian so favourably that, before being escorted to his room, he swallowed a raw egg well laced with Worcester sauce without demur except for an astonished choke when he discovered that the innocuous-looking egg that made its way with such cool ease down his throat was followed by a draught of filthy fire-water. He looked reproachfully at Thomas, saying:

"'Ere now, look 'ere, Tommy boy. Wot was in that glass? Sh'd've washed it, reely you sh'd've. Mi' be weed-killer." Then he stumbled towards the stairs, supported by Thomas's unobtrusive arm. "Good ni', all; good ni'. Nighty-night, Marion, old duck. Cheer up. Brother's back."

When Thomas had rejoined them and they were together again, banded against the invader who was already snoring upstairs, it was Kate who spoke first. Marion and Piers were too stunned, and Bess was worried in case this apparition would turn Piers against her; in some curious way she felt this might happen.

"He is a bit tight, isn't he? But he'll probably recover in an hour or two."

Rachel could not bring herself to such a mild acceptance of the situation: "My opinion is that this is all a practical joke," she said firmly. Then, seeing the disbelieving faces, she added: "Still, boys will be boys."

"Adrian can hardly qualify for that, Aunt Rachel. He must be nearly fifty." Bess surprised herself by such a contradiction.

"My children will always be children to me. Adrian is young in heart. In that respect we are alike." Rachel hoped that Bess was not going to become high-spirited.

"Bess is absolutely right, Rachel darling. And you know it," Piers said.

Bess's eyes expressed her gratitude at this unexpected championing of her cause. Perhaps he did care for her, after all? She was not so very much older, and she would feel younger, look younger, away from this house. Already in her mind they were married, but her imagination baulked at the reconstruction of their everyday living. How could she think of Piers coming down every morning to a breakfast which she had prepared? How could she see him, neat and business-like, reading the morning papers before giving her a husbandly kiss of farewell and going off to his daily work? Could she chain him to this routine six days out of every week? No, he and such an orderly existence would fall out almost before they had met. Piers was at home in ugly rooms, filled with books and papers, where he could sit and work all night and sleep half the day, waking in time to begin all over again. She sighed. Her face was blurred by the irreconcilement of these images.

"Day-dreaming?" Rachel cackled harshly. Adrian was beyond all hope, but at least Bess could be tormented in his stead. Just because a boy—for, after all, what was Piers but a boy?—who had nothing better to do kissed her now and again! At Bess's startled expression, Rachel attacked openly: "We know all about it—oh yes, we do. You needn't think that we are all blind. Love's young dream!"

Piers jumped up, his face dark, anger-filled. "I can't stand any more of this. I'm going out. What about you, Thomas?" Piers was not sure whether he was referring to Adrian or to Rachel's words.

"All right. I'll come with you," said Thomas. Surely, he thought, you are not going to leave Bess here to be sucked by that old vampire? Poor kid! She does ask for it, though. Why must she appear so vulnerable? He saw Bess's white face, and said kindly, "Why don't you join us, Bess? Do you good."

"I don't know—I mean—that is——" Bess stammered, refraining from glancing towards Piers.

"Oh, come if you want to," Piers said roughly. "Shall we all go?" He looked enquiringly at Marion and Kate, who were hesitating.

Within a few minutes they had gone out, and Rachel was left alone in the room. One of them might have stayed to talk to me, she thought. When one is old, one is treated like a child. But a child knows that childhood won't go on for ever. Now I am old I cannot grow backwards. So I shall always be treated like this. She cried a little. Adrian, too, whom she had counted on to be a comfort, her especial ally. It was too much to bear. She gulped, self-pity filling her eyes with tears. If only Jonah had lived—her dear, handsome, clever Jonah. He would have protected her from such cruelty. A woman with a husband cannot be relegated to a second childhood, but the status of a widow is different. A widow is more alone in the world, she thought, than a woman who has never married. Because when one expects to live alone one becomes self-sufficient, but getting used to a husband and then being without one, and at her age, that is worse than anything.

They walked out into the slate-blue winter afternoon. One or two lights could already be seen in the village below. At first they kept together, a line of five wavering people, uncertain, when they reached the crossroads, whether to walk along the village street or to turn towards the sea.

Although the air was colder than it had been earlier in the day, the sky shone with a promise of warmer hours. The grey, egg-shaped clouds edged with fire rested still against their darkening background. The disappearing sun looked new-minted, over-bright.

Piers swung round towards the sea, and Marion followed him, not because she wanted to be with Piers, but because she particularly disliked the sharp flatness of the undercliff road and believed in choosing the harder way.

Bess would have trotted after them had not Thomas, who was determined that Bess should be prevented from following sheep-like after Piers, taken her arm and pulled her in the opposite direction, up the narrow village street.

There was a shuttered desolation about the village, usually so busy, now silent, the shops closed.

"See you later," Thomas called over his shoulder, in casual discouragement.

Kate, who had lagged a few steps behind, stood for a second or two wondering which way she should go. Thomas and Bess obviously did not want her, and although Piers looked back to wave, the sea-front was too large, too overpowering for her liking, fit only for a summer's day.

She was worried, too, about Rachel. Perhaps one of them should have stayed with her. Would Mrs. Page be there to prepare the tea? What a tyrannical woman Rachel was! Worse and worse as she became older. But it might not be entirely her fault: there is no domination unless there are obedient people.

Slowly Kate turned back along the road she had come. She let herself into the house by the garden door, and found Rachel dozing with an expression of discontent: as if even in her sleep people were thwarting her, getting the better of her, refusing to be intimidated, and then slipping off before she had had a chance to tell them to go.

Kate moved softly, trying not to awaken the sleeper. Rachel opened her fine dark eyes, pulled herself upright in her chair, pretending that she had not slept.

"I was just having a nice quiet think," she said. "As soon as I begin to think, I am interrupted."

Kate laughed good-temperedly. "It was too cold for me, so I came back to talk to you."

Rachel was pleased. "That's a good girl. Sensible, too. They'll all come home sneezing and shivering and expect us to fuss around them. Which way did they go?"

"Two by two. I was odd man out."

"Which two?"

Kate told her.

"Ah, that's just as well. Thomas will talk a little sense into Bess's romantic head, and Piers's nonsense will brighten Marion up."

What a wonderfully simple solution, thought Kate.

"Now that you and I are here together, Aunt Rachel, tell me why you are so bitchy to Bess."

"Kate! What are you saying?"

"Bitchy was the word," Kate said gently.

Suddenly Rachel laughed, rocking to and fro. "Have it your own way."

"You make fun of her whenever you can, and that is pretty often. You're doing your best to make Piers hate her, and altogether you are making her life hell." Kate thought that this was the best she could do, although not at all what she wanted to say: too crude, too easily refutable.

"The whole thing is most unsuitable," Rachel said primly. "Piers is a mere boy, almost a child, and Bess is a middle-aged woman."

"If you can call Adrian a child, Bess is certainly not middle-aged," Kate said angrily; "and, anyway, Piers is no child—why, he must be about twenty-five."

"He isn't as old as that." Rachel was sullen.

"The point is that you don't care a damn about their ages;

you just want to keep Bess to yourself, so that she will stay here with you."

"I have lived many more years than you have. You may be clever, but I understand people. Piers may have thought that he was attracted to Bess—although the very idea is beyond my comprehension. But you know as well as I do that it wouldn't work out. Nothing would come of it. Nothing."

"I don't deny that——" Kate began, but Rachel interrupted her.

"And Bess would be very, very miserable. What should I do with her, just the two of us alone in this house? Better to nip it in the bud."

"Bess's feeling for Piers is stronger than you think. I am sure of that. Bess will be unhappy either way. So she might just as well exhaust herself emotionally on Piers as stagnate here and feel nothing at all."

"Her life here is exceptionally comfortable and she has many varied interests." Rachel was hurt by the implication that her behaviour towards Bess was motivated by selfish designs. "A lot of rubbish, too, all this falling in love," she said. A little less of that, she thought, would make the world a better place. "Not only a waste of time and energy, but it's useless. Never lasts."

Kate sat silently. That was true, it did not last. But one soon learned to accept the impermanence.

"You can't tell me that it goes on for ever, this being in love, and all the rest of it!" Rachel was truculent.

"What does that signify? Personally I don't want such a

turbulent state to go on for ever. It's fun, but I am always glad when it is over."

"What did I tell you? Everybody rushing about, killing each other, committing suicide—oh yes, they do, you needn't smirk—upsetting their families, turning everything upside down; and what for? To catch at something which will be gone before they know it, and which they won't want when they do get it." Rachel spoke in the manner of one who has finally summed up.

"Can't you remember what it was like?" Kate asked tactlessly.

"I was married when I was eighteen. So naturally I have had my little peccadillos—nothing serious, of course—but I was very beautiful, or so I was told. I have certainly never created the chaos that people do nowadays. Not that I have not had provocation, and plenty of opportunities. Mine has been a hard life, but I've made the best of it."

"Why won't you let Bess make the best of her life? Or even the worst?" Kate asked.

"Because she is a little ninny," Rachel said impatiently, "who couldn't be trusted to drive a goose to market. As long as she stays under my roof I shall reserve the right to act as I think fit for her own good."

"But where else could she go?" Kate asked hopelessly.

"Don't be silly, dear. She could live anywhere she fancied."

"It is not easy to find anywhere to live at all."

"Bess should have thought of that before, and made her plans accordingly." Then Rachel thrust with a swift counter-attack. "Perhaps you'd like Bess to come and live with you?"

"No, I wouldn't." Kate was shocked into betraying her dismay. "My flat is far too small. She'd be in the way."

"There! Now you'll realise what I have done for Bess. I've given her a home, and that's more than most people would. Even those who are kind enough to interest themselves in her welfare," Rachel said emphatically. "Bess must cut her coat according to her cloth." With this meaningless finality, Rachel shut her eyes and appeared to doze again.

Kate went into the kitchen, where Mrs. Page was preparing the tea-trolley.

"The others are still out. Perhaps we had better have tea, and not wait for them?" Kate asked.

"Whatever suits, Miss." Mrs. Page cast off any responsibility.

"I am sure they won't be long."

"Just as you like." Mrs. Page was not interested.

"And we will all come out and help with the washing-up after dinner. Then you'll get away at your usual time."

"Oh, no. Thank you all the same. I've had some of that, and I don't want any more. When the washing-up is finished, what happens? Why, you're tired, fit to drop, after all that work. So what do you fancy? A nice cup of tea and a snack. So you start making tea and cutting sandwiches, and then there's another lot of washing-up. No, thank you."

What a puking, puling household, Kate thought, as she climbed the stairs. She rapped sharply on Adrian's door.

After a few seconds a muffled voice called out:

"Ongtray!"

Kate sniffed as she entered the bedroom. There was a smell that she could not recognise. Whisky? No. Neither was it gin nor brandy. She looked curiously at the large-faced man who lay on the bed staring vacantly at the ceiling, not even letting his eyes follow her advancement. She sat on the edge of his bed, where the spirituous smell was strongest, hoping to discover what it was. He must have spilt some, she thought.

"K-k-k-Katie. Fancy coming to see if yer old nunky wants anything? I could do with a cuppa tea."

"It will be ready in five minutes. You'd better come downstairs. What have you been drinking?"

"Just a nip of the Water of Life. Have some?"

Kate shook her head, and afterwards accepted the silver flask. The liquid had a hot, yet bitter taste. She handed the flask back to him, saying, "You'd better wash and pull yourself together before tea." Guiltily she wondered if she herself would not be infinitely happier if she were not pulled together, and if she had a flask filled with the Water of Life? Certainly a drop more of that would liven up the household.

"Quite the little madam!"

"What have you come back for?" Kate laughed. She did not intend to, but the sight of Adrian's large face, like an outsize egg, was so absurd that suddenly she felt her irritation tempered by fondness.

"Wot a poser! wot a poser!" He looked at her in pretended reproof, wagging a thick, admonishing forefinger. "Why, ter see me dee-ar Mother."

"You've struck unlucky. She hasn't much to spare nowadays."

"My ambitions are very modest," Adrian said primly, in accents that were his own, yet remained false and affected. "I aim to set up for myself. Nothing pretentious. Just a little business. Something of an advisory capacity with plenty of scope. Ask Adrian to Aid you in Your Problems—along those lines."

"I don't think we can afford you."

"Better think again. I'm staying."

"We shall see about that—after Christmas. Get up now—that is, if you want any tea," Kate said as she left the room.

Stiffly he began to move, feeling the cold air of the room against his aching body. He remembered the heat of the sun that he had left, and the light on the waters of the lake. Remembered how warm the Adriatic could be; the sand that burned his feet. Remembered how the country had flattened with each mile that had dragged him away from the heat to the dreary docks, to the boat that had brought him across the Channel. Remembered the waiter's cold contempt at being addressed as "me boyo".

"It's hard cheese," he rehearsed softly as he bathed his face with cold water, "to be called back to England at me age. Not getting any younger, don'cher know? Italy is me home, don'cher know? Shall never cease to regret it. But me poor old Mater's gettin' on, and I'd never forgive meself if. . ." He looked closely at his face in the mirror, then stepped back a few paces to regard the effect of a swinging gesture as a fitting end to the sentence. To whom could he say all this? Living here was going to be bloody, and no mistake.

He straightened himself, licked his finger, tweaked a lock of hair that hung over his forehead, and tripped downstairs singing *Valencia*.

There he found Rachel sitting in her usual chair, looking rather cross. She was stabbing ineffectually at a large, unwholesome piece of canvas which she had pulled out from her workbox. This was her tapestry work, which she produced occasionally when she felt that the backward and forward thrust of the needle would be soothing. Not that it was, because after each interval she discovered that moths had eaten farther into the pattern: when they kept within the background she did not greatly care, but to lose first a piece of a peacock's tail, next the stem of a rose, was most upsetting.

What was it that Kate had asked her? Whether she remembered what it was like to be young, or some such nonsense. What Rachel could not tell these insipid young people if she chose! But she had not given in. Or had she left a piece of her life unfinished?

Rachel looked up at Adrian. She supposed that the nasty, humming whine he was making was his idea of singing.

Kate's words had brought back to Rachel a year that she wanted both to retrieve and to forget—a year when she was in Copenhagen, when she had everything: beauty, admiration, a husband who was handsome enough, a new city before her, a new air to breathe; new streets leading to unknown gardens, to gay restaurants, to cafés by the water's edge, to statues that were there only for her to look at. There had been no end to the joys, all new, and all hers.

"I hope you are feeling better now?" Rachel asked Adrian. Her tone was that of a polite stranger; for, being a young woman, how could she have a son who was middle-aged?

Copenhagen, she thought to herself, with conscious melodrama, was the traitor. Copenhagen nourished the serpent that ate into the flesh of Rachel's self-satisfaction. For to her the city meant only one man. His name was Miles. His features had become blurred in her mind almost before he had gone from her sight. She concentrated on remembering him. Yes, he had been short rather than tall. She could see a small-sized, square figure. Not fragile. His head was oddly shaped: a wide forehead; heavy cheek-bones cutting down to a pointed chin. Eyes that were red as a fox's; a mouth too wide, too delicate for the rest of his face. An ugly face? Yes, she admitted to herself, except for the peculiar quality of goodness that had settled over the features, so that whether he laughed, or teased, or disregarded her, the goodness remained, as if his human emotions were thinly covered by a skin of purity. She could not have altered him. She had made no difference to his life. When she arrived in Copenhagen he was there, and there he remained, serene and undisturbed, when she left. Yet, was it purity, when he himself was incorruptible, and yet he had corrupted her by his ideas? That was not good; it was cruel.

"I said, Mother," Adrian repeated, "I feel as right as rain."

"I am very glad to hear it. I am not deaf." Rachel, unaware that she had been spoken to several times, regarded the present moment with displeasure.

And yet, thought Rachel, pushing Adrian and Kate's entry with the tea-tray out of sight, Miles was no mysterious being. Merely the younger brother of the manager of the Copenhagen office, who had been asked to look after Rachel and to keep her amused while Jonah, her husband, was occupied by business affairs.

Miles spoke English well, but without ease and slowly, as from disuse. Either his Mother or his father was English, but Rachel could not recall which: factually she knew so little about him. Day after day they had spent together. He had asked interminable questions, and always he had smiled at Rachel's replies, and when he smiled his eyes became thin, bright lines. Neither before nor since had Rachel been treated with such heedless ridicule.

"Yes, dear"—Rachel spoke to Kate—"you pour out, will you?" Then added, to explain her preoccupation: "I have just got to a very difficult bit, and I must go carefully." Rachel held up the moth-eaten canvas.

Adrian opened his mouth preparatory to speaking, then thought better of it. How many years was it since he had seen his Mother? And now that he was home, she had got to a very difficult bit.

If I told them about Miles? thought Rachel. Sometime, perhaps—not yet. All she had left was his name, and if she spoke of him—Miles, Miles, she tried the word out in her mind—she would have nothing. Had his eyes ever looked lovingly upon her? No. She could see them, obstinate, flatly red and brown. Perhaps he had not dared? She had been, after all, a young married woman accompanied by her husband. Not dare? With those fox's eyes? If thinking could have brought him to England, kept him by her side, he would never have left her.

Suddenly Rachel felt exhausted: this was all Kate's doing. "I'll have a piece of cake. Yes, that piece with the icing." Seeing that Adrian was preparing to totter across to her, carrying the Christmas cake on the heavy silver dish, Rachel added impatiently: "No, no. Just put it on my plate."

Rachel nibbled at the icing. The cake wasn't as good this year as last. Not rich enough. She must speak to Bess about it. How had Miles, she wondered—that small, unremark-able man—how had he, without a word of personal regard, made her life ragged, sent her back to England unsure of herself, uncertain of Jonah, wanting to live two different lives at one and the same time? And Jonah? Why had he remained placid and unnoticing? Jonah's attitude had renewed Rachel's fretfulness. For her secret preoccupation with Miles was a pride as well as a sorrow. And she would have been pleased if her secret had been discovered. All Jonah had said was that he hoped she had not been too bored: and "that little chap—Miles didn't you call him?— wasn't a bad little fellow. Worshipped you. I could see that."

Even now Rachel could blush at the thought that she had written to Miles: a clever, careful letter, thanking him for looking after her. A letter that conveyed her unhappy affection. A letter of vague, unfinished sentences, of words that were not too thoroughly crossed out. The letter of a virtuous woman whose sense of decorum only just held her passions in check.

"Aren't you going to give me some more tea?" Rachel imagined that she was being neglected, kept waiting, remembering how, all those years ago, she had waited for the longed-for letter from Miles. She had lost her temper and accused the postman of carelessness; accused Jonah of picking up her letters with his own; suspected the charwoman of deliberate malice, and the frightened young maidservant of criminal deception. After several weeks Jonah remarked with unforgivable nonchalance: "Forgot to tell you. Had a charming letter from Miles. Delighted to hear from you. Quite delighted."

Rachel had refused to return to Copenhagen. Even years later she would make excuses for not going back. For, once there, she would find Miles: and she would never leave him. There would be no question of whether he loved her. She would stay regardless of his wishes. And what would have happened to her? For when she knew him, Miles had had hardly enough money to live on, and, worse still, he had lacked ambition. So she would have been a penniless woman in a foreign country. She had cried whenever she had thought of it.

After this decision Rachel had set her heart upon finding another more pliant Miles in England. There had been many candidates, for not only was she beautiful, but her husband appeared disinterested and was moderately well off. One by one came, smiled, talked to her, kissed her and borrowed a few pounds. None of them qualified.

And now, at last, she thought, she was left with Piers, the only young man in her elderly world. She had made up her mind that Piers should remind her of Miles, refusing to admit that Piers was a poor substitute. He should not escape. And surely day by day he resembled Miles more and more? Why in a few years' time Piers would be the same age as Miles had been all those summers ago. By then, she assured herself, she would hardly be able to tell them apart—the Miles of her mind and the Piers of her old age. Piers was taller, of course: his eyes were unfortunately black, lacking the essential reddish lights. His face was weaker, but later generations breed less prominent bone-structures.

Rachel put down her tapestry.

"Pull the curtains, dear," she said to Adrian. "It's nearly dark." Then she turned to Kate: "The tea will be quite cold. I don't know why they want to go traipsing about in this weather, especially at this time of the day." She picked up her tapestry, and handed it to Kate, saying: "Put that away for me, will you? The moths have been at it." She looked around her, but there was nothing to hold her interest.

"Haven't you anything to say?" Rachel asked teasingly. "What a silent couple! Tea-time is meant for talking. And you, Adrian, should have a lot to tell me, after all these years." Rachel waited, ready to be amused.

Bess and Thomas sat in a tea-shop facing the village green. The café was called *The Prince's Parlour*, and was famous not only because the waitresses were dressed as Dick

Whittingtons, but because it was extortionately expensive, and was lit by large, perilously placed candles, so that it was very dark.

As they ate slabs of dough that could be pulled and stretched into any shape, but defied cutting, Thomas said:

"What do you really like?"

"Being left alone," Bess replied unhesitatingly.

"Does that mean you wish I wasn't here?"

She shook her head. "No. In my mind. I prefer not to have to feel or worry about people."

"That is impossible."

"Yes, I know. But you asked me."

"You can't pretend that it is not an effort for you to concentrate on me. I don't believe you have stopped thinking about Piers—not for one second."

"I'm sorry."

"It beats me what you see in him."

Bess looked bewildered. This belittling of Piers was a conspiracy. For how could anyone fail to realise his charm, his enchantment? Every movement found her heart. The way in which he walked, even when he walked past her, stayed in her mind's eye. He was Piers and she was Bess, and nothing could be explained.

Thomas looked at her gloomily. He saw her eyes darken. He wondered whether it was worth it, trying to help others. She's just a soft little fool, he thought, yearning over that lout, that bad-tempered, flashy fellow. Amazing how women can be so taken in. She'll grow out of it, and nothing can hasten the process. What does it matter whether she needs days, or weeks, or even years? Even supposing I could dig her out of this, she'd only fling herself into another mess. He saw that Bess was looking at him with apprehension, wondering whether his was the hand that would strike her.

"You must try not to look frightened," he said kindly; "it's enough to make anyone treat you badly. You do ask for it."

"So you think that Piers treats me badly?"

"It's pretty apparent, you know."

"That is an act put on for your benefit. He's quite, quite different when we are alone. You ought to see his letters——"

Can't she realise, he thought, that whatever Piers has said, he is finished now, longing to be quit of her?

"If you held Piers there," said Thomas, taking and curving Bess's hand so that the palm was a small hollow which he touched, "you would not want him."

"Oh, what's the good of your talking like that! I cannot force myself to believe what is unrelated to my present senses!"

"What do you think of Marion?" Thomas asked abruptly.

"In what way?" asked Bess. She was confused by this sudden breaking off. What had she to do with such a question, shrouded as she was in herself, careless of what happened outside her repetitive thoughts?

"Generally," Thomas said, feeling disloyal, yet telling himself that he must make her realise that Piers had not eaten into all their lives.

"She is very efficient, very masterful," Bess said

reluctantly, visualising Piers being cut off from herself, taken away by Marion.

"Kate asked me why I married Marion," said Thomas.

"Did she? What an extraordinary thing to say!" Bess was shocked by this exposure. For although she did not like Marion, Bess would fight against the undermining of the solidarity of two who were joined in the sight of God. She could always imagine herself as Piers's wife. Supposing someone asked Piers such a question? Might he not begin to wonder why he had married Bess? Even though he had previously been content with his choice? A dreadful doubt to place before any man.

"And what did you reply?" Bess asked anxiously, telling herself that she would accept Thomas's answer as a sign that Piers would, in a similar position, answer likewise. Bess often played such agitating games.

"I said that I married her because I was fond of her. As I still am fond of her," said Thomas.

His mind shied away from the word "love," although he had used it when speaking to Kate. But to Bess the word could convey only the mawkishness she now suffered. Fond was, too, the more apt word, implying a detached attention that matched Marion's plump cheek, over which the skin stretched so that his kiss was thrown back at him. How unlovable Marion had become! Marion in the mornings, dressing with the relentless urgency of a fabricated monster regulated to certain movements; Marion eating her breakfast with precision—just so many tablespoonsful of cereal, the same number of slices of toast, three cups of tea: sufficient to sustain her until luncheon, but not enough to give her either indigestion or the burden of lethargy. Such planned perfection encouraged Thomas to be more slapdash and slothful than his nature willed, feeling as he did that life is made tolerable by incalculable possibilities, and as Marion's mechanism did not admit of anything outside her routine, Thomas threw away all rules and rotas to effect a balance.

Even Marion's spare time was divided into hours of studious self-betterment. She was a member of a local society that aimed to teach hard-working adults snippets of information that they would have felt freer without. Marion was often worried because the salient points of a lecture, such as the one on the Civilisation of Ancient Greece, had gone from her mind, effaced by the Minutes of the last week's Board Meeting. Years ago she had complained to Thomas about these lapses:

"My dear girl," he had said, "give up sweating in that office. We'll both take a long holiday. Go away for two or three months; damn what comes after. We'll go to Greece, we'll go everywhere, see as much as possible. Do you more good than all the evening institutes. And you won't be able to forget any of it."

"That would be very nice. Later, perhaps. We couldn't afford it yet." Marion had tried to hide her exasperation.

"Please don't dismiss the whole idea." Thomas had felt an urgency alien to him, knowing that this might be the only solution, the apparent madness, founded on sanity. "I could arrange a mortgage on the house. Get as much as we can, so that I can take a few weeks afterwards to look around—if my job isn't kept open for me." He had slurred the words, making himself say them in spite of Marion's obvious disgust.

"A fine scheme! I suppose I shall have to keep both of us while you 'look around', as you so tactfully put it." She had known that Thomas had meant nothing of the kind, but her insinuations came from her horror of such a project. She had been terrified in case, once having suggested itself, this profligate plan should end in Thomas throwing off the safety garment of yearly routine with which she had carefully cloaked him. The idea of mortgaging the house, the complete possession of which was her constant pride, had been unthinkable. If they could have afforded such a holiday without any sacrificial offering, Marion would still have suspected that if Thomas saw too much of other less-disciplined countries, where feckless people, so she had heard, lolled about in the heat of the day, untroubled either by obligations of conscience or fact, he would not easily be persuaded to return to his normal life.

Thomas remembered that instead of answering her he had swung out of the house, striding along a path bordered by beds of geraniums, through a wooden gate into the neighbourhood of neat suburban houses, daintily arranged in circles and triangles around open grass plots, making pretty patterns for the lives of easy-going, conforming people: one had to conform, there was no room for violence.

Marion had been surprised to see him go. She was sorry

that she had hurt him. But she had not feared his continued absence. He would come back.

Sitting in the small, dark tea-shop, drinking tea, he thought of how he had walked on that day: miles across London, until he had reached Hampstead Village, and from thence to the gravelled path leading to the grasslands of the Heath, sparsely tree-set, crowned by one small wood, broken by chill, flat ponds.

How silent it had been on that winter's day! For by the time he had reached the first pond the afternoon had nearly gone from the sky, and the glitter of the evening star and the soft, thin rind of the moon were already reflected in the waters. One or two women called to their dogs, but most of the walkers of the neighbourhood were indoors. Those few who were still out hurried towards their homes, to hide away from the evening that had crept upon them unawares.

He had kept in mind, so as not to walk too aimlessly (for that Marion abhorred), that he should climb to the highest point of the Heath, from where one could look across at the chimneys of Highgate Village. An engraver's scene, coldly beautiful. But the evening had been quick in taking over from the day, and the darkness had soon masked even the nearest clump of trees. He had been robbed of all purpose, and he had not known what to do with himself in that far-off place. Too dark, he had thought: dark, darkling, Keats listening to a nightingale, and the roads leading into and about Keats Grove. Of course! Happily he had turned towards a friendly welcome. Eugene lived here, one minute away. Eugene, whom Thomas had not seen for years; Eugene, whom Marion distrusted because of his ability to exist without providing for the future—or for the present.

Thomas remembered finding the small house squashed thinly between more imposing ones; remembered walking up the narrow stone path, noticing that a light shone from a back room. He rang the bell, but heard no sound. The bell must be out of order. He found the knocker, which left a surface of gritty rust upon his palm. Heavily unwilling steps came towards him.

As the door was slowly drawn back, Thomas saw the figure of a tall, plump man in a dressing-gown, tied round the waist with a piece of rope. In one hand the man held a thick slice of bread out of which a bite had been taken.

Self-consciously Thomas announced himself to Eugene, for this large, unhappy-faced man, although at first unrecognisable, was Eugene. In spite of Eugene's altered appearance, he welcomed Thomas as of old, with generous heartiness, as if such a visit was the most welcome interlude in his otherwise dreary life.

"I do hope"—Thomas was conscious of the dressing-gown—"that I have not made you get out of bed. You're not ill, are you?"

"Why, bless us, no," said Eugene. "I like to feel comfortable, that is all."

Thomas followed his host along a passage to a small room overlooking the garden. Thomas glanced around him, and immediately realised that this room could hardly be called untidy, for that would be judging it by inapplicable standards. This was no room: rather it was the nest of some giant man-magpie who had snatched at everything that he wanted and thrown the resultant heap into a small space bounded by four walls. Quite impossible to see what was there. Thomas had an impression of books, papers, fire-irons, unwashed cups—but no saucers—opened pots of jam, a soap-dish, more papers and books, a lot of paint-brushes of different sizes stuck in an empty jam-jar, a piece of crimson velvet lying with an air of rich abandon on the floor. The air smelt of turpentine. On the crimson velvet was a woman's hat, a hat fit only for such occasions as meeting Mr. Wilde, made as it was from tiers of yellowed lace, over which curled a sweeping plume of purple-pink feathers; by the side of the hat were some screwed-up pieces of paper, the stub of a cheque-book and a blue-print.

Thomas walked towards the velvet and leaned over it with a fascinated, almost hypnotised expression.

"You won't touch anything, will you?" Eugene said anxiously. On being reassured, he explained, "It's for my next still life. Took me months to work out the exact symbols."

Suddenly Thomas felt very lonely; not only wifeless, homeless, as he was, but lacking even the consolation of a symbolic refuge. He looked away from the objects on the floor, and saw on the wall opposite him a sight of magnificent absurdity. An enormous picture in oils; a riot of fruit, as if oranges, pears, apples, cherries, plums, tomatoes, had been tossed into the frame. The picture was slashed from corner to corner, and there, in the very centre, proclaiming responsibility for this vandalism, was the point of a sword that protruded more than an inch from the canvas.

"What do you think of that?" Eugene's voice was full of pride.

Thomas said nothing.

"I know. I know. Affects most people that way. Terrific, isn't it?"

"Has it got a name? I mean a title?" Thomas asked dubiously, hoping that this would guide him.

"I call it *Miching Mallecho,* because it means mischief," Eugene said, and, far from looking unhappy, as had been Thomas's first impression, his face was that of a man who had won through.

The rest of the evening Thomas could not clearly remember, except that other people had come in, making the room's disarray more confused.

Thomas had been battered about from one conversation to another: unacceptable opinions were forced on him, and his beliefs derided.

Courteously he said his farewells, although nobody listened. As he walked away from the house, down the hill, citywards, he saw himself as a man who had lived securely, protected by the ferocity of Marion's convictions. While enjoying his immunity from attack, he had convinced himself of his exceptional capacity for living fully, freely, if he had had the chance. Now he knew that he was either too old or temperamentally incapable of being anything except Marion's husband.

Obedient to the controlling power of his weakness,

he returned home. The following summer they went to Denmark, which Thomas had found very flat.

"What about your inattention?" Bess asked, cutting across Thomas's re-living of the incidents which shadowed his self-confidence.

"That was awfully rude of me." Thomas summoned a quality of youthful charm which nowadays his voice seldom possessed. "But one is apt to take advantage of a restful person like you."

Bess was appeased, not wholly believing, but basking in his words.

"Shall we walk home by way of the front? We might meet the others." Thomas was anxious to please her.

Meanwhile Marion and Piers had walked very quickly along the undercliff road, not discouraged by the spray, as the foaming sea, nearing high-tide, occasionally beat against the promenade or breakwaters, to fling a wave skywards, to fall in large drops upon their heads and shoulders.

Marion battled on, looking, with her wet fringe, not unlike a stocky terrier. Piers walked swiftly, not because he cared for such wild weather, but because Marion was evidently determined to reach a certain landmark before turning back, and the sooner it was over the better. He wished, too, to present himself as an ordinarily sporting, robust young man, and as such he supposed that he would enjoy being thrown about by beating spray. There was no particular reason why he should choose to ingratiate himself with Marion, but there was no knowing when an ally might be useful. As she was proud of her straightforward outlook, she would easily accept what he pretended to be for what he was.

"Sure you aren't getting too wet?" he asked in his role of masculine protector.

"Nonsense! I love it. Can't be too rough for me!" Marion replied heartily.

"What superb energy!" Piers said admiringly. Tireless as a horse, he thought fastidiously. What women are bred nowadays! This puffing fool, who makes everything into a marathon; Kate, sharp-tongued and unsympathetic; Bess, who has no idea of how to clothe her mind or her body. All those soft, swishing materials.

"What are you thinking?" Marion's question was a friendly bark.

Of all questions, this was the one he most resented.

"About Bess. Why does she dress so unsuitably?" He could see her as she should be, tall and slim in tweeds (expensive ones, of course), but when he turned his attention to the face, it was not Bess at all, but a woman with harder features and predatory eyes.

"Some man once made fun of her," said Marion—"told her she looked like a hockey-girl. Ever since then she dresses herself up for a garden-party."

They sniggered, for once in accord.

Marion slackened her pace to turn to the right and to climb a flight of steps steeply cut out of the cliff. Piers, much relieved, followed her. This showed him that they were to return by the grass-covered path of the downs, and would at least be out of reach of the waves.

"What do you think of your Uncle Adrian?" Marion's voice was strident, demanding, determined neither to spare herself nor her companion.

Piers was shaken; he had carefully not thought of Adrian.

"Ashamed of him, aren't you?"

"If you must know, yes, I am." How could anyone fail to be, he thought, confronted by a vulgar old soak?

"No good having finer feelings, my boy. He's my brother, and I can't do anything about it. Hope he goes back soon. He will if I've any say in the matter."

Piers was not comforted, knowing that however much Marion might roar and bluster, she had in fact no say.

"Perhaps Thomas might have a word with Rachel? She'd probably listen to him," Piers suggested tactlessly.

"What? Thomas?" Marion discounted the idea of her husband being able to accomplish anything.

"He is quiet, and logical, too," Piers said, unaware of any danger. To advance his cause he added quickly, "To be frank, I do not like him, so I am quite unbiased with regard to his good qualities."

"Oh, so you don't like him? That's a nice thing! To tell me that you detest my husband!"

"I said nothing of the kind." Piers realised that he had gone too far. That is the worst of the whole lot of them, he thought: they can't be trusted for a minute; always one has to be on guard. "Merely that I did not very much like him."

"Impertinence! You know nothing about Thomas, and never will," Marion said with vicious formality. Thomas may be difficult at times, lethargic, uninterested; but how dare this puppy criticise a man twice his age? And, more-over, a man who is my husband?

Walking stiffly, angrily, they reached the cross-roads. Two figures could dimly be seen coming slowly along the village street. Marion peered until the figures came within the circle of a street lamp.

"That's them," she said, with splendid disregard of grammar. "We'll wait."

Piers wondered how long his symptoms of influenza would take.

"So there you are!" Marion said loudly as Thomas and Bess came nearer. She managed to convey that she had dis-covered them in a guilty secret.

Piers, humiliated by Marion, was ready to hurt someone else, for only in that way could he reinstate himself.

"We've been talking about Bess as a hockey-girl," he said.

"What do you mean?" Bess was unprepared for this greeting.

"Do you play hockey?" Thomas asked innocently.

"Of course I don't," Bess snapped.

"But you used to look as though you did. Don't you remember, dear?" Marion asked.

Bess blushed. "Let's go back, Thomas. It's so cold. Let's go back quickly." She spoke desperately, taking Thomas's arm and drawing him away from the others. The absurd incident did not trouble her, but she was sure now that Marion and Piers had been discussing her, sneering at her, making fun of her. That was why they had gone off together.

"It's all right, Bess. Nothing is the matter." Thomas spoke gently, feeling her arm tremble beneath his hand.

"And don't forget," Marion called after them, "that's my husband you're going off with!" She laughed boisterously, to show that this remark was almost a joke.

Rachel was supervising Kate, who was hanging the smaller presents on the Christmas tree. Adrian sat staring moonily, drearily, at the preparations for the festival of dinner.

"I don't think those lower branches are quite strong enough, dear," said Rachel.

What she wanted to say was very different—as different as all things were when she was young. She remembered herself as a girl, decorating such a tree; but she could hardly recall the sense of gladness she had then felt: a sense of all being well and certain. She had known with her mind, but never with her heart, that all must change. That her parents would die, that her husband might die, that her children would leave her, that she would lack even a sharp reminder of those days. Now she was too old even for tears. Besides, among all the wrongs she saw and knew of, which one should she choose to weep for? There were too many. Ah! that was the time, when one could say, "And next year I shall . . ." ; or "When Marion is ten we shall send her to. . ." ; or "When Jonah retires we shall live at . . ." Such plans were casually mentioned, because one knew that if next year and the year after continued their smilingly gentle ways (and why should they not?) one had a perfect right to plan for half a century ahead, always with the addition of the half-superstitious proviso, "if God should spare me."

Now, she thought fearfully, one had to reckon not with a righteous God, but with man: man, death-giving and dreadful. For she had planned to be a softly spoken, kind old woman. She had planned that her parents should live for ever. And why not, if she dare not consider otherwise? She had planned that her husband would grow more dear, more dependable, and that they should be together, linked by warm affection until . . . no, not until, for farther than that she had not forced herself to see. Now all her plans were gone, all dead as those others had died, without warning, without giving her time to begin anew. What is there to build? What is there to scheme for? Every day I hear of a future that will be darker, more terrible. My bones chill now, to think of what I have lived through. Now they talk of another war, of annihilation, of the wiping out of this world, which, however sadly altered, has some semblance of that earlier world. It is cruel, she thought, cruel that such things should be said, that they should come unbidden to the mind of a woman such as I am. Even her God had gone away: the God she understood, the God who pandered to her. Her life was full of terror, muted yet persistent. If these young people knew what she felt, if they knew, they would treat her considerately, would look after her, and, above all, would comfort her.

Irritably she said, "No, no, Kate! Don't put the lights over the top of the tree like that!"

What is the matter with her? Kate wondered. Rachel

used not to be quite so difficult: sometimes she had been gay, had sung half-forgotten songs, had liked the sound of a piano and would tap her feet to the tunes. Perhaps that is just what happens when one is old. Perhaps even a year can make all the difference. Will it to me? No. I shall always remember how it felt not to be old. But perhaps I shall not be able to. And I have nothing yet—have not even made up my mind what I would do if the choice were mine. Will there be time? Is there still time? Does it still matter?

Rachel sighed as she suddenly noticed that Kate did not look particularly happy. There is little fun, thought Rachel, even in being young today.

"That is very pretty, darling," Rachel said gently. "Come over here, and you'll see how lovely it looks."

Kate smiled, trying to forget her momentary panic. "Yes the tree is rather nice. What do you think, Adrian?" She tried to draw the three of them together, if only for an instant, so that they would be united against a future which was already eating them away.

"Fine," said Adrian abstractedly. He knew that he had shocked and upset his Mother, that everyone hated him, everyone was ashamed of him, however much Kate might pretend otherwise.

Rachel looked disapprovingly at her son: she might uphold him publicly, refusing to admit her deep disappointment, but she could not deceive herself. How differently she had imagined his homecoming!

"Tell me about your job, dear," she said, making believe

that she would regain the pleasure she had anticipated at having him home. "Your letters were not very informative."

"Which job?"

"Why, the last one. The one you're doing now. I do think that you might have been given leave before this."

"I haven't one now," Adrian said weakly, his jokes, his digs, all out of hearing, left as he was, a meek, unhealthy-looking little man.

"You're taking up a new position when you go back?" Rachel did not choose to understand.

"I'm not going back. I want to stay here. Italy's all right, but jobs aren't easy there. Fare is expensive, too."

"What do you plan to do over here?" Rachel asked, her thoughts muddled and uncertain. Supposing she gave him his fare? But how much over would he need? If he stayed here, could he be persuaded to work hard? To live frugally? But what could he do in this regimented country? Italy, she imagined, would put up with a great deal of nonsense that would not be tolerated here. And, so she had been told, very little work was, anyway, ever done on the Continent: there were always strikes, people marching with banners, which no doubt suited Adrian very well.

"My idea is to look around in the new year. Nothing will come along until well after Christmas. But by the end of January . . . or perhaps February would be better . . . ?" Adrian's voice trailed off.

"Well, well, we must have a long talk about everything." Rachel realised that the problem necessitated some hours of working out; if Adrian continued now, she might let herself be trapped into a careless phrase which he could snatch at and use for his own ends.

"Yes, we mustn't talk about serious matters until after the holiday," Kate said, understanding that Rachel needed time to weigh one disadvantage against another.

Adrian smiled. The difficult part was over. How could he be disregarded? Here he was penniless, and there was his Mother with enough to keep him. He had done his best: he had brought gifts for them all—beautiful Italian brooches, rings and bracelets, set with semi-precious stones. What more could be expected of him? Indeed, nothing more. They knew, he reminded himself—they knew all along that I should have to come back. If one of them, just one, had taken the trouble to think about me, even for five minutes, I could have been put right, I could have fitted in. No. They are either ashamed or amused. They push me away as a bad penny. None of them has tried to feel what it is like to be me. They pretend that I do not exist. I have to snatch a few words before someone comes in or before someone else goes out. But I got my piece in this time, he thought, as from the opened door, soon closed, blew a sharp, clean air, salt, reviving.

Thomas and Bess were the first to arrive.

"I hope you've had tea," Rachel said. She hoped that they had not, for that would be a minute revenge against their sudden departures.

"Yes, thanks," said Thomas.

"And where are the others?" asked Rachel.

"On their way," he replied.

"And did you have tea all together?"

"No, just Bess and I."

Rachel sniffed suspiciously. Gadding about in cafés on Christmas Day. Not only thoughtless, but faintly disreputable, especially as they might have enjoyed themselves.

"What can I do?" Bess was anxious to prove herself part of the usual pattern.

Before Rachel could allot some trifling unnecessary task to Bess, Kate interrupted: "Nothing at all. Go upstairs and get ready, so that I can use your bathroom later when I come up to change."

Bess smiled gratefully, and slithered upstairs with the air of one who expects to be recalled.

Marion hurled herself into the room. She looked storm-tossed, healthy and energetic. Piers was just behind her, pale and inclined to shiver.

"Good God, Mother!" said Marion. "Isn't tea ready yet?"

"Tea has been cleared away long ago." Rachel spoke with placid satisfaction. "I thought you had tea together. The four of you."

"Tea for two,
Burburbledee doo,"

sang Adrian, who was thrown back to his former self by Marion's presence.

"That will do, Adrian." Rachel's voice was cold. She spoilt the effect by adding vaguely, "We have had quite enough of that sort of thing." The young Adrian she had been able to control, no matter in what slum alley he had learnt his tricks, but this middle-aged man confounded her.

"Always one for a laugh, my dear old Mother is," Adrian said loudly, treating Rachel as though she were in her dotage, hinting at affectionate contempt for them all.

"Ter-hee for ter-hoo,"

he sang in a high falsetto, afterwards screaming with laughter at Marion's outraged expression.

"Rachel, darling, it's a bit thick," Piers began, and then was furious with himself for using such a schoolboy phrase.

"And what do you consider you have to complain about, young man?" snapped Rachel, provoked to the extent of attacking her handsome nephew.

"I am cold. Perhaps we could have one cup of tea each, darling?" His voice coaxed.

"I'll go and make you some," Kate said.

"Don't bother, I'll do it," Piers replied: "By the way, where did you get to? We missed you."

"I came back."

Piers smiled fondly on her. Why, he wondered, had he not stayed with Kate? He moved towards the kitchen door.

Kate stopped him, saying: "I'd rather make the tea, if you don't mind. Mrs. Page is a bit touchy today."

"All right." Touchy? he thought. No wonder. This is the kind of place to drive everybody mad.

As quickly, as unobtrusively as possible, Kate prepared a tea-tray. This pandering was against Mrs. Page's principles;

she believed that those who chose to be absent from meals should go without.

"That's all, isn't it?" Kate asked placatingly, holding up the tray for Mrs. Page's approval.

"Yes. You've got everything. More than they deserve. More than he does, at any rate."

"Who?"

"Why, Mr. Piers. Not very pleasant, but I suppose it's just his way."

"I hope he hasn't made you lots of extra work?" Kate asked, wondering if Piers flung his things about the bedroom, or spilled ink on the carpets.

"Work!" Mrs. Page was contemptuous. "That's not the only thing. I can't stand trouble in the air. Never have been able to. There'll be a bust-up, mark my words. Sets me all on edge."

Kate put down the tray. What on earth is the woman getting at? "You'd better tell me, Mrs. Page; then we can try to put it right."

"We can't do anything, Miss." Mrs. Page's voice was thickly ominous, and, seeing that Kate was preparing to depart, casually to dismiss these prophecies, added, "Fer instance, Mrs. Marion and Mr. Thomas were going at it like boiling kettles."

Kate was startled by the simile: her mind pictured Thomas and Marion, their faces attached to the bodies of kettles, rushing at each other. She brought herself back to reality: "That is probably nothing—trifling differences between husbands and wives."

81

"Not like that!" Mrs. Page was triumphant. "Another thing. Miss Bess is getting that silly about Mr. Piers. Just you watch her. Don't admire her choice."

"There is no reason why they should not be fond of each other." Kate hoped to end the discussion.

"Cousins shouldn't feel that way," Mrs. Page said emphatically, implying that the family was already near enough to insanity. "What will Madam say when she finds out?" Mrs. Page produced Rachel.

"We shall see," Kate made one last ineffectual effort to prevail upon Mrs. Page not to confide in anyone else.

"That we shall see!" Mrs. Page agreed with greedy anticipation.

Kate left the tray in the sitting-room, thankful that she could go to her room and stay there until dinner-time.

After Kate had had a bath, brushed her hair, painted her lips and was happily reading and smoking with a whole hour to enjoy alone before she need go downstairs, she jumped at the sound of a gentle tap on the door.

At Kate's resigned invitation to enter, Bess sidled into the room.

"May I come and talk to you?" she asked urgently.

"Yes, I suppose so," Kate said ungraciously, staring at Bess's yellow crêpe-de-chine frock, badly cut, too large for her and, above all, the wrong colour.

"Would you like to try on a frock that I have brought with me? It's too small for me, so it might fit you perfectly."

Bess nodded. From where she sat on the end of the bed she could see the reflection of herself in the mirror, and even the dim lighting showed up her pallor, greenish-tinged against the yellow material. Her eyes stared dully back at her.

Obedient to Kate's instructions, Bess scrambled out of her frock and into another of soft wool, grey, severe. The folds of the dress accentuated Bess's thin figure, making her nun-like, contrasting with the deeply crimson lipstick with which she was prevailed upon to redden her mouth.

"That is much better," Kate said proudly to the tall, remote woman standing before her.

Bess was shocked, yet delighted. She allowed her hair to be pulled up from her shoulders and coiled high, Grecian-wise, at the back of her head. Her head felt heavy and uncomfortable, but she was happy.

"Will you keep the dress? Please. You look much nicer in it than I do."

"Thank you. I'd love to." Bess forgot for once that she must guard against being patronised and despised.

Kate took a bottle of sherry out of a cupboard and they sat by the electric fire, smoking and drinking.

"What do you want to talk to me about?" Kate asked.

Bess did not reply.

"Tell me now. That is why you came in here. Tell me now, and don't tell anyone again. Not even yourself."

Bess shook her head. "Not yet. There will be more to tell before all this is over, and I shall have to say it to you."

Kate looked at her curiously, thinking that Bess had more intelligence than she was credited with; more, perhaps, than she was permitted to show.

"Very well. Let us leave it for the moment."

"The worst of it all," said Bess, in angry remembrance, "is that Piers begins to talk to me and always we are interrupted, or he deliberately breaks off before he has really said anything."

"For God's sake," Kate said, "don't try to force him to any point."

You are right, of course, thought Bess. People like you never try to force anything. You shy away so that you are pursued and made to listen. In the end you get everything. Whereas I, who long to hear, am told only in the past tense.

After a second glass of sherry, Bess said: "I could understand if Piers had never loved me. That would have been natural, and I should have thought no more about it."

"Wouldn't you?" Kate tried to sound interested, tried to concentrate wholly on Bess's problem. From Adrian's room came a sound of banging and of drawers being opened, then shut again. Whatever Adrian hunted with such desperation he had evidently found, because soon there was silence, except for his voice singing happily for his own amusement *After the Ball was Over*.

"Very little more, anyway. But why should he have begun only to stop, and for no reason?"

"Reason has nothing to do with it," Kate said solemnly, as if from the experience of an old woman.

"He used to write such wonderful letters. He wrote first, too. I would not have dared." The sherry, the warmth of the scented room, herself sleek, new-born—all these combined to make Bess feel light, rootless, confidential and a little drunk.

"Letters!" Kate pounced triumphantly on the word.

"I have kept them." Bess was emphatic.

"I'm not doubting you. I am sure that you have dozens of them. Did you reply?"

"Of course I did. I wrote every evening for hours, absolutely all that I had done during the day, and exactly how I felt."

"You did?" Kate laughed softly.

"Yes. I spend my life writing. If I had not answered, I could have understood."

"You are wrong. If you had taken no notice, Piers would still be the same. Always, always remember not to say what you feel—if you are apt to feel too much." Kate thought herself remarkably clear-headed.

"That is not my nature," Bess admitted miserably.

"It had better be. That is, as long as your taste remains so deplorably low."

"I'm not ashamed of loving Piers."

"Set your cap at someone different, and you'll be able to behave naturally."

Bess sighed, thinking, You do not know the half of it. How can you see what this exhilaration was, what it was in its prime? How can you know the way in which we walked together when October was in the leaves, the sky, even in the very air? Not much more than a year ago. You were not there, so how could you notice Piers, whose eyes were black, bright, whose presence was all living creatures? You,

Bess thought, with your slick theories of how to get and when to discard. What do you know about me? How can you imagine me as I was then. So rich my life was for a few months that I could not consider a past that was bare and a time to come when my finery would be gone. Piers, serious-faced, telling me what his future would be. Not that he ever said 'we'; for him it was always 'I'. The pointed words that he once used to tell me that I could not now or ever become part of his plans, that the essence of his scheming was the carrying-through of his work alone. 'Oh no, Bess, oh no, my sweet. That wouldn't be your kind of life. No matter how you deceive yourself, for you it just would not do.' Gaily, as if this final dismissal was of no moment, he had continued to read, sure that although Bess was, as it were, under notice, she was still there. Well, she had lost, but better that than be a vulgar plotter like Kate.

Kate was conscious of Bess's regard, stern, disliking. "Let us have some more sherry before we go down. Then we can face them."

"No, thank you." Her voice was formal, her manner that of one who has been forced to recognise a chance acquaintance. She wanted to get away from the room as quickly as possible. "I must go now." She turned back from the door. "Thank you again for the dress. It is lovely."

Kate's astonishment appeared to hang about the room, so nearly tangible it became. How contradictory people are, she thought; friendly and relaxed, giving and demanding security, and all for no purpose, leading merely to an abrupt going away. She pitied herself that this should have happened today, plucking at the rawness of her nerves, making her remember what she had tried to forget. That she had had bad dreams. How childish the simplicity of thought. Yet how unchildlike the night had been. These conscious fantasies are not dreams; they come in that half-light of the mind when one's body lies heavily, unable to move, upon a familiar bed, and when one's eyes can see the details of the room. An ancient terror of death, of extinction and, above all, of an implacable fearfulness still to come, flows into one's blood, edges along one's bones. Now she was left to anticipate the idea of the quiet house and of herself alone, vulnerable to attack, before the time came.

Kate's face was palely set, her eyes widened, her hair fell flatly round her cheeks. It was the face of a woman who looked for a talisman to hold against the dark and dreadful hours.

There in the corner of the room stood the Christmas tree, frosted, present-hung, with lights twined in and out of the boughs. Silver charms dangled among the pointed leaves.

"After dinner, my dears," Rachel announced, "Adrian will be Father Christmas." She turned towards Bess. "You had better lead the way, because you look so splendid this evening. Not that such an unusual costume would be suitable for everyday wear. A trifle *outré* perhaps?"

"I chose that frock for Bess," said Kate. "I think it makes her look distinguished."

"Quite right," Thomas agreed, "and Bess will be herself when she looks as attractive as she does now."

Bess waited for Piers to speak, but he did not: although his stare might be admiration, not necessarily for Bess, but at least for Kate's cleverness.

"Personally I'm all for comfort," Marion said.

"We know that. Although how you can be at ease in a skirt which is far too tight, I can't imagine," Rachel said critically.

"With the years one broadens in mind and body." Thomas spoke carelessly, the first words that came to mind.

"In that case your scragginess denotes a static condition," Marion turned upon her husband.

"Here, here, old girl! steady, steady," Thomas said, with casual disregard.

"Could you refrain from talking to me as if I were a horse?"

Thomas looked blankly at her. That is my wife, he told himself—that square, hard woman lacking either intelligence of mind or flexibility of action. Only this morning I said that I loved her. That is what I said. For I had not considered the matter farther, accepting as a fact that what one used to feel automatically continues to be a present truth. But that is not so. Praise be to God and to man, who, given time, recovers; who, given time, throws away the ass's head. He bent down to give Marion a boisterous, unloving kiss. How fond he was of them all, of Marion, too, now that he had discovered his stupendous release.

Marion pretended playfully to push Thomas from her. Fancy! she thought, at his age. It is a proof that men respond to the influence of good, uncompromising women. If

Thomas had married a weak, doting girl he would by now have gone quite to pieces.

"That's my dear old boy," she said fondly.

Was it possible, Thomas wondered, that Marion had noticed nothing? He felt a dangerous breath of excitement, almost of intoxication, at the precariousness of his position: a breath that came from his stomach, rushing to his throat, threatening to force itself out in a burst of laughter. He put his hand quickly to his mouth, biting his forefinger in an unfamiliar gesture of repression. But he was unable to stop a grunt of amazed delight. Then he saw Kate's eyes upon him. Eyes that did not warn, neither did they enquire; but they watched, knowing, he was sure, that they looked at a different, wilder man. Her face, unemotional, interested to see what would happen next, stopped the crow of laughter. Not that he minded about Kate; but what she saw now, the others might recognise soon, and that he would rather put forward to another day.

Adrian swayed unsteadily around the table to reach the chair that his Mother tapped imperiously as a signal that everyone else was seated and they awaited him. To show his recognition of the importance of Christmas and his homecoming, he had changed into a suit of pale blue linen, obviously intended for the tropics.

Rachel regarded her son grimly. In what part of Italy, she wondered, could such outlandish clothing be the customary attire?

"Will you be warm enough?" she asked disapprovingly.

"Should say so," Adrian spoke carefully. Jolly fine effort. All those s's.

"What are you hissing for?" Rachel asked sharply.

"Was I? Must've bin talking out loud." Oh, definitely blurred, he reprimanded himself.

Rachel sighed gustily. Adrian had been out of her sight only for half an hour.

"Talking of glad rags." Adrian giggled and pretended to peer across at Bess. "What have we here?"

"I think Bess and Adrian make a fine pair. Fit for the circus ring." Marion was complacently contemptuous.

"You're so damned satisfied with yourself, aren't you?" Bess's voice was controlled. "Just as well, because you're past any improvement."

Marion flung down her table-napkin with dramatic effect.

"Mother! Either Bess apologises or I shall go. This very minute."

Rachel put her palm against her forehead—a delicate gesture of despair.

"I do beg of you to remember that this will most likely be the last Christmas that I shall see. Surely you can refrain from making me nervous and unhappy?"

"Mother, please." Marion spoke more quietly. Against her judgment, she was taking her Mother seriously.

"Well, darling, if it comes to that, it may be the last one for all of us," Kate said.

"Now, Kate, it's your turn to upset me!" Rachel quavered. "With the world as it is—that is all the more reason for us to live peaceably."

"Talk of war and ultimatums and crises becomes part of us," said Thomas, "and we bring these into our homes."

"Why should you complain, Aunt Rachel? You set us by the ears, and then sit back and say how difficult we are," said Bess.

"As for you, my girl, you are getting thoroughly above yourself. Dressed up like that! It goes to your head." Rachel fought well, snapping first at one, then at another, completely self-possessed.

Kate laughed in time to stem Bess's angry words.

"It seems to me——"Adrian began.

"You've been out of England so long that you cannot have anything of interest to say. You are quite out of touch." Marion was decisive.

"I'm staying here now, and I shall have plenty to say, and you'll listen." Adrian gulped claret.

"That will be something for us to look forward to," Piers sneered.

"You're all very fine, all very pleased with yourselves. Christ knows why. Sitting on your bloody behinds putting the world right, scratching at each other like a lot of cats."

There was a shocked silence.

"Adrian, never, never use such disgusting phrases. I will not have it. Do you understand? I will not have it!"

"No offence meant. I wasn't speaking to you, Mother."

"So you find us unpleasant?" Marion was ominous. "Perhaps you remembered us differently? We are certainly rather poorer than when you went away."

Adrian pushed his face nearly inside his glass. He could feel the angry redness that made the tips of his ears throb. The cow! he thought. Might have known she would not leave the past alone.

"I couldn't help it, could I, if the company didn't do as well as I expected?"

"I should imagine that it did better than you expected. A tidy little sum you cleared altogether."

"Stop it, everybody! Otherwise Mother and I will go off into Seaford and leave you to fight it out." Thomas smiled ingratiatingly at his mother-in-law. His head had begun to ache.

"I'll come with you. You'll have two escorts clamouring for your favours, Rachel darling." Piers's gallantry was belated.

Rachel smiled coldly upon him. He had missed his cue.

"I hope that will not be necessary. I should hardly appreciate the humour of being driven out of my own house—by my own family." Rachel spoke relentlessly.

"We'll be perfect lambs, Aunt Rachel," Bess attempted to soothe.

"We ought to have gone to church. That would have made the beginning of the day right, and it would have continued well," Rachel said primly.

"But you have not been to church for years," Marion reminded her Mother.

"Perhaps not. But I know that I would often like to go. I miss going. I should feel better for going. So would we all."

"Then why don't you go?" Adrian asked in bewilderment.

"When you are as old as I am you'll find that there are many things you want to do but have not the strength for."

Adrian grunted. He was more absorbed in the claret, which everyone else disregarded, but which he found to be surprisingly good.

"Rachel, darling, if I'd known, I would have taken you to church this morning." Piers was anxious to make amends.

"Thank you, dear boy. I cannot begin again. I lost the habit of pleasing myself when Marion and Adrian were children."

"Did they prevent your going to church? Couldn't you have taken them with you?" asked Kate.

"Things are not as simple as that, my dear." Rachel was condescending. "Marion was invariably sick long before the sermon. As for a cathedral, she was often sick at the sight of the outside."

They all laughed. Marion blushed, partly pleased at having provoked some merriment.

"The smell of churches is too rich, too old, for me," she explained. "I believe I would have been more suited to chapel-worship."

Rachel sniffed. "That I had no intention of trying."

Bess and Marion exchanged half-smiles as a sign that they had agreed to forgive each other.

After dinner Rachel produced from a locked cupboard a bottle of liqueur brandy. They trooped like obedient animals, well-fed and docile, from the dining-room into the hall-sitting-room, to group themselves in chairs around the fire; to drink coffee and brandy.

Rachel looked enquiringly at Adrian. Was he steady enough to be trusted to distribute the presents from the tree?

Adrian caught his Mother's eye and winked back at her. Rachel decided that Thomas should undertake the task.

Piers brought Bess her coffee. His unusual solicitude amused her. Someone else's frock, she thought; is that all I have ever lacked?

"Darling," he whispered, "you look wonderful tonight." He balanced himself on the arm of her chair. "My present is not what I would have liked to give you. But I promise to write inside it later, just for you. Not for other curious eyes."

"What are you talking about?"

"Wait and see."

Rachel sneezed—a soft, self-induced sneeze. "Piers, my dear, will you bring the screen from the other room and put it round the door? There is such a draught here."

Piers grinned as he rose obediently to do his aunt's bidding.

"You'll forgive me, Bess, for taking your young man away?"

Bess smiled as uncaringly as she could.

"But he will come back. That was my experience when I was your age," Rachel said smoothly.

When Piers had arranged the screen according to Rachel's instructions, she beckoned to him. "Come and talk to me, dear boy."

Piers glanced towards Bess, who looked away.

Thomas came over to Bess's side. "He's not worth it, you know," he said softly.

"Oh, you've said all that. And what's the use of my knowing? That only makes matters worse. Don't tell me that I shall get over it, either. Because I know that, too. But it does not help me now."

"Yes, that's true. It's impossible to move people's lives forward. If you could skip five years, then you'd have no more anxiety."

"What makes you think that I shall learn all that wisdom in a few years?"

"You won't learn it. It will be forced upon you. I could try to explain. But you don't want me to. Do you? Whatever I say is a nuisance, because I am distracting your attention from Piers."

"I am becoming quite horrible."

"You look very lovely. I shall just stay here and not say a word."

Across the room another softly spoken conversation joined the general babble. Piers sat on a footstool by Rachel's side. She patted his head affectionately.

"Now, dear boy, you must tell me all your news. You are not thinking of finding yourself a beautiful young wife to spend your money for you?"

Piers shook his head. He wondered how much Bess could hear.

"Well, well, perhaps that is a good thing. A wife is an expensive luxury for a man who is setting out in life. Your career must come first."

"A few debts are all that I have collected since we last met." He grimaced, glancing up at her with deliberate appeal.

"That is not so serious. Perhaps we can find some way out of your troubles." Rachel glinted with a sidelong, almost imperceptible movement of her eyes towards Adrian. Piers understood the wordless warning. Rachel might take pleasure in helping her nephew, who was attractive and youthful enough to be a careless spend-thrift, where Adrian, penniless and without a job, was a profligate, middle-aged man.

"No need for you to think of marrying for a long time." Rachel was determined that Piers should not misinterpret her. If he was freed from debt, he must realise that there was a condition attached to his release.

"In all things, darling, you shall guide me."

Rachel purred, well satisfied. She would have to keep an eye on Piers, for her influence depended on proximity, and could not withstand many miles between them.

Thomas's voice, louder than he had intended, sounded through a momentary lull in the several conversations: "I have always wanted to go to China."

"Why China?" Bess asked.

"Anywhere, really. But China has always been a far-off, impossible place. Different from anywhere that I have ever seen."

"Don't encourage him, Bess," said Marion. "He is full of fairy tales. Why, he even wanted to go to Russia just before the war." This, her voice explained, was an undeniable proof of irresponsibility.

"Aah, just like I used to be." Rachel was enthusiastic. "I wanted to see the world, once."

"And when you've seen as much of it as I have you'll thank God not to go out of England again." Adrian spoke feelingly. The brandy had saddened him.

"As for Russia today, that is a disappointing country if you like!" Rachel snatched the conversation back into her hands.

"In what way? Politics or scenery?" Kate asked vaguely.

"In every way. I have not been there. But I know very well what Russia used to be." Rachel sipped her brandy with the air of an exiled princess.

No one questioned her, so she had to continue without any assistance from her apathetic audience.

"How wonderful it was! The balls, and the jewels, and the music; and all that food, too." Rachel's eyes shone because of the glory that she had not seen. "And the uniforms, and everybody speaking French."

"But, Aunt Rachel, that was only one small part—" began Bess.

Thomas put his arm against her shoulder in gentle reproof. It was not the time, he felt, to educate his mother-in-law about conditions in Russia before the revolution.

"That's all very pretty, Mother. Have you just read *War and Peace*?" Marion asked.

"As a matter of fact, I have. More to it than most books nowadays."

"Now we are on safe ground. We can't argue against that," Thomas said.

"Although, as for Russia now, the title of the next book will be just *War*." Marion spoke loftily, thinking herself the only one in touch with international affairs.

"Surely," said Piers, "something can be done?" As he spoke he lifted his head with a quick movement. He thought that he must look rather fine; his cameo profile was the study of a young man fighting against the powers of darkness.

"Naturally there must be Something, as you so lucidly put it. Our only little problem is to find what that Something is."Thomas's voice had an undertone of contempt.

Piers flushed. "You tell us, then.You're so damned clever, Thomas."

"I think that we should wipe out Russia." Marion spoke without hesitation.

"How ridiculous! How cruel! We tried to do that to Germany; now we have to help them to get back again," Kate said.

"Why should we? And how on earth could we do that?" Thomas was irritated. "Quite apart from the destructive futility of such a suggestion, how would we set about it?"

"If we haven't the means, then it is up to America," Marion said decisively.

Thomas sighed and scratched ineffectively at the faint nicotine stain on the nail of one forefinger. He thought them all quite intolerable.

"So it is left to Piers's Something to work the miracle." Bess was affectionately teasing.

"Piers may not be far wrong. It all comes down to what

I have always said. God is the only solution." Rachel's voice swept away all obstacles.

"Yes, but who can pull God down from each ceiling? Or out of the sky? Who can give God to the people in every house in every country in the world?" asked Kate.

"People in houses are not as difficult to convince as people in sheds. And we must not forget those who have nothing at all," said Thomas.

Rachel was affronted. "God in ceilings! God inside each of us, that is what it should be."

"You are still speaking of ideals, Aunt Rachel. But there is a lot in what Thomas says. Perhaps nowadays we can only believe in God to the extent of our goods. So they are synonymous."

"God is in church," Rachel snarled. "That is where God was when I was young. Why should God move, just to suit a pack of irreverent creatures such as you!"

"But, Aunt Rachel, that is not what we were saying," Bess interrupted anxiously.

"Besides," said Kate, "if you believe in God, then God is everywhere. Not just in church."

"If you believe in God," mimicked Rachel. "That is the bedrock of our differences. I cannot imagine that such an impertinent supposition exists."

"Oh, Mother, must we start on that again?" Marion sounded tired. "You say God, we might say another name, but it is the same thing in the end."

"So if you worship the devil, that is just as good as praying to God?"

"No, of course not!" Marion snapped.

"That was what you said. Now, wasn't that what she said? You all heard her say it!" Rachel demanded in exasperation.

"Bless your heart, Rachel darling, you are too quick for us," Piers said placatingly.

Rachel was not to be pacified so easily.

"Just because I have caught you out, each of you, challenged your nonsense, you want to change the subject."

"But, Mother," said Marion, "you never keep to the point."

"And none of you has a point to keep to. What I say is, that God is in church, and you have to go there to find Him. You cannot have God unless you take the trouble to find Him first."

"We do try to find God," Kate said. "Each in our own way."

"There is very little evidence of that." Rachel swept their possible faiths aside.

"Rachel dear, you must not be so stern with us," Piers said.

"You should take yourselves to task." Rachel still felt angry, and determined to give one final stab: "The world is no better, as far as I can see, for all your un-Christian ways."

"Aunt Rachel, please forgive us if we have expressed ourselves badly." Bess could envisage many hours of tormented argument when Christmas was over.

"What you need, Mother, is another little drop of brandy," Adrian suggested hopefully.

"Yes, dear, perhaps I do." She smiled upon her son, who had at least refrained from talking disrespectfully about God.

That is perfect, thought Thomas. We try to understand and to explain, however crudely, and Rachel claws at each of us in turn. Adrian merely offers her brandy, and immediately she is as smooth as silk.

"Shall I switch off the lights, so that we can just have the bulbs on the tree?" Kate had been waiting for an appropriate moment.

"Yes, dear, if you like. That will be very nice."

Thomas moved towards the electric-light switches, while Kate stood by the tree. When the room was in darkness except for the firelight, Kate bent down to plug in the flex attached to the coloured lights, blue, yellow, pink, purple, green and white, that were entwined in the branches. There was a loud explosion. Kate jumped backwards. Rachel screamed. The bulbs did not light.

"Fuse," said Thomas briefly. "I'll see if any lights work."

"I knew it," Rachel was dramatic. "I knew it. That is what I have always expected. Every year I have said to myself, 'This year it will happen. We shall be blown up.'" She turned accusingly towards Kate. "But you will have them. You insist upon having them. It doesn't matter what I say. I knew that this would be the end of it all."

"If you were so certain," Marion asked, "why on earth did you let Kate switch the things on? Why didn't you say that there was something wrong, and that they must not be used?"

"How can you expect me to know? I am not an electrician. But I felt something here, inside me." Rachel touched the jet necklace that she wore.

"Indigestion," Marion said disrespectfully.

"I may have a weak heart. But I have never had indigestion."

"You're jolly lucky," said Marion.

"While you sit here talking about indigestion I will try to find some candles," Bess said impatiently.

"Shall I come and help you?" Piers was eager.

"If you like."

"I wish we had flambeaux." Kate was looking out of the window. "How magnificent they would look, one on each side of the steps, streaming and blowing their lights into the dark!" Kate spoke regretfully, remembering how lovely they were and how seldom she had seen them.

"Where's Mrs. Gage or Rage or whatever her name is?" Adrian's voice was thick. He had helped himself lavishly to brandy and was incapable of any movement or coherent thought. He was afraid that his Mother might suddenly ask him to co-operate in finding this, that or the other.

"Mrs. Page has gone home half an hour ago. She only comes back to wash up after dinner. If you think that we have a staff of servants here, then you are very wrong," said Rachel.

Bess and Piers returned. Bess carried a saucer on which rested a candle-stub.

"This is all there is," she said, holding up the fragment.

"Don't be absurd," Rachel snapped. "You have not looked properly. We have dozens of candles in the top cupboard. You know that as well as I do."

"They aren't there, Rachel. I looked very carefully," Piers said.

"Well, where have they gone?" Rachel demanded, seeking for a possible culprit.

They shook their heads.

"She must've eaten them." Adrian gave a throaty giggle. "You starve her. That's what it is. Starve her."

"Adrian! Pull yourself together. Remember you are not in Italy now. We are not barbarians." Rachel spoke distractedly.

"Mrs. Gage. Has to eat candles. You're a cruel, heartless woman," he goggled in playful drunkenness at his Mother and waved a reproving finger.

"People have eaten candles, haven't they?" asked Kate, who was interested in the idea, and who already saw Mrs. Page sitting down to a breakfast of candles and marmalade.

"In 1918 the Belgians ate candles." Marion sounded sure of her facts. "But that does not seem to have any bearing on our present dilemma."

"I remember the Boer War, when things were very bad indeed, but I have never had to eat candles. I wouldn't have done it. I would rather have died." Rachel was belligerent because although she had lived through the Boer War she could not recall that time.

"Rachel, darling, don't be so terrifyingly brave." Piers gave an affected shudder.

"I would have eaten anything. What does it matter? You always were fussy about your food," Marion said contemptuously.

"What is all this about food?" asked Thomas, who had just come into the room. Without waiting for an answer, he continued: "Everything is fused. There isn't a light in the house."

Bess stretched herself contentedly. This inadequate firelight and Piers's nearness were all that she could ask for. Tomorrow would never bring this. Nor the day after, nor any day that she could imagine. For tonight it was perfect, because it was accidental, but a contrived repetition would cloy.

Rachel sensed rather than saw Bess's expression. "What are you grinning at, child?"

Bess did not realise that she was being spoken to.

"Lost your tongue, too!"

"Wake up, Bess," said Marion.

Adrian cackled. He had just noticed Bess's preoccupation with Piers.

Bess smiled. She could afford to disregard them. For this one evening their jeers had no power.

"Get a move on, Thomas. Mend the fuses," Marion instructed her husband.

Thomas saw how the firelight softened the thin lines of Bess's face, and realised that her mood of self-satisfaction might depend upon such a trivial matter.

"Sorry, dear. Can't be done. Not with this fuse-box," Thomas answered, with deliberate stupidity.

Marion's heavy breathing denoted exasperation. "Well, surely somebody else can?"

No one replied.

"We had better make up the fire. That will have to do for us. Then we can save this little piece of candle for Aunt Rachel's room," Kate suggested.

"This is quite cosy, and very seasonal." Rachel was contented. Her chair had been moved nearer to the steeply banked redness of the coals, and she could admire her rings, shining in the light from the flames.

"Some new people are staying next door. Just over Christmas. A very pleasant young man and his Mother," Rachel said irrelevantly.

"When did you meet them?" Bess asked without any real interest.

"I haven't met them yet. I have seen them from the window," corrected Rachel.

"How can you know that the young man is pleasant?" Marion deplored such vagueness.

"Because I have seen him. He looks so very English." Rachel pushed away nebulous memories of another young man who had neither looked nor been English. As for pleasant——?

"That is hardly to be wondered at." Marion's voice rasped at the senselessness of her Mother's remark.

"If you used your eyes, Marion, you would see that most men look as if they belong to no country at all." Rachel stared meaningly at her son-in-law. "In fact, I can recall a Dane who appeared very like a Frenchman." She must speak of Miles, however indirectly, however falsely. She must bring him into the room. She must turn and twist the conversation to make irrelevance relevant.

"Is that a riddle, Mother?" Marion laughed.

"Certainly not. It is a very sad story." Rachel did her utmost to resemble a frail old lady whose life had been wrecked by a romantic moment.

"Come along, Mother. You cannot leave us in suspense. What happened?" Thomas asked, glad of a breaking up of the discord.

"I bet you were wicked, darling. Tell us how you broke his heart." Piers smiled at her from across the room.

Yes, of course; that was how it had been, Rachel thought. Poor Miles! pining after her. Not even daring to write, for fear of cracking the edges of her smooth, polished, safe life. She sighed, then looked down at her hands, pink and soft, folded in her lap. She spoke in a low voice:—

"I will not tell you his name. For it would mean nothing to you. He was young. I was young, too. He was an . . . enchanter. I do not know how I withstood him. He had ideas, too. Oh, how we used to talk for hours! And about everything under the sun. He had an exceptional mind. In every way he was . . ." She paused effectively, as if the memory was more than she could bear. "If I had not been married; but it is no good thinking of that——" She waved the words away as if they still had power to tempt her.

"Darling, what a tease you are!" Kate said affectionately, knowing that Rachel was waiting to be persuaded to continue. "We all believe that he was extraordinary, otherwise you would not have remembered him. But we want to hear the whole story."

"Don't hurry me; I shall tell you." Rachel was enjoying

herself and wished to prolong these moments of her solo performance.

"But we must know his name." Bess felt that a young man who had once been wonderful and clever and adoring was fitting for such an evening.

"Well, if you must." Rachel did not know why she had not spoken his name. A fair enough name it was, too. And one that suited him. Miles. She said it over in her mind. Yet she could not say the word aloud. Miles had for so long been the cherished property of her thoughts that she feared to lose him by sharing even that particle: yet she wished to tell them of the glory of renunciation.

"His name"—she hesitated slightly, then continued with decisive defiance—"was Maximilian. I called him Max."

Thomas, who had noticed the pause and the flatness of her voice, interrupted: "Max? A surprising name for your strange young man."

Rachel looked shrewdly at her son-in-law. Who would have expected Thomas to have such perception? "There you go, Thomas! Always saying something ambiguous." She turned challengingly towards him. "Do you take me for a liar? Or perhaps an old fool who is losing her wits?"

Thomas grinned back at her. This was anger in jest. She could not catch him in that way. Rachel was pleased at his disbelief.

"What does it matter? Max is a perfectly reasonable name. If he was called Max, he was called Max, and there is nothing more to be said." Marion glared at her husband. A man who cannot mend a fuse, she thought, should have the grace to keep quiet and to refrain from adding to an old woman's confusion.

"Thomas is very discerning. Max was not what he should have been named."

Adrian yawned—a long, loud gasp ending in a groan; so violent was his physical reaction that he nearly fell off the chair. "Hey ho, the holly," he sang softly to himself in an attempt to cover his yawn and to cheer himself up.

"What I am talking about happened before you were born." Rachel turned a displeased face to her son. "So if you find it tedious to listen to anything that does not directly concern yourself, you have my permission to go to bed."

Adrian mumbled apologies and protestations of intense interest. After which effort he slept soundlessly and happily under cover of the darkened room.

"Now perhaps I may be allowed to finish?" Rachel resumed her story-teller's voice, deep and emotional.

"We met, Max and I . . ." she paused effectively, "in Copenhagen."

Bess sighed, a small gasp of relief. Subconsciously she had feared a nearer, drabber place. Supposing, she asked herself, it had been Hendon? Or Croydon? Or Seaford? How pointless the story would have become!

"When did you meet?" Marion was greedy for facts.

"In the summer," Rachel answered irritably.

Marion was not satisfied, but decided that there was little hope of extracting reliable information from her Mother.

Rachel chuckled to herself. Imagine the Miles she had known as Maximilian! Miles. A name as cool as the water that had licked the sides of the flat-bottomed boats in that hot summer. Max. Hot and furious. Everything that Miles was not. Is not? Surely he still lived? Living or dead, she had no part in him.

"What is Copenhagen like?" asked Kate.

"A lovely city. Clean and calm. Wide streets. Gardens to play in. Gardens with theatres and cafés. And statues, and a water-front." Rachel was astonished to find how little she could remember about the city. "You must go there. I cannot describe it. You must all go there." Rachel's enthusiasm surmounted all practical difficulties, and for one second they believed that they were free to go wherever and whenever they wished.

What misplaced tenderness, thought Marion. I have seldom had a gentle word from Mother, certainly not a helpful sentence, and yet there she sits with tears in her eyes romanticising about a place that she has not seen for over forty years, and of which she can recall only a pretty young man.

How rich Rachel is, thought Thomas, with all these frivolities for her mind to feed upon. How protected she is! For what would it be to her if the atomic age of fear should begin tomorrow? How much she has—enough to last her for another lifetime spent in a cellar living without daylight or sun or stars or any other than artificial means of keeping her body sensate. Whereas what would we take with us? Very little. Adrian might not fare too badly; surely he has at least a small sin or two to keep him company? Marion would have only her everlasting sterility of mind and body to lie by her side. And Bess? Bess would sit hand in hand with her unfledged self. As for Kate, her changefulness, her uncertainty would be a cold bedfellow for all the nights spent without expectation of morning. Piers would have one staunch, never-failing companion: an arrogant sense of being himself.

Rachel, Thomas realised, had nearly ended her story. Her eyes were bright and young as a child's as she confessed:

"But there was Jonah. So I told Max that we must never see each other again. Never."

"That was hard and implacable of you, darling." Piers gave a sympathetic moue. "And that lovely city, too. You had to give that up as well?"

Rachel smiled her thanks to her nephew, so quick to respond in the right key.

"Yes. I could never return. I could not trust myself to. Besides, Max would have kept me. He wouldn't have let me go a second time."

"More fool you," Marion said brusquely. "No man would keep me away from a place that I liked."

"That I can well understand." Rachel looked sourly at her daughter. "Surely such a choice would never arise? You are safe from distractions of spirit."

"Out with it, Mother!" Marion spoke with careless good humour. "I'm too damned plain. Isn't that what you're trying to say?"

Rachel shook herself with the delicate movements of a bird-of-paradise whose plumage has been sullied by the splashing of a heedless common fowl. "I see that coarseness is the customary speech nowadays. Well, I shall learn. I shall learn."

Adrian was sufficiently awake to hear the finality in Rachel's voice. The tale must have been told. Some comment would be expected of him. He struggled to formulate a remark that would impress his Mother, show how attentive he had been.

At last it came. From the remote corner where he had slept his voice croaked out in blurred syllables: "Thas' ony one of 'em. What about the other chap? The Frenchman?"

Rachel stood up. "The very essence of the stupidity of countless generations has solidified into one person. And that person is you, Adrian." Rachel sat down again.

Adrian closed his eyes. What have I done now? There's no pleasing them. Better leave it alone, old boy; leave it alone. Always the best thing when in doubt. Having counselled himself, he drowsed once more.

"I can remember a time," said Thomas, anxious to distract his mother-in-law's attention, "when we used to sing songs on such an evening as this. A long while ago, of course. When I was still at school." His voice trailed off as he became self-conscious. *We'll go no more a-roving* had been his favourite, the one he had always chosen. How appropriate, he thought, how prophetic. What a sorry rover I should make!

"Songs?" Adrian roused himself. "My word! The songs I've sung! Christmas, Easter, Sundays, holidays, Feast Days. Or just any day at all. They loved it. Couldn't understand English, poor blighters!"

Unsteadily he rose out of his chair, put an imaginary cap on his head, swung an imaginary cane, and danced a little jazz step. They recognised the charm he had once had; this figure that recalled a 1914 ragtime revue.

"If you've never been the lover of the landlady's daughter, then you cannot have another piece of pie," he sang as he pranced about.

Even Rachel laughed.

"Thomas, will you please give out the presents?" Rachel was gracious. "Now that we are comfortably settled—and awake," she added warningly to Adrian.

After Thomas had peered about for some minutes, taking each parcel to the fire to read the label, this proved such a slow process that everyone, excepting Rachel, groped among the branches to distribute whatever packages could be easily found.

How beautiful, thought Bess, the coloured wrappings are, as one by one falls to the ground, or, folded by careful fingers, is placed on the arm of a chair. Surrounded as she was by small, pretty trifles, useless trifles, she looked towards Kate to tell her that nothing could equal the dress which had brought a new if transitory self. Bess put her hands to her hair to touch the unfamiliar knot and to feel the tortoiseshell combs that Thomas had given her. She beckoned to him.

"They are perfect. Look." She turned her head so that he might admire. Her neck was young and thin.

Marion called to her husband. "Can you really see me in this, Thomas?" She held up a hat, a foolish, spring-like hat with a bunch of pink flowers high on the shallow crown.

Thomas had had a wild theory that a hat such as this might persuade Marion to fit herself to the irresponsibility of the flowers. He wondered now how he could have let his fancy so mislead him. Instead of Marion's transformation, the hat had suffered a change, and appeared neither *chic* nor expensive—merely vulgar and tawdry.

"I bought it in Grosvenor Square." Thomas was apologetic.

"That's no excuse. Do I look as if I could be bought in Grosvenor Square?"

Thomas turned away. Not that he minded Marion's contempt, but he disliked the commotion that she was creating. Rachel's bright, inquisitive eyes darted from husband to wife, maliciously summing up.

Bess fumbled through paper and string, anxious to discover the one present that she really cared about. A small, flat box. That would be it. With quick, furtive movements she felt inside to bring out a card, "*For Bess with love from Piers.*" She threw the card down. It meant neither more nor less than the other cards. Inside the box were two pairs of nylon stockings. Pleasure left her face.

Piers came over to her side. "My sweet, that is only one, just for show. Look again."

This must be the one secret present for her. This small packet that she had left unopened. A book. The green leather cover was soft and warm to her hands. The rubbed thin line of gold pleased her. She held the book towards the flames to read the title *Œuvres Complètes de François Villon*. She smiled up at Piers. Her face was shaded, screened by his shadow as he leaned over her.

"I want to write inside it. Just for you."

She nodded, holding the book with affectionate fingers. "I have never seen one like this." She would have preferred *Toi et Moi*.

"I found it in Paris. A heavenly morning last summer. I remember every moment of that day." He sat down at her feet, speaking in a whisper, his face half turned away from her. "I walked about, seeing everything, talking to lots of people, drinking in all the cafés, going into all the bookshops." When he thought of himself as he had been on that day, he fell in love with himself again.

Bess put the book down by her side, suddenly losing interest in it. Why should she not have been there to share those hours? She had nothing to keep her here. She could see Piers, jaunty, expectant, ready for whatever or whoever came his way, walking along the banks of the Seine in the freshness of the early morning, before the sun is too hot, before the air is dusty and stale, when the city is at its best. Alone? Not for long. Piers would have friends, would make friends, wherever he went. Easy, meaningless friendships. More than that? Would he have a girl, who walked springingly by his side? Perhaps. If so, he would not have her company only in the mornings. She could imagine a hotel bedroom, even hear Piers's laughter and an unknown lilting voice.

"It is different for me. No one ever speaks to me. I could live my whole life in a foreign city and no one would notice me."

Piers frowned. What is she talking about now?

"Were you alone in Paris?" Bess could not resist the question.

"No one is alone in Paris?" Piers allowed himself a boyish swagger. "I went round with the usual crowd."

"Wherever you go, I suppose you have a usual crowd?"

"What's wrong in that?"

"Nothing. Except that I envy you. I have no usual crowd. Such a sociable state is beyond my wildest expectations. Even here, where I have lived nearly all my life, I know nobody at all."

"Am I to blame for that? Do I want you to emulate Robinson Crusoe and shut yourself away on an island?"

"It is nothing to do with you. Nothing at all. I am just trying to explain what my life is like."

"Why do you put up with it?"

"Can't you understand that it would be the same no matter where I lived?"

"You are getting so touchy, Bess. I like you when you smile, but not when you preach at me." Piers's face was sulky.

"I just want you to realise how lucky you are."

"If people like me, what is lucky about that?"

"All very fine for you. A young man needs nothing except to be a young man."

"Now you are talking Kate's nonsense. Did you put on her opinions with that frock?"

"Can't you remember who I am and what you felt about me? You used to know me better than this."

"I loved you when I knew nothing about you. Now you insist on telling me far too much."

"But love is knowing and understanding more and more." Bess's whisper was desperate.

"You are thinking of forgiveness—not love." Piers smiled bleakly down at her. Always wanting and wanting, he thought. Digging their nails in, snatching and clutching; women are all the same. Taking time and energy, demanding words that stick in one's throat. Love and understanding and screens to keep away the draught—always wanting something or other, but never wanting quiet or to be left alone.

"Pretend, pretend," Bess said childishly, "that we are at the beginning. Write what you would have written then."

"I will. I promise." What else was there in this ghastly place? Bess adored him. What else was there but downland and sea? Would he ever meet a woman, he asked himself dramatically, who would realise that he had a thousand different decisions and indecisions within the space of an hour?

Rachel's voice trilled across the room: "It is difficult for me to remember how poor I am. If only I could give each of you the exact thing that you ought to have."

Obediently they clustered around her.

"Darling, you've given us all cheques, and what could be nicer than that?" Kate laughed at her aunt.

Adrian thought of the piece of paper in his pocket. Ten pounds. Does she call that money?

"That is nothing to what I would like to give you, my dear child. You should have emeralds. Large, lovely emeralds to wear on your hands, round your neck, in your ears." With a delicate gesture, Rachel touched Kate's hands, her throat, the tip of one ear.

"Whenas that emerald that you wear shall live to be a precious stone when all your beauty's gone . . . Or something like that. Is that what you mean, Mother?"

"Lately, Thomas, you are becoming excessively morbid," Rachel said.

Really, thought Marion, Thomas is getting worse and worse. Perhaps he is going out of his mind. For what could be madder than this continual trotting out of bits and pieces of poems that he read when he was at school? For surely he could not have read them since; certainly she had never caught him at it. Such a bad impression Thomas made with his affectations and studied unconventionalities . . .

"I would prefer sapphires, please." Kate was willing to play at this make-believe.

"Sapphires would never do. Not with your hair."

"What about Bess? What shall we give her?" Piers was determined to be noticed. "Rubies. Don't you agree with me, Rachel darling? Rubies would be just right."

"Good gracious, no! She should have pearls—strands and strands of them."

Was it a shiver? Or was it the coldness of those pearls around Bess's neck?

"What nonsense this is, Mother. You have given us quite enough."

"As for you, Marion, my present would be a trip around the world to show you less limited backgrounds."

"Waste of money." Marion was unmoved. "I am past such benefices."

Piers took Bess's hand and drew her back from the others.

"Tonight may I come to your room?" Then, as Bess hesitated, he coaxed her: "I'll write in your book and bring it to you."

She nodded uncertainly. The practical side troubled her. Piers was clumsy, and without electric light he was sure to fall over in the passage, so that everyone would be awakened.

After several often-repeated good nights, one by one they went up to bed, stumbling and shuffling, by the yellow gleam of the torch which Thomas had found. Thomas stood at the foot of the stairs to light them on their ways. At last only Marion remained. She had waited for her husband.

As they climbed the stairs, Marion hissed: "It is really most disgusting. Under our very eyes, too."

"What's disgusting?"

"I don't know what you do with yourself most of the time. You never have the least idea of what is going on."

"Do wait a minute before you list my numerous failings."

Stonily Marion clumped ahead.

When they were inside their room, Thomas turned up the gas-fire and sat down on the end of his bed to smoke a last cigarette. His wife stood stiffly, uncompromisingly, by the fireplace.

"All right, tell me if you must," Thomas said.

Marion tapped her foot on the polished floor: "Aren't you going to offer me a cigarette?"

"Sorry. Here you are. Let me light it for you."

"I am relegated to the countless details of your background which you no longer see. I am only your wife. Why should you be ordinarily courteous to me?"

Thomas stared bleakly down at the toe of his shoe, which caught the glow of the fire.

"As you do not smoke more than one cigarette a year, how am I to know that this is the annual occasion?" He tried to speak good-temperedly. Her Mother, vixen that she was, he thought, at least had charm.

"I shall have to keep my eye on those two." Marion spoke at last when it was evident that Thomas did not intend to question her.

"For God's sake say what you want to."

"Your Bess isn't such a sweet little innocent," she sneered. "Piers isn't to blame. He'll just take what he can get. All men do."

Thomas refused to be goaded. Precious little you had to give, he thought.

"They were whispering and petting all the evening. It really is disgraceful. And, from what I could catch, they meant"—she looked slyly at her husband—"what you might call country matters." She was rewarded by Thomas's slight recoil.

"I don't know what you mean." He spoke with deliberate blankness.

"Well, you used to, my lad." Her voice was a threat.

All I need to know now, he thought, is how to extricate myself. Otherwise night after night, all the four seasons, I shall be shut up in a small room with this woman. Night after night. The dark seemed to close in upon him, drawing them nearer. The room, in spite of the cold winter air, was hotter than it had been yesterday evening. He felt that if he stretched out his hand he could touch each wall in turn, so near were they brought by the thickly grouped shadows.

"Look here, Marion." He made himself speak softly, reasonably, but go towards her he could not. "This will not work. You and I. It hasn't for a long time." That will never do, he told himself. I must be firm, not pleading. "We would be better apart. Just for a bit, anyway." How foolish that sounded!

"You're tired, old boy. A good night's rest, that is what you need." Marion was indulgent.

Thomas tried to protest, to strengthen himself against her will, but while he hesitated, choosing and discarding phrases, Marion had begun her evening ritual. First she emptied the contents of her large handbag on to the bed: counted her banknotes and silver, checking them against a note of expenditure.

"Must you do that now?" Thomas was becoming furious. "Must you do everything at the same time every night of your life?"

"You've been drinking. Wine doesn't suit you."

"Besides, you haven't spent anything today."

"What I do and when I do it is my affair."

"What do you look forward to?" Thomas tried despairing to bring the conversation back to general terms.

Marion clucked as she brushed the lining of her bag.

"Look forward to?" She was bewildered. "A long, healthy life, I suppose. Not that I have ever thought about it."

"But what do you want to happen?"

"As little as possible. I like my life as it is. Do you expect me to prance about in a state of continual expectancy?" Marion looked at her husband, a tall, thin form outlined by the light from the gas-fire.

Thomas did not answer. There was nothing left for him to say. Whatever he said, Marion would either disregard or misinterpret.

"I am not a girl, Thomas. I cannot behave as if I were eighteen."

"Can you remember what it was like to be young?" Thomas was irritated by the futility of his own question.

"No, I can't. Apart from a vague discomfort. And I am certainly not going to try."

"Surely you see that we must have something to break up our lives. That we can't just continue for ever and ever until we die?" Thomas's voice was uncontrolled.

"We come down here. We go away in the summer. What more can you want?"

"I want everything to be changed."

"Including your wife?" Marion's voice was harsh with the realisation of danger. She sat upright, a square figure, stiffened against disaster.

"The first thing I want is to give up my job. I hate it. You've always known that. You wouldn't want a jobless husband."

"And for how long do you propose to remain idle?" Marion was wary.

"Until I have no more money. Then I'd go off and get myself something. All I need is just enough to live on."

"Very interesting. I have worked all these years, kept myself, paid my share of the house, so that now I am at an age when I ought to take life more easily, and my husband leaves me. Leaves me because he hasn't outgrown an adolescent longing for the open road. Leaves me to work for the rest of my life. Leaves me unprovided for." Marion spoke softly, but the triumphant undertone could not be disregarded.

Once again, thought Thomas, as he pretended to busy himself with the unloosening of his tie, I am routed. For what she says is partly true. Except for those twists and twirls of circumstance which I cannot explain. So here I am, left standing stupidly against the hard surface of Marion's logic.

Without another word, Marion undressed. Clad in woollen pyjamas, she was a compactly formidable figure as she walked heavily over to the wash-basin, where she cleaned her teeth with unnecessary ferocity.

Curtly she grunted good night to her husband as she threw herself into bed. She breathed loudly; the only sign that she had been disturbed.

Marion shut her eyes, willing herself to sleep immediately, so that Thomas should know how little his tantrums affected her. She looked forward to the end of the Christmas holidays. How good and settling it would be to return to work! One luxury she would allow herself. She would tell Miss Winter what she had had to put up with. Miss Winter was an elderly woman who for many years had been Marion's secretary and assistant. Miss Winter was discreet. Miss Winter was wise enough to see Marion's point of view. Contentedly Marion rehearsed her part, saying over to herself the carefully selected words: 'As you can testify, Miss Winter, I like to deal fairly with others, as I expect fair dealings from them.' She could imagine Miss Winter's moistly sympathetic expression. 'I have always made every allowance for my husband, Miss Winter, as you know. What would have become of both of us if it hadn't been for me I just can't imagine.' At this point Marion would pause to allow Miss Winter to agree fervently. 'As for money, Miss Winter, in the strictest confidence, I have never had a penny from him.' After a brief outline of Thomas's remarks and behaviour, Marion planned to say: 'I shouldn't complain. I am well aware of that. But I can't help feeling bitter sometimes when I think back over the last few days.' By that time Miss Winter would have put the kettle on and they would sit drinking tea, cupful after cupful, and eating biscuits while they discussed the problem of Thomas. Naturally they would have to work overtime to make up for the wasted hours of the afternoon; but what of that?

Thomas prolonged his undressing. Even if he had bowed weakly before his wife, he would show her that he was still sufficiently a free man to risk keeping her awake while he smoothed the creases out of his tie, and manipulated the heavy old-fashioned trouser-press, a relic of Jonah's dandy ways.

By the time he had turned out the gas-fire Marion was asleep. Thomas pulled the curtains away from the window nearest to his bed, so that he could see the brightness of the windy winter night. The moon shone coldly over the still colder sea. If only, he thought uneasily, as he stretched himself between the stiff linen sheets, if only I wanted to do one thing for myself, instead of wanting merely a negative state. My whole ambition is to be unmarried. To leave Marion, even if I could, would not be the solution. To wake up to find myself twenty years younger, and to know that I had not married her, that is what I long for. Yet he could recall the months of nights and days, all confused and incomplete, because Marion was not with him. Had he really wanted her so insistently? The idea was abhorrent. That was why he could find no peace even if he ran away, because the consciousness of his own instability would go with him. But what one yearns for at twenty, one loathes at forty. That is natural progression. Still, he was not comforted. He felt a cool draught from the uncurtained window, and wondered whether that would mean a return of his rheumatism.

Thomas's dreams were always of his home. He was a boy again. His Mother was telling him they could not afford university fees. His father stood in the background, a gentle, ineffectual figure, coughing sadly, dissociating himself from his wife's explanations. Thomas gave the same smiling answer to calm their fears. Lacking ambition, he had not greatly minded facing the world without the protection of a degree. But after that his dream deviated from the recorded happenings. He never met Marion, and he continued to live the effortless life of a young man who works in the daytime to earn a living, but who returns

home in the early evenings to take up his true vocation—
that of a son. After such a dream, when he was still caught
between sleeping and waking, he had often wondered why
his Mother had not warned him against Marion. Surely his
Mother, all-knowing, not wise in a worldly sense but with
an essential knowledge of heart and spirit—surely she must
have seen to what hell of subjugation Marion would bring
him? Restlessly he turned, conscious of his wife's presence,
to search for a sign that his Mother had tried to lead him
away from the trap. She had said very little about Marion,
except, 'She appears a trustworthy and reliable girl'.
Hardly sufficient recommendation: yet Thomas had con-
strued these words as a joyful blessing upon his marriage.
His mind chased half-forgotten images and endeavoured
frantically to recall the contented certainty that for a short
time he had once possessed.

The thickness of one wall away, Rachel was lying in fat
contentment under a mound of blankets topped by a soft,
silk-covered eiderdown. She was wide awake. Her eyes
stared into the room's blackness. Every few minutes she
put out a plump hand towards the bedside table, to take a
peppermint cream from an open box. She shook the paper
container on to the floor, crammed the chocolate-covered
sweet with greedy pleasure into her mouth. Her one
disappointment was that the house was too well built.
She had heard anger in the voices from the neighbouring
room, but she could not distinguish the words, try as she
might. She considered creeping out into the passage and

lingering absentmindedly there to see whether the wind would blow the sounds in her direction. After all, she told herself virtuously, I am an old woman now, and nobody tells me anything. Not even my daughter. I ought to know what is going on, especially in my own house. But young people nowadays have no stamina. Bloodless, that's what they are. Thomas certainly looks anæmic, and Marion is pasty enough. They haven't the strength to finish what they begin. A couple of minutes and it is over, and they fall exhausted into bed. Now, she and Jonah could have taught them a thing or two. She giggled to herself.

Piers sat in a large armchair in his bedroom. He, too, stared into the surrounding blackness. On his knee was the copy of Villon. There he had sat for nearly half an hour, fountain pen in hand, waiting for inspiration. What should he write in Bess's book? What would satisfy her without compromising him? His thoughts had wandered away from the immediate problem. The ash from his cigarette dropped on to the carpet. That he was smoking a cigarette, late at night in his bedroom, showed his troubled state of mind. By this time he had almost forgotten the blank page awaiting an inscription. His mind was busily chasing exciting fragments of a continual source of pleasure; the jig-saw of his achievements which would eventually be brought together into a complete pattern. The finished picture would be commensurate with his boundless ambition. That he had never doubted. Behind his appearance of romantic charm and youthful overbearing was a sharp stone of personal ambition—a stone that was gradually working upwards, pushing through the triviality of his daily contacts, making him impatient of this time of waiting until the moment of departure came. He would go far away, where his efficient brain and strange knowledge of rocks and stones and trees should take him: that, too, he had never doubted. From one country to another he would go, limited only by the boundaries of the smallness of that part of the universe which is available to the travellers of this age. He dreamed of the day when he would set off, never to return to Europe, where nothing remained for him to discover. He could do as he pleased in this restricted phase of his life. Nothing that happened to him here would remain for one second after he had begun his journey towards wider, richer explorations. This unformulated certainty made these people and this puppet life a separate sideshow which he enjoyed momentarily. But soon he would go from these. Soon he would be called to do the work he lived for. He would not fail, or, if he did, he would never know it. Failure would kill him even before he realised that he had not succeeded. His behaviour, his half-hearted love-making, his clever, smooth sentences, his willingness to merge himself in Rachel's idea of what a nephew should be—all these were unimportant preliminaries to his true life which had not yet begun. An impersonal destiny was his. These chattering, scheming creatures of his present surroundings were figures under the sea.

Restlessly he stirred, conscious of his cramped position and the fumes from the gas-fire that tightened his eyelids and swamped his power of concentration. He felt lonely.

His work was his belief, his future, his religion, and his continual burden of silence. He could not blur the broad sweep of his thoughts by the explanation of first principles to ignorant children. What else were they—these people, this family that tripped and squeaked in the house? The hidden life that must not be spoken of twitched his nerves, made him into a gaoler.

He would take nothing with him; that knowledge was his support. He could marry Bess. Yes; even that would not scratch one line upon his monument of achievement. What could one woman do against his block of applied learning? He was free with a freedom which was inexplicable. In spite of this limitless air, in spite of the beating of wings telling him that his prison was a temporary one, he wanted to talk to someone, to feel a human presence in the room. He yawned. Not even a light to read by . . . He pitied himself, isolated now in body as well as spirit. Bess would be expecting him. He could not go to her for solace unless he presented her with the book suitably inscribed with a lover's words. Even if he could have seen well enough to read the poems, would he find a quotation to please her? From what he could recall, there were mostly loving references to thieves, pimps and bawds: except for an occasional few lines of filial affection. Bess would not care for a son's remembrances. He yawned again, gulping the stale, smoky air. Perhaps he would go to Bess's room, not necessarily as a lover, but as a young man who was willing to be enfolded in a cloak of affectionate kindness. He was unprepared to go meekly to bed in his own room. Yet to go empty-handed would put him in the wrong. Irritably he shook himself out of the chair, stumbled across the room, splashed his face with water, brushed his untidy hair. He picked up the book. Poor little thing! he thought; I must go to her. I'll write in this damned book in the morning. Before he turned out the gas-fire he looked at himself in the mirror. Against the background of the nearly dark room his reflection appeared taller, almost menacing. The black dressing-gown which he wore over his silk pyjamas was most effective. He smiled at himself, then pulled his mouth down and raised one eyebrow to add a satanic expression which, although he could not see clearly, he was sure suited the imposing figure that was mirrored before him.

With unusually careful movements he opened the door. As he crept along the corridor he saw a glow of light under the door of Kate's room. He stopped. Certainly no gas-fire could give out such a radiance. If Kate could have all that amount of light, why should he be doomed to roam the corridors because his room was in complete darkness? He hesitated, then his annoyance overcame his caution and he scratched upon the door: a slight almost soundless touch of a fingernail drawn along the polished surface. A faint breath of an answer reached him. The hinges were silent, smoothed with oil. Rachel was careful to exclude the possibility of a noisy guest crashing his way to the lavatory, and so awakening her from her first and sweetest sleep.

Kate was sitting up in bed. Her face was pale, her eyes startled and staring. An open book rested on the eiderdown. On the table by the bed were four long, thick candles standing on a small glass tray which was already covered with lumps of candle-grease.

She beckoned to him. Piers closed the door and walked towards her. Kate's expression had changed from fright to furious uncertainty as she wondered whether this was a mere whim or a desperate summons.

"What's the matter?" Her whisper was urgent. "Are you ill? Is Rachel all right?"

"Do be quiet!" Piers breathed hissingly. "I saw the light and wondered how you'd managed it. Why didn't we all have some candles? I've been sitting in absolute darkness."

"I found them in the drawer. Probably Rachel put them there herself."

"The old eagle." Piers spoke with affection.

"You do love her, don't you? Yes, that is your redeeming feature."

Piers was unable to disregard this challenge.

"May I sit here? Otherwise I shall collapse under your disapproval."

Kate pushed herself up in the bed, buttoned her blue satin jacket with coquettish circumspection. She had forgotten her sleeping tablets, and the night was before her—long, conscious hours to spend in a quiet house while others snored and stretched their heavy, sleep-filled bodies.

"If you like you may take some candles back to your room."

"Why? Do you want me to go?" Piers was already seated on a chair, which he had placed alongside the bed.

"No, not particularly. I can't sleep."

"Couldn't you pretend that you like my being here? No tact." Piers's whisper was mocking. He leant forward to look closely at her. "How different you look without the kohl on your eyes!" The word fascinated him. It meant Arabian Nights, warm air, coloured silks, a different richer light. It was both an insult and a compliment.

"Mascara. Yes, I suppose I do. Bald and blank."

"I like you better when your face is made up." Piers spoke seriously, reaching the decision with detached interest.

Kate yawned. "You are very immature."

"Only in trifles. I have other things on my mind."

"Such as?" Kate was bored.

"My work."

"Do you want your name to blaze from star to star?"

Piers fidgeted, twisting his body in the low chair so that Kate could not see his face. He was hurt, because the fame that he wanted was even harder to achieve: that of a power behind the scenes. So that the few people whose knowledge he respected should acclaim him.

"I'm sorry. This house brings out the worst in me." Kate was surprised to find that anyone as over-confident as Piers could so easily be disconcerted.

Piers took hold of Kate's hand, holding her fingers with gentle firmness, admiring his own finger-tips and carefully filed nails. On the whole, he thought, men's hands are much more attractive than women's.

Kate tightened her fingers, gripping his hand, as she said, "Tell me, Piers, what about Bess?"

"Oh God! What a ghastly yapping family you are!" Kate

did not reply. "Kate, I'm not at all like this. You only know me here. You must not judge me." Suddenly the house had become full of enemies, plotting against him, tripping him up, waiting behind doors, knives in hands.

"I never judge."

"I know that." He was contrite. "But you're different here, too."

"I am not much better at home. Living alone isn't easy. Not at first."

"You will soon get over that. All you have to do is to forget that you are living alone. Pretend that someone is coming back, until you find that you don't want anyone. At least, not often." Piers's face brightened with enthusiasm. This was one point on which he was qualified to advise.

How utterly callous! she thought. Telling me to pretend that somebody is returning. Just when Alec has gone and there is no one at all. For weeks I have schooled myself not to think like this. Now a young fool pushes himself uninvited into my room so that he may upset me with his bland nonsense. She bent her head to stare resolutely down at the eiderdown, so that Piers should not see that self-pity had ousted her will. Two fat teardrops fell on to her still-open book.

"My sweet!" Piers was horrified. He jumped up to sit beside her, so that he could put his arm around her shoulders.

Kate groped about for her handkerchief, and, not finding it, was forced to accept one from Piers. She blew her nose vigorously. Then her small, dark unhappiness rushed back, refusing to be dismissed. She cried with uneasy, squeaking noises, snuffling into Piers's shoulder.

"Listen, my pet." He rocked her clumsily. "Listen, darling. You don't want to wake everyone up. That would be damned awkward." Women, he thought, take every word personally. He longed for logical problems without the shadow of a face between him and his conclusions; to be able to see the way to the truth without the intervention of strands of bright hair waving and blowing before his eyes.

He swung his legs on to the bed. Kate's head was pressing uncomfortably against his arm. An occasional sniff and the pink, shiny tip of her nose were the only reminder of her crying.

"Shall I blow the candles out? I'll stay until you are asleep. Then I'll slip back."

Kate nodded docilely, afterwards digging her head more deeply into his shoulder. She was exhausted by her bout of sorrow. "What were you doing, anyway, prowling about in the middle of the night?"

"If you must know, I was on my way to Bess's room."

Kate wanted to laugh. It was an unworthy thought, but pleasant, that she was still attractive enough to waylay Piers, however sexless her hold might be.

"Won't she be waiting for you?"

"No, of course not." Piers lied firmly, because he could not believe that Bess would desert her vigil. "Anyway, it's too late now. You go to sleep."

He shut his eyes. Holidays were extremely tiring festivals.

*

Piers was right. Bess no longer waited. She was fast asleep; one hand clutched the bedclothes around her ears, shutting out the world, protecting her against the trials of yesterday and tomorrow. She had waited for Piers, but soon the anticipation had tired her, and her last waking thought was to hope that he had changed his mind. She longed for sleep.

Her room was primly tidy. Her clothes were folded away in a drawer. Her grey frock hung in the wardrobe. She had arranged the setting with precision. The nun-like correctness was a defensive barrier. The sterner part of her nature insisted that the sinfulness of desire should not only be apparent, but even horrible, seen against this uncharitable background. Having made everything as difficult as possible, she slept peacefully.

CHAPTER THREE

The Day After Christmas

KATE stirred drowsily in the large bed, happily conscious that the night was not yet over and the soft, dark warmth would be hers for several hours to come. She put out her hand, aware that Alec was beside her. Yes. Satisfied, she pushed her head deeper into the pillow, ready to sleep again. How absurd! she thought. I dreamt that this was over and that Alec had gone away: that I had told him to go, but I could not be sure whether he was glad or not. I can remember the silly little jokes I made about him, so that everyone should know how little our parting affected me. It is comforting to hear his breathing that breaks up the thickly encroaching night. What a family fantasy she had slept herself into! They had all been there: Aunt Rachel, Thomas, Bess, Piers, Marion—oh, and suddenly she recalled Adrian. Adrian, whom she had not seen for years. How amazing dreams were! Was it a warning that she must leave Alec? In the darkness she felt for the ring he had given her: small rose diamonds set around the miniature of a girl's face, broad-browed, oval-shaped, brown hair in long, fat curls, all the attributes of a Stuart beauty. It was not on her finger: she must have put it on the dressing-table. A ring given by Alec as a sign that they would be married. But they were not yet married, and probably never would be. What had it felt like without him? The dream seemed to have sprayed itself over the surface of her mind and insisted on colouring every thought. She had not been here at home, but in Rachel's house. She had had a dream within a dream, too. Now her waking and sleeping lives were so intermingled that she could not tell one from the other.

Kate tucked the bedclothes closer around her back. What could be more delightful than being just sufficiently awake to realise how cold and unpleasing was the world beyond the bed? She turned towards Alec. He was very far away, and she had to push herself up in bed to reach him, and then prodded at his arm before he put it around her. She could lie back safely protected against whatever evils the black room contained. How extraordinary Alec is tonight! she thought. Perhaps he has had a dream like mine. And is he sorry to find himself here? She put this slightly disquieting idea aside: that could be faced in the morning. Now all was well. All was as usual. Soon she slept again, resting within Alec's arm, so that her head sank more heavily, until his arm suffered first prickles of pain and finally complete numbness.

Some hours later Kate awoke with a startled jerk. Had she heard a click of a door being opened? Perhaps the bedroom door? She tensed herself against the shock, listening for the horrid creeping sounds of someone, something, in her room. Her own heart-beats were audible, and the lighter sound of Alec's breathing. There! She had not imagined it. There were sounds of quiet footsteps; but not, she thought, thank God—not in the room. Footsteps that dragged along the carpet outside the door. Footsteps—her breath was a sigh of partial relief—going away. What menace had they escaped? Escaped, yes, but only for the moment.

"Alec!" she whispered, "wake up! Do wake up!"

"Hush, Kate, hush. You'll have the household about our ears."

What a meaningless remark! They were in the flat, just the two of them, with some crawling monster outside the door, and he talked about waking a household.

"You are dreaming," she whispered impatiently. "Someone is outside. Quick! Get up."

Alec's hand touched her cheek. "It's all right, Kate. I'm going to pull back the curtains a little. Now don't move, don't jump." He spoke so softly that she could hardly recognise it as Alec's voice.

She heard the sound of metal curtain-rings tinkling a little, until a strip of window could be seen and the early light between night and morning came greyly into the room. The figure who turned and came towards her, walking quietly, was taller than Alec. Was not Alec. Swiftly reality relegated her waking thoughts to a dream, and the dream to what had happened. Alec was not here.

"You've been wandering, Kate. Do be careful. It is getting light already," Piers said as he sat down on the bed by her side.

"Will you give me a cigarette?" Her voice was hardly a whisper, so that although he bent towards her he had almost to guess her words.

Piers felt in the pocket of the dressing-gown that he wore over his pyjamas, and brought out a crumpled packet of Camels and a box of matches. The striking of the match and the quick burst of flame were like an explosion in the hushed house. They waited silently, expecting to hear voices demanding entrance.

The familiar taste of the cigarette, and the sight of Piers as he sat looking down upon her, calmed her nerves.

"I thought that I heard the door being opened, or somebody trying the handle. And then footsteps creeping away."

Piers looked worried, trying to assess whether or not Kate had imagined this.

"Are you sure?" he asked doubtfully.

"Fairly. I must have heard something that woke me up."

"Damn. If there's somebody prowling about already, how shall I be able to get back to my room?"

Kate laughed, a short grunt of amusement which made Piers frown warningly.

"It's quite absurd really. The whole situation is ludicrous. Anyway, we both behaved most properly. Nothing has happened."

"Nothing. Except that you insisted on sleeping on my arm. You were very heavy, too."

"Was I? I'm so sorry."

"What is the use of your continually saying how sorry you are?" Impatiently he stubbed out his cigarette. "It must be getting quite late. And here we sit indulging in trivial conversation. By the way, what is the time?"

"My watch has stopped. Aren't you wearing yours?"

"No, it's in my room."

"Suppose you walk out boldly, making as much clatter as possible. We haven't anything to hide. This is Rachel's fault . . . If she'd remembered where she put the candles———" In her excitement Kate's whisper became louder.

"You are a child." Piers felt paternal. "Who is going to believe that story? If anyone sees me coming out of here, within a few seconds we shall have a screaming pack of accusers. We shouldn't have a chance to explain. We'd be shouted down."

"Yes, perhaps." Kate sat upright in bed, wrinkling her eyes at the thought. "My God! We must see that no one knows about this, if only for Bess's sake. She has always anticipated something really nasty, and this would be it."

"Why should I be saddled with a ghost of Bess, just because I was fond of her—still am, in a way? She did look magnificent last night."

"Do stop behaving in that lordly manner. You did feel this, and you do feel that. Just think of other people for a change. You must have told Bess a pack of lies. You probably wrote them, too. Then you are bored because you have succeeded in making her what you wanted her to be." Kate jumped up and down angrily, shaking the bed.

"What a creature! Sitting up in bed lecturing me because I do not propose to devote my life to Bess!" Piers was amused, irritated, disturbed.

"Oh, I know that I have no sense of time and place. But please do promise me one thing. In return I'll do what I can to smuggle you out of here."

"That's a noble offer." He grinned at her. "Why should this secrecy matter more to me than it does to you?"

"Because you adore Rachel. She'd be terribly hurt and shocked. You'd have a hell of a time talking her round. And then there is Bess. You still care for her a little."

"Come on. Be quick about it. What do you want me to say?"

"That whatever happens, if there is a bloody row about tonight, you'll make Bess believe you."

"Why are you so concerned about Bess?"

"Because she might do something frightful. Cut her throat, or throw herself over the cliff."

"That is rather melodramatic," said Piers. He thought of Bess's letters; in particular the last ones. How violently she had reproached him for his long silences. How lengthily she had assessed her life as worthless, hopeless, if she did not at least hear from him. And how over-joyful her replies had been to the few notes that, latterly, he had written. If only she had remained gentle, remote, undemanding, inaccessible, as she had appeared when first he had noticed her. If she had not taken him seriously; if she had had the wit to pretend an indifference. If he had had to follow, to find her—that would have kept him happy and alert. But instead of that, one word of encouragement, and she had rushed to give in exchange a thousand sickening expressions of eternal devotion. Women should be elusive.

"You are still very young"—Kate's whisper had an undertone of menace—"so please do as I say." Idly, for her mind was still sluggish, still half embedded in the night, she revalued Piers from an uncousinly point of view: a young man with possibilities, one who might be moulded and reshaped, not certainly to her heart's desire, but at least to lighten the lagging moments. Freed from the presence of Bess, who expected his love; of Rachel, who wanted him to play up to her; of Marion, who disapproved of him; of Thomas, who turned his back; of Adrian, an unknown humiliation—away from all these, Piers would become a person in his own right. Abruptly she focused her thoughts on Bess. Certainly Piers was not worth slashing and slaying for.

"I promise," he said at last, nearly convinced that her forebodings could not be discounted.

"I'll go out on to the landing and let you know if the coast is clear. Then you can slip into your room. Open the door carefully. I'll go downstairs and ask Mrs. Page for an aspirin. Tell her that I woke up early with a bad headache."

"Mrs. Page? Surely she is not here yet?"

"I think so. I heard vague scufflings just now."

"And if you do see someone outside?"

"I shall go straight down, and you'll have to lurk here for a while."

"All right. This is unbelievably crazy. Where else would it be necessary? I mean any other family would be reasonable. Besides—oh, what the hell!" Piers was appalled by the need for such manœuvres. He would prefer to swagger out, but he was not prepared to bear the possible consequences of such bravado.

Kate slithered out of bed, put on her dressing-gown and

slippers, powdered her nose to give herself confidence, waved encouragement to Piers, who moved towards the door, so that he might be ready to depart without delay.

Outside all was dark—the windows on the staircase were still curtained. Swiftly Kate looked about her. There were no open doors, and up here, apparently, everyone slept, yet someone had tried to open the door. She turned to beckon to Piers, and then moved towards the staircase. As she began the short ascent she heard behind her the faint click of a latch. He was back in his room.

Downstairs in the kitchen Mrs. Page, still wearing her hat and coat, sat drinking tea.

"My gracious!" Mrs. Page gave a small theatrical scream. "You did give me a fright. Anything up?" Her eyes glinted at the prospect of disaster.

"Good morning, Mrs. Page," Kate said primly, her voice weak, as befitted one whose night had been tortured by migraine. "I'm sorry if I startled you. There is nothing wrong. Except with me. I've got an awful headache. Could you find me some aspirins? I forgot to bring any."

"Aspros." Mrs. Page fumbled in her handbag and produced a flat packet. "That do?"

"Marvellous."

"Have some tea. It'll buck you up."

"Yes, please." As Kate sipped the strong, over-sweetened liquid she shook two tablets into the palm of her hand and ostentatiously muzzled them into her mouth. That would authenticate her story, and she could do with them. She was surprised to realise how jumpy she was.

"You're very early, Mrs. Page," Kate said as she drank a second cup of tea, then added, for want of something better to say, "Does your husband mind? I mean, does he get his own breakfast?"

"This isn't my time really, but I oblige Madam when there's company. My husband, did you say?" Mrs. Page cackled shrilly. "Should be Miss by rights, but Mrs. makes for more respect."

"Does it?"

"Makes a world of difference. Otherwise you get treated like dirt. Wait till you're older, then you'll see."

"Maybe I shall," Kate said absently. "I'll let you know." This literal acceptance confused Mrs. Page, who suspected mockery.

"I know what I'm talking about, and you'll know, too, when it's too late," Mrs. Page said warningly.

Perhaps, thought Kate, we shall all be far too knowledge-able soon: somewhere about breakfast time.

"Shall I tell Madam to let you lay? Say you can do with an extra hour or two?" asked Mrs. Page.

"Yes. No, perhaps not. Yes." Kate wavered, wondering if it would be safer for her to appear at breakfast, conforming to customary routine, and also to curb Piers, in case he could not resist ambiguous hints. As against that she was exhausted and could sleep until luncheon.

Mrs. Page stared curiously at Kate. "Doesn't do to take notice of Madam; she doesn't mean half of it." She tried to work out what had frightened Kate. Was it her aunt? Not she. She stood up to them. Must be something brooding over the family that Kate had felt. Unless she had been privileged by a Visitation.

"Seen anything peculiar in the night, Miss?" Mrs. Page asked suddenly in a hoarse voice, taking Kate completely off her guard.

Quite unnerved, Kate let her cup bang down on the saucer. She could feel herself becoming pale at the unexpectedness of the attack.

"No-o. I d-don't think so." How could this wretched woman have found out? Unless she slept here, after all, and perhaps it was she who had crawled around on the landing? But, if so, why the hat and coat? Oh, if only, Kate thought, we had not begun this ridiculous deception. It's too late now. We shall have to go on with it; otherwise we shall both look fools—or worse.

"Well, I can see you don't look yourself," said Mrs. Page, who was fascinated by Kate's behaviour. She was always so sure of herself—too much so at times. "I can tell when Something's up," she added with awful emphasis.

Kate made an effort and managed to regain her self-possession, saying with precise articulation: "Thanks again for the tea. My headache is much better. I'll go back to bed for an hour, so that I shall be quite fit by breakfast time." She smiled with false sweetness and walked with dignified steps from the kitchen.

Mrs. Page looked astounded as she muttered to herself: "They're all alike. Potty, the lot of them." She allowed herself the luxury of a forbidden cigarette while she considered the mysterious ways of families who meet for the purpose of making each other miserable and bad-tempered. She screwed her face into a mask of ferocious cunning as she told herself that nothing could be hidden from her for long. Whatever had happened—and by this time she had convinced herself that something was Going On—she would make it her business to find out.

Thomas rose early, and so quiet were his movements that he was able to leave Marion sleeping soundly in the twin bed so near—too near—his own. He was conscious that he had not slept well. There had been, so he remembered, a sense of unrest in the night. Noises of footsteps, coming and going. Kate must have had nightmares. He had heard her talking in her sleep, and once she had laughed. Lucky Kate, whose dreams were amusing.

There was no one about downstairs, except Mrs. Page, who stamped in from the kitchen to waylay him by saying:

"Morning, Mr. Thomas. Happy Boxing."

"What? Oh, yes, Happy Boxing," he replied politely, thinking that this must be the usual greeting.

Mrs. Page grimaced maliciously at his back. Silly fool! she thought. They say anything. Like parrots. No sense at all. She hummed gaily to herself, pleased that her first trap had been successful. One up to me, she thought. On her good days—and this was one of them, for she had an enquiry to conduct, and of a kind which she most relished—she played these little games. She always won. Every time she tricked one of them into saying or doing something downright dotty, she scored a point. Up to now twenty had been her highest for one day.

What an old monster she is! thought Thomas. The mental discomforts that people will endure rather than accept the physical necessity of looking after themselves! Although might not Mrs. Page herself be merely the product of Rachel's tyrannical rule? Thomas had been brought up to regard women as gentle creatures whose domination was concerned only with the trivia of living. He would have understood a wife who screamed at him for entering the house with muddy shoes. She might have occasional tearful rages because her marmalade had not set, and he would have been prepared to soothe her. Such a woman had his Mother been, and so lasting were the memories of her that all women today were unnatural—that is, all who did not bring her to mind, and very few did. He had not discovered that Marion was quite unlike his feminine conception, because he had no precedent for thinking that women could be otherwise. He knew, of course, of a few fanatics, but these were either geniuses or were at any rate not met with in his middle-class environment. His Mother had died before she could see that her undeviating goodness had let her son marry a woman who had planned merely to acquire a husband. Why should he question the fresh-complexioned, bouncing young girl who obviously had set her heart on marrying him? Planning and arranging as she already did, that was the very hallmark of youth. That she might not eventually settle down to the customary womanly occupations had never occurred to him. Marion remained obstinately interested in those affairs and problems which he had hitherto regarded as existing solely for masculine minds. She continued to work, flaunting this as her first banner of victory. Soon their joint banking account was completely controlled by Marion, for it was she who added up how much they could afford to draw out each month, and what proportion of their incomes should be put aside for household bills, and what sum each should have for personal expenses. Thomas would gladly have worked to provide for a wife who was incapable of keeping herself. He would have managed to buy those luxuries which women are supposed to desire. As a kindly mentor and guide he would have excelled, but as the stumbling-block to the ambition of a wife who was rapacious for security and then for greater security, he was a failure. He needed the ballast of responsibility: now nobody depended upon him. His capacity for an intelligent and balanced life would have had a chance to become strong-rooted if only he had chosen a wife who required such qualities. As it was, he knew that every day he leaned more on Marion's protection. Wishing as he did to leave her, yet he could not envisage what he would be without her. Perhaps he was too old? Yes, that was the answer. But he was not wholly satisfied.

Thomas had wanted this hour, before the day had properly begun, to be by himself, to walk along the downs, and to urge himself to a point of courageous self-assurance.

He was annoyed to see Piers sitting on the low sea-wall, waving. Of all people, thought Thomas, Piers is the one that I do not wish to see: Piers, who has every reason to be sure of himself; Piers, who is young, and who has a career ready made, put into his hands by the money that has been spent on his education.

"Are you just walking? Or are you fleeing from the foul fiends?" Piers called out as Thomas approached.

Thomas laughed, realising that he had been hurrying, perhaps with the idea that the farther away he was from Marion the less hold she had over him.

"I'd thought of going on to Seaford and having breakfast there," said Thomas, who had just decided on this. The exercise would do him good, and he hoped Piers would consider the distance too far.

"Do you mind if I come part of the way with you?" Piers asked, with unusual diffidence. He was weighing the cold walk against the possibility of a solemn breakfast hour presided over by Rachel. Ought he to desert Kate, who might be in need of support? No, she was capable of doing quite well by herself. "In fact, I'd like to join you for breakfast. Oughtn't we to telephone and tell them that we shan't be back?"

"If you like," Thomas said resignedly. When he had made up his mind to disappear, if only for a few hours, he disliked being led back to the fold of courteous behaviour. "You can do that in Seaford. They won't miss us for an hour."

"Shall we get there so soon?" Piers was appalled.

"If we stir our stumps a bit." Thomas was pleased. I'll teach him to tack himself on to me.

Piers shuddered. What a peculiarly unpleasant expression!

"You'd better make your apologies. No one will bother about me. But you are Rachel's white-headed boy."

Piers scowled. "I think that, for a woman, Rachel is most intelligent, and I am very fond of her."

"You have a low opinion of women?"

"Well, yes, I have. Their influence is obstructive."

"Surely you would not allow anyone to stand in your way?"

Piers chose to disregard the intended sarcasm. "I prefer to avoid obstacles. My work means more to me than any woman could."

Thomas suffered a quick, hurtful envy. To be able to dismiss so effortlessly all other considerations, and to concentrate on an impersonal end, that was surely the sum of every man's desire. Curtly he replied:

"You are in a fortunate position. A specialised training has given you something to work for. Supposing you had to earn your living at a routine job, such as adding up columns of figures all day?" Without allowing Piers to answer, Thomas continued quickly, "You'd sing a different tune then." Thomas had sickened himself by these platitudes, to which envy had driven him.

"People have been asking me that damn-fool question as long as I can remember," Piers said in arrogant dismissal.

"And you still can't answer it." Thomas was goaded beyond caution.

"The question itself is so elementary that no reply appears necessary. I should not do the kind of routine work you have in mind. No matter what education I had had. I should somehow manage to make myself fitted for work more suitable to my temperament and capabilities." Piers's voice was deliberately bored. He lengthened his vowels affectedly, so that he should not be betrayed into apparent anger.

"Thank you for showing me so clearly that you regard me as an uneducated driveller. I may not have had your advantages, but in the harder school of everyday contacts I have been taught to give polite answers to well-meant questions."

It seemed to Piers that he had suffered a dastardly personal attack. He did not realise that at this moment Thomas regretted bitterly his background of private schools and inefficient tutors. Piers could not speak because his voice would show that he was vulnerable, and that, he reasoned, would invite further brutality.

Thomas accepted this silence as contemptuous disregard. "I wonder that you condescend to mix with middle-class bores like us."

This so exactly described Piers's attitude towards Thomas and Marion that Piers was sure his guilt was unmistakable. To control his expression, he put his hands in the pockets of his overcoat, tightening his knuckles until the fingers became white and bloodless. This, he thought, is a beastly mess. He grudged the energy that must be spent either in pacification or in letting his sullen temper have its way. When he said that his work meant more to him than people, this was a true, if clumsy, expression of his natural instincts. That was why he was occasionally frightened of Bess. Not that he did not find her fragilely attractive, but he recognised in her the tenacity of a woman without purpose, except to make him or some other man the focus of her loving nature. This, he had thought to himself many times with self-conscious wisdom, can be immediately recognised in a woman. The pity of it was that Kate, for instance, who would not present a problem, did not attract him. He knew her worth, liked her, but with a brotherly regard. How loosely Kate would hold another's life, not wishing to entangle herself in the grip of that devotion which counts the world well lost. But, then, Kate had herself to consider; she was one of the seekers—as he was. No matter what one sought, the hoped-for discovery was the very core of one's life, and would not permit the forming of any other than a casual link. Piers had tried, without any great hopes of success, to re-fashion Bess to his ideals. She should be loving towards him and yet retain her detachment; she should admire him, but such admiration should be tempered by disdain; she should need him always, but realise that such heaven was not for her; she should have enough pride to hide the misery which his absences in mind and body might inflict upon her. In fact, she should thankfully take what she was offered, and, as for the rest, she should wear her rue with a difference.

"You completely misunderstand me," Piers said at last.

"So you are misunderstood, too!" Thomas jeered. "I suppose that's the privilege of youth. When you get older you will find that you are understood only too well."

Piers suddenly stopped. "Look here . . . What have I done? You'd better go on and have your breakfast alone."

"Yes, perhaps so. It's not your fault, just that anyone

would ruffle me this morning. The only way to deal with problems is to work them out alone."

"Your generation hasn't a corner in problems, you know." Piers was by now thoroughly angry.

"No. You have a big one to tackle. Let me advise you to leave Bess alone. She has had enough. She'll soon come to her senses if you give her a chance."

Already Piers had swung around, and with a mocking salute began to walk away. A tall figure in a flapping tweed overcoat, he typified not assent, but derision.

Piers arrived just as Rachel was complaining about his absence. She and Marion were at breakfast in the dining-room.

"Frightfully sorry to be late." Piers rushed to kiss Rachel.

"So provoking of you, dear. Your egg has been waiting nearly five minutes."

"As long as you have waited for me, what do I care?"
Rachel chuckled.

"Good morning, Marion." Piers bowed exaggeratedly, laughing at Marion's glum-faced distaste. He had got the better of her nondescript husband and, after all, he thought, one must be generous.

"Where's everybody? What a select little party we are!" Piers began to eat with furious appetite.

"Adrian is having breakfast in bed, as a special treat. Kate has a headache and doesn't want anything, and"—Rachel taunted her daughter—"Marion can't keep an eye on her husband. He's gone. Just disappeared." Rachel waved a still delicate, white hand: a theatrical gesture that purposely reminded them how beautiful the young Rachel must have been.

"Is it my job in life to know where Thomas is?" Marion asked sullenly. She could not stomach such remarks at breakfast.

"When I was a girl, Jonah would not let me out of his sight. He even insisted on accompanying me to the dressmaker. There he would sit outside in the carriage, for an hour or more. The dear boy. Of course I had then a certain attractiveness." Rachel's voice insinuated all that she did not say.

"You have often told me that you did not know where your next meal was coming from," accused Marion, "and then you expect me to believe all this rot about carriages."

"My dear child, you really must try not to be so devastatingly literal. Be careful, or you'll find that you've lost all the fun in life."

Marion puffed with exasperation and purposefully poured herself another cup of tea, as if she hoped that the taste would wash away her Mother's nonsense.

"Thomas has gone to Seaford for breakfast," Piers said.

"Gone out for breakfast!" Rachel was shocked. "Very peculiar. Most thoughtless, too. Although I ought to expect bad manners in this uncivilised age. Sometimes I think that a long life is a misfortune. One is out of place."

"Where's Bess?" asked Piers, who had just realised that someone was unaccounted for.

"Nowadays we consider that husbands and wives need not be together every moment of the day," Marion interrupted. "I don't want to keep Thomas tied to me."

"Tied to you! Bless my soul, child, you obviously couldn't do that. It's no good crying for the moon," said Rachel.

"Where's Bess?" Piers asked impatiently.

"Where's Bess? where's Bess? where's Bess?" snapped Rachel. "I'm not allowed to eat in peace without someone asking me where's this, that or the other."

"Oh, leave her alone!" Marion spoke to Piers. "And now perhaps you'll tell me why Thomas favoured you with the information that he was going to Seaford?"

"I met him on the front, and he just told me. I did not ask why. I'm not married to him," Piers said viciously. How bloody clever of Kate, he thought, not to put in an appearance! We shall all have headaches soon.

Pleased with Piers's snarling tone, Rachel rewarded him, "Bess is seeing about Adrian's breakfast and trying to persuade Kate to eat a little something."

"Better let her sleep her headache off," advised Marion.

"Fancy staying in bed for a headache! In my days we kept going uncomplainingly. People are weak because they pamper themselves." Rachel looked virtuous as she imagined her early slavery.

"Why should Bess have to do all the donkey work? Isn't Mrs. Page here?" Piers thought that Bess's presence would lighten the atmosphere. Even Rachel had already treated him off-handedly, and Bess, if she had not stayed awake too long waiting for him, would prove constant.

"A most selfish and thoughtless remark." Rachel spoke haughtily. "There's a lot to do in this house, and Mrs. Page has only one pair of hands. Besides, she's not a strapping young woman"—her gaze rested on Marion—"and when you get old you'll find that you can't tear about as you do now."

Mrs. Page stamped in from the kitchen. "Anyone call me?" she asked menacingly, suspecting that her name had been taken in vain.

"No, thank you, Mrs. Page. I was only telling these young people that they do not realise how much work there is to do in a large house like this."

"Don't s'pose they do." Mrs. Page sounded bored. "Now I'm here, Mr. Piers, what a mess your bottle made! Couldn't you have taken it out?"

"Did it?" Piers asked abstractedly, hardly listening.

"I should say it did." Mrs. Page was indignant at being disregarded.

"Has he been a naughty boy, Mrs. Page?" Rachel asked playfully.

"Seems to have slept in a pool of water. Bottle leaked, and he didn't even trouble to take it out. Tch! tch!"

"Then it must have leaked after I got up," Piers said firmly, at last realising the implication.

"That it didn't. I was in your room just after you left, and your bedclothes was pulled back, all soaked in water, and it 'ad gone right through to the mattress."

"I can't understand how it was that I didn't notice," Piers said miserably, conscious of the flaws in his defence.

Mrs. Page intended to have her full share of attention. "I thought ter meself that I'd better go round your room quick before breakfast like, to get one job outer the way.

An wot 'appens? Wy, more work than ever. Even 'ad to 'ang the mattress out. Tch! tch!" Mrs. Page usually remembered to model her speech on Rachel's, whom she admired, but in the excitement relapsed to her old ways.

"I'm very sorry, Mrs. Page, that you should have had such a disastrous morning. We must all endeavour to make it up to you." Rachel was honeyed and condescending. She was showing her audience how to treat the lower orders.

O Lor', thought Mrs. Page, it's one of her airy-fairy days. Then she produced her trump card, giggling coyly before she spoke: "'Course, I used to be chambermaid at the King's 'Ead, and, my word, if it 'ad 'appened there I should've known wot ter think." Still giggling, she departed.

Rachel and Marion stared at Piers.

"How can you bear to have that filthy old woman around all the time? She's a maniac. Probably a murderess." Piers spoke angrily, although he knew that he should have laughed.

Before either Rachel or Marion had recovered from the encounter with Mrs. Page, Bess came into the room. She looked unusually gay and bright. She had convinced herself that Piers had tried to keep their nocturnal appointment, but that he had started out and been forced to return owing to watchers on the threshold.

"Oh, hullo, Piers," she smiled at him.

Piers grunted a subdued greeting.

"What's the matter with all of you? It's a lovely morning. I'll have some tea, please, Aunt Rachel. And more toast, too. I'm awfully hungry."

Marion sniggered.

"You are very different this morning, Bess. Not at all like yourself," Rachel said sharply.

"Do you object to my being hungry?" Bess's tone was almost pert. She did not feel the same, for knowing that she had been beautiful last night had made her feel almost beautiful now.

"My word, you are on top of the world." Marion gave a hoot of laughter, making Piers jump nervously. "I must have picked a wrong 'un. Poor old Thomas doesn't have that effect on me! And Piers"—she rocked to and fro, laughing cruelly—"well, who'd have thought it!"

"Stop that, Marion! Stop it immediately!" screamed Rachel.

Bess's face was flushed, she was quite unable to follow any of this, and was conscious only that Piers was looking at her pleadingly, expectantly.

"Why do such things happen to me?" Rachel took a small square of lace out of the pocket of her silk bodice and pretended to wipe her eyes. She sniffed softly. "To think of the Christmases I have seen—happy, carefree times—and now this!" She flung out her arm, spilling her tea, and at that she sobbed—choking, heart-broken yet lady-like sobs.

Bess patted her on the arm, saying: "There, there, Aunt Rachel. You stayed up too late last night. Don't upset yourself, there's a darling. Let me settle you nicely upstairs so that you can have a little rest."

"You see, you see"—Rachel had not made up her mind how to deal with the situation, nor whether there was one to be dealt with. She shook off Bess's hand—"she dares to tell me, she dares . . . so brazen . . . I shall never get over it." Then Rachel straightened her back, looking like a woman who was bearing all without flinching, and said with magnificent dignity, "I shall go up to my room now. I am not feeling very well. And you"—she spoke to Marion, ignoring the others—"you may bring me a fresh pot of tea and the bottle of sal volatile from the cupboard in my bathroom."

Rachel's exit, tottering, bowed, but still unbroken, was superb. Marion followed, awed into silence by the splendour of her Mother's perfect timing.

Piers slid the palms of his hands along his trouser legs to wipe off the sweat.

"Do you think," Bess asked anxiously, "that she is perhaps a bit?" She tapped her head significantly. She wondered whether the excitement of Adrian's return had been too much for Rachel.

"Probably. Her age, you know." Piers hoped to delay the crisis indefinitely.

"She's not as old as all that." Bess was irritated by his apparent lack of concern.

"She must be well over sixty. Nearer seventy, I should say."

"You're mad, too, this morning! What a thing to say! Why, some of the most intelligent, the most alive people I know are over sixty." Bess was annoyed, feeling herself relegated to the near senile.

"All depends what you call intelligent. They might trot out the same old stuff, but if you'd never heard it before you'd think it was wonderful," Piers said bitterly, remembering the elementary textbook on physics that Rachel had inexplicably given him on his birthday.

Bess shrugged his words off. She buttered another piece of toast and piled it thickly with marmalade.

He looked at her with condemnation. Why did she have to be argumentative this morning, just when he felt nervous and ill at ease? Usually she was timid and self-effacing.

"Good Lord!" he said, "you're going it. Aren't you ever going to stop eating?"

"If you're poorly," she mocked, "and can't stand the sight of a normal appetite, you should have had your breakfast in bed. Most of them did."

"For Christ's sake shut up!"

She stared at him, her eyes misty, ready for tears.

He was satisfied. That was more like Bess. He bent down and kissed her nose in charming forgiveness. "How can one stop people nagging on and on in this household? I mean when they have got hold of the wrong end of the stick?"

Bess looked bewildered. "Has Adrian run riot and insulted Mrs. Page?"

"Why are you so flippant this morning?"

"What is there for me to be serious about?"

"Please, Bess, just listen, and don't ask questions. Darling, I need your help."

Bess looked lovingly at him as she nodded encouragement.

"Mrs. Page is a mischievous old bitch. And you are not to take any notice of what anyone says."

This enigmatic pronouncement so surprised Bess that

159

she forgot that she should be the silent adorer, and asked excitedly: "What kind of thing? What who says?"

Piers flapped one hand angrily at her. "You are a fool, Bess! Just take no notice of anything. Surely that is simple enough? Mrs. Page is trying to start trouble."

"Oh, she has threatened to leave again? She always does every so often. But she never will. We have to pretend to be frightened," Bess said kindly, pleased to be in possession of superior knowledge.

"This is quite a different matter." Piers sounded as if he had reached a point of utter negation.

"I'm sorry, darling. I want to understand."

"Well, stop talking, then."

"How insufferable you are! You come whining for help and then you insult me."

"I adore you, you tiresome woman." His voice coaxed. "That is why I don't want any unpleasantness, because then I wouldn't be able to come and stay here."

"That need not prevent your seeing me. I am single and a free agent, although you choose to forget it. You could even marry me."

"Ye-ee-e-s, I suppose I could. Perhaps I will," Piers said vaguely. He remembered that he had wanted to marry her once, but that was a long time ago. Sometimes the idea repelled him, on other days such a marriage was a possibility to consider in general terms. He knew that he would continue to change his mind about this, as about everything else, several times an hour. He smiled secretly. Rachel would be livid. Serve her right, though, for treating him badly. Besides, he could always talk her into a good humour whenever he put himself to the task. And of course it need never happen; promises were given, but words could be retracted.

Bess was gazing at him with an expression of incredulous joy. What did it matter to her that she knew Piers to be irresponsible and untrustworthy? As long as he married her, what did it matter if he proved as unsatisfactory a husband as he had been a lover and a friend? She could flaunt her marriage as she would a rare jewel, knowing that she would wear it only for a short while before she lost it, had it stolen, or the giver merely decided to take it away. This was her priceless reward for refraining from asking Piers why he had not come to her room last night. Her eyes shone, her cheeks pinkened, and her nose twitched with the strain of waiting for Piers to speak again.

She is not at all bad looking; Piers considered her earnestly. Properly dressed she will make quite a sensation, and she would do anything for me, she would look after me. He was excited by his power over another human being: excited because he alone could make Bess happy. He became dreamily remote, seeing himself as a fairy godmother turning this Cinderella into a Princess. He did not imagine farther than Bess's cries of thankfulness. That he would be expected to live with her, to work for her, and to sleep with her, did not for one second take shape in his mind. He of all men could transform Bess's life, and to draw back now would surely be sadistic?

"We will get married. Of course we will." There! He was triumphant. His supreme gesture had been made.

"Darling!" She pranced towards him like a thin, leggy puppy. "We'll get married next week. You must get a special licence. Do something now. Telephone somebody and find out what one does."

"I say, that's a bit quick, isn't it?" Piers was appalled yet delighted by his success.

Marion called out from the top of the staircase: "Do stop shouting! Mother is trying to get off to sleep."

"We're going to be married! Do you hear? We're going to be married!" Bess wanted to say this over and over again, the magic words of the spell that meant not only Piers but self-justification for the humiliation she had accepted as a temporary measure to bring her this achievement.

"So I should think," Marion said chillingly. "Now perhaps you will stop screaming. I do not want to tell Mother what the fuss is about. She is upset enough as it is. And you will probably have changed your minds in half an hour."

"They are all so horrid to me." Bess spoke childishly. "Piers, darling, you will look after me, won't you?"

"Of course I will. But you'll have to look after me, too." Piers was anxious.

Thomas arrived at this moment, letting himself in by the front door, which was fastened only by a latch. He was in time to see Bess resting her head lovingly on Piers's shoulder and gazing up at him with an expression of idiotic contentment.

"What's going on here? Oh, sorry I interrupted." Thomas spoke roughly. His breakfast had been disappointing, and he had returned by bus along the coast road. He could remember when Seaford and back had been a mere stroll. He felt old. His thighs ached with the unaccustomed exercise, and the wind had brought a sharp intermittent pain in one ear.

"Piers and I are getting married next week," Bess said condescendingly, forgetting that Thomas had been her confidante in sadder times.

Thomas stared at them both. What trick had Piers played on this guileless creature? For, in God's truth, Thomas thought to himself, Piers does not mean to marry her.

"*Sans blague?*" Thomas jeered. The warmth of the room had increased his earache.

Piers's face reddened angrily. "Perhaps you had your eye on her yourself? Just as a little bit on the side? Marion isn't terribly, terribly interesting, is she?" He controlled his fury sufficiently to drawl the words so that the sneer was given full measure of insult.

Thomas's face was white, the skin taut and shining, his cheekbones over-prominent. He advanced towards Piers so that they stood close to each other, Piers half a head taller, looking down on the other silent man.

Bess retreated behind Piers. That she should be the cause of this desperate encounter was her moment of glory. Piers would surely speak soon, a short, witty phrase which would vanquish Thomas, and also join Piers and herself together in an alliance of affection against all ill-wishers. She waited ready to applaud. She saw Thomas sway slightly, and then strike swiftly with clenched fist at Piers's forehead—an ineffectual blow with little force behind it.

The unexpected attack came upon Piers as he was standing awkwardly, his weight upon one foot, making him lose his balance and topple over backwards. As he fell, his head thumped upon the carpet. Lying sprawled on the floor, Piers was not only dazed by the blow, but mentally stunned by the ignominy of his defeat. He decided to close his eyes and to faint.

The commotion brought Mrs. Page rushing to the scene. Thomas stood stupidly staring down at Piers. Bess was unable to move.

"He's killed 'im! He's dead. He's killed 'im!" screamed Mrs. Page while she jumped up and down. The best Boxing Day she could remember. What a lark!

Thomas shivered. He looked wonderingly at his hand. Had this frailty of skin and bone really done such a deed? No, such distinction was not for him.

"Now, now, Mrs. Page. He'll be all right. Bring some brandy, will you?" Thomas hoped that he sounded controlled and guiltless.

"You've killed 'im. 'E's dead. Dead!" Mrs. Page did not intend that Piers should recover. Jolly good job, too, if he is dead, she thought. I wouldn't lift a finger to bring him back.

Bess gave a hysterical howl: an inhuman sound that made Piers wince slightly, although in the general clamour this was unnoticed.

Rachel appeared at the top of the stairs. At the sight of Madam, Mrs. Page ceased jumping up and down. The room quietened. Only Bess's voice could be heard sobbing:

"Married. My fault, all my fault." Then, as she noticed Rachel, Bess's sobs became choking snuffles.

Mrs. Page whisked off, and returned carrying a small jug of cold water, which she threw energetically over Bess, saying as she did so: "You'll feel better soon. Mustn't give way. Just as good fish in the sea." That's one for her, thought Mrs. Page.

Bess, bedraggled, whimpered softly, conscious that she was behaving ridiculously.

Rachel's silent descent was awe-ful, personifying as she did inescapable doom.

"What terrible thing has happened here?" Rachel's voice boomed. She saw Piers lying on the floor. "Wretched woman! Murderess!" She turned upon Bess.

"I did it," Thomas said, although he knew that no one was listening. "I did it," he repeated feebly.

"My own boy." Rachel bent down to stroke Piers's fore-head. "So white. So cold."

"Here, I say," shouted Thomas, suddenly frightened, "where's the brandy?"

"'Ere y'a." Mrs. Page was resigned to these attempts to bring Piers to life. "Not that 'e isn't past it."

Rachel cradled Piers's head on her arm, and gently, very, gently, lifted him so that she could pour brandy into his lips, A few drops trickled down his neck.

"Do be careful, darling; you are soaking me." Weak though it was, it was Piers's voice.

Mrs. Page sighed and turned her back on the others, ready to return to the kitchen. The situation had become commonplace, and no longer interested her. As she passed Thomas she croaked, "Nev' mind. Better luck nex' time." If I'd hit the la-di-da young swine, she thought, he wouldn't be guzzling brandy.

"Why are you shielding Bess?" Rachel turned so violently upon Thomas that he retreated. "No, don't tell me. Because you are dominated, you are all dominated, the whole world is dominated"—she paused impressively—"by sensuality, not of action, but of thought. You, Thomas, are a man, not perhaps the most virile of your species——"

Marion called out from the doorway: "What's that, Mother? Are you accusing my husband of impotence?"

"Marion, what an abominable expression, and at a time like this!"

Marion now saw Piers, whose head was still supported by Rachel's arm. Marion's eyes widened. "Has he passed out?" she asked.

"Let me continue!" Rachel bellowed. "As I said, it is disgraceful that just because Thomas is a man and Bess is a woman——"

"Shut up! They fought because of me," Bess screamed.

"And you're proud of it. Oh, yes, you are. Proud of it. Borgias, both of you, trying to kill Piers. Borgias!" said Rachel.

"Good Lord! Is he poisoned? Have you sent for a doctor? What did you give him? Let me see, for strychnine it's potassium bromide, then for arsenic you make him sick and give him lots of castor oil, and for something else it's white of egg and strong tea." Marion was competent.

"You needn't bother, Marion. I tapped him lightly on his brow and he collapsed," Thomas said in a faint voice.

"Did you, by Jove?" Marion's tone was respectful. "Wish I'd been here to see it."

"Can't we," Thomas asked pleadingly, "lift him upstairs and put him on his bed?"

"Only if you are very careful." Rachel welcomed the suggestion, because she was suddenly rather weary now that her fury had lessened. Perhaps next Christmas she and Bess would stay at some expensive hotel, away from her family, away, too, from the sea, for of late years the tireless movement of the waters exhausted her. Sometimes she could not sleep for the crash of the waves on the shingle and the noise of the smaller pebbles being sucked back into the monstrous greyness of the sea. Bess, she thought, and Piers. Marry? No, it was absurd. Of course she had heard it all. Nothing but talk. Only words. Piers, as she well recalled, was too lethargic to stoop to pick up one of the small pearly shells that are to be found half embedded in sand when the tide is out. How, then, could he snatch Bess from her home, from Rachel's powerful hold? Besides, Piers would not care, whereas she had an urgent need of Bess. The whole thing was nonsense. Just talk. None of them had enough to do, that was the trouble: idling the hours away, talk, talk, talk.

"Don't touch him. Don't touch him! We must fetch a doctor." Bess stumbled forwards. As she bent down to Piers, her hair flopped over his face, making him sneeze loudly.

"Oh, my head, my head! Where am I?" Piers whispered. He opened one eye, keeping the other closed, which was difficult, but essential, otherwise he might be considered convalescent. "Where am I?"

"Lying on the sitting-room floor. Thomas says he knocked you out. That sounds a bit far-fetched. You probably tripped." Marion was calmly informative.

Piers opened his other eye to regard her with hatred. "Everything is blurred. All gone from me." He shut both eyes. Lot of half-wits, he thought. Why can't they make me comfortable? There is such a draught coming under that door. I shall get pneumonia. I know I shall.

"Don't you know me, Piers? Oh, say you know ME," Bess cried.

"You are a voice in the wilderness," Piers said sepulchrally.

Rachel took her arm away from Piers's head, so that he fell back again on the floor. Rachel felt that this had continued long enough. Most of the morning was already gone, wasted, and she had had no coffee. At her age she could not afford to dispense with mild stimulants.

"Get up, Piers, there's a good boy," Rachel said briskly. "You can lie for a little while on the sofa, and when you feel stronger we'll help you upstairs and you can rest until luncheon. Bess will bring you a nice egg beaten up in milk, and Thomas will apologise. Won't you, Thomas?"

"All right. I'm sorry," Thomas said sulkily. Anything, he thought, to put an end to this farce.

"Rabbit," Marion said with contempt. Firmly she grasped Piers's limp hands as she shouted encouragingly, "Ups-a-daisy, ups-a-daisy. Whoa there! Whoa!" Pulled by Marion's strong fingers, Piers was forced to stumble up and to allow himself to be draped along the settee. Bess covered him with a pink woolly blanket which she had fetched from her bedroom, while Rachel pressed a bottle of smelling-salts into his hand. Thomas turned his back and looked gloomily out of the window, blowing cigarette smoke down his nostrils.

"Come and sit down, all of you. Come near the fire. And you, Bess, stop moaning. The worst is over. We might as well compose ourselves. But"—Rachel glared at the three of them—"let this be a lesson to you to keep your angry passions in check. Perhaps, Marion, as Bess does not appear to be capable of carrying out her customary duties, you will ask Mrs. Page to make us some coffee. It is long past my usual time."

"Don't bother, I'll go," said Thomas.

Within a few seconds he returned from the kitchen. "You'll have to wait a little while, Mother. I'll get the coffee myself. Mrs. Page is sitting with her feet up on the mangle eating lumps of sugar. She says the fright has turned her stomach, and that her knees are watery and she can't stand," Thomas repeated with obvious enjoyment.

"Eating my sugar!" Rachel snapped. "Why is she eating sugar? My sugar?"

"She says it's the only thing that will pull her together."

"Marion, will you kindly go and tell Mrs. Page to stop pulling herself together? I can't spare the sugar. And while you are there perhaps you would make the coffee?"

"All right, Mother." Marion got up. "Mangle? I did not notice that you had a mangle in the kitchen. What do you want a mangle for? Surely you don't do all the washing at home?"

"It is a very small one. Besides, that is neither here nor there. Hurry up, do. Otherwise there won't be any sugar left."

"I'll come and help you," Thomas said as he opened the door for his wife. He followed Marion into the kitchen, only to return immediately and whisper conspiratorially to his mother-in-law:

"Don't worry. She's left quite a lot of sugar. She's gone on to jam. Ladling it up with a tablespoon." Such a trivial revenge, Thomas thought, for what he had endured.

"I rely on you, Thomas, I rely on you to DO SOMETHING ABOUT IT AT ONCE," Rachel barked.

Thomas went back to the kitchen.

"Dear boy!" Rachel waddled over to Piers and patted his hand. "You stay here quietly."

He kept his eyes closed, but grunted an affectionate acquiescence.

Rachel turned her attention to Bess. "You look very damp. Surely you cannot have cried all over your hair?"

"No, Mrs. Page threw some water over me. Just as if I were a mad dog."

"Dear, dear. Go upstairs this minute and change your blouse and dry your hair. Otherwise you'll be ill. A fine state of affairs. And who do you think will look after you?"

"Mrs. Page. I wouldn't expect you to. After all, I'm not Piers, am I?" As Bess said this she began to run up the stairs.

"Wait a minute, wait a minute," Rachel called after her.

"You might tell Kate to come down. I cannot understand how she can stay up there with all this commotion going on. For a woman she certainly lacks curiosity."

"Would you like Adrian, too?" Bess asked mischievously.

"No. No, I think not. He has had such a tiring journey. Better let him be." They were all getting out of hand, thought Rachel, and Adrian's presence might provide just that unknown quality which would completely undermine her authority.

Within a few minutes Bess returned, alone.

"Where is Kate?" Rachel asked. "Surely she cannot have slept through all this? Kate! Kate!" Rachel called in a penetrating voice.

"Coming," Kate said in muffled tones as she groped her way on to the landing. She was still in her dressing-gown; her eyes were heavy with sleep.

"Don't you care what is going on? No doubt all our throats could be cut and you would not trouble to get up." Rachel tried to focus Kate, who remained a blur almost out of sight.

"Why, what is going on?"

"Come down and see. Don't stand yawning there. I know you are yawning, by your voice, even if I can't see you properly. Didn't you hear anything?"

"Vaguely. It sounded as if you were all playing Animal Grab."

"Is it likely, is it likely, that at my age I should indulge in such foolishness? Look!" Rachel pointed dramatically at Piers.

"Poor old Piers! Is he ill?" Kate was too sleepy to appreciate the value of the tableau.

"Thomas attacked him," said Rachel.

"They were fighting over me." Why do I have to say that? Bess wondered. Of course they were not; they were ready to kill each other for no reason at all. But I cannot help pretending that I was the cause.

Thomas came into the room carrying a tray set with cups and saucers and a coffee-pot. Marion followed him, managing to give the impression that although Thomas carried the tray, she alone was responsible for this achievement.

Kate looked puzzled. What had happened between Piers and Thomas?

"Well, have you lost your tongue?" Rachel now thought that everybody was behaving far too calmly. Kate ought to be shocked by such a revelation of family disaster.

"I can hardly express an opinion unless I know what it was all about. Can I?" Kate was feeling kindly disposed towards Piers, and not prepared to believe immediately that Thomas had been in the right. Piers opened his eyes and winked at Kate.

Bess saw this wink, and felt that there was a peculiar bond between them.

"What an awful lot you are!" Kate yawned again. "Except you, Thomas. Coffee is the only sensible thought anyone has had. Can't we keep the peace for these few days in the year?"

"What do you know about it, clever-box, when you were not even here?" Marion asked.

"Your remarks, Kate, are most uncalled for." Rachel was pontifical. "Piers might have been killed. Then Thomas would have been a murderer, and Bess an accessory for allowing it to happen."

"Shall we"—Thomas sounded tired—"leave that subject and drink our coffee?"

"Piers seems to be recovering. Come on, sit up, Piers, and drink your coffee; otherwise we shall have to listen to interminable stories of your escape from death," Marion said brusquely.

They sat in silence. Bess was pleased to notice that Kate looked most unattractive this morning, stuffed up in a woollen dressing-gown. A man's dressing-gown, which was too long for her. Had it once, Bess wondered, belonged to Alec?

"May I have another cup?" asked Kate.

"Of course, dear." Rachel sniffed. "If I had my time over again, if I were young, I would not live like this. That I would not." She looked around defiantly.

"None of us would. But, as we are weak, we have no choice. Except for you, Mother; you are the powerful one," Thomas said.

"That is a preposterous statement, Thomas, coming from you, in the prime of life. Fancy saying that to me, old and feeble as I am."

"Thomas is right, Mother. None of us has ever known what it is to be in the prime of life, whereas you have never been out of it."

"That is a very clever remark. You have adopted your

husband's confusion of statement. But you cannot make sense out of nonsense."

Piers sipped his coffee with conscious invalidism. "I wish you would all keep quiet. My head hurts. There is so much noise in here. Everyone is angry, and that makes me feel worse. After all, I am the only one who has been hurt."

"Bess, please come upstairs with me while I dress. I would like to talk to you. Please," Kate said, disregarding Piers.

Bess looked uncertain. Although she despised herself for accepting domination, she was unaccustomed to going away from Rachel without tacitly asking permission to do so. Now she had two loyalties: Rachel and Piers, although Piers hardly appeared to notice whether she stayed or not.

"All right, I'll come."

Kate dressed quickly, while Bess ambled around the bedroom looking at Kate's books and clothes. She had brought so many things—far too many, surely—to read or to wear during three or four days.

"Why do you bring so much stuff with you?"

"Perhaps because I haven't anybody to bring, and so I make up for it by having my own things around me."

"What do you want me for?"

"Because you were making such a fuss. It is time you thought a little, instead of screaming and panting when you're upset."

"I do think. I am not the fool everyone takes me for."

"If Piers were not here you would be very different."

"Well, he is here. What's more, we are getting married next week."

"Are you?" Kate spoke with careful disinterest. There was a conquering gleam in Bess's eye. "So you are sure of him at last? Then why do you bother still to behave as if I were your enemy. He is all yours. Anyway, I want none of him."

Bess forgot to be haughty. "I am not certain of him. And I never shall be. You know him. You cannot believe that he will ever belong to me?"

"No. But you'll soon tire of him. He will be impossible to live with."

"Why are you telling me this?" Bess was curious, yet exasperated.

"Because I know that Rachel will do her damnedest to keep you here. Better Piers than that. So I advise you to go away and take Piers with you, as soon as possible."

"We shall go tomorrow."

"No, go today. Otherwise you will not go at all. And you had better make up your mind to leave him. Oh, marry him if you must—it is as good a solution as any——but plan your escape."

Bess laughed. "A few hours ago I would have hated you for saying that."

"That is one step forward. Perhaps all this cafuffle has cured your midwinter madness?"

Bess shook her head. "You cannot expect me to have such strength. Besides, mine is not a seasonal malady. For years I have adored Piers. For years I've thought of no one else."

"Yet only yesterday you told me that you would marry any possible man."

"But that was when I did not consider Piers as anyone's husband—certainly not as mine."

"Now that you can see yourself as his wife, is he still so godlike?"

"I'm tired. It's been an exhausting morning. First of all I was so surprised when Piers asked me to marry him that I felt quite sick. Then Thomas came in and was rude and Piers was most unpleasant. That was when Thomas knocked Piers over. I got excited, and Mrs. Page joined in, and altogether there has been too much of everything."

"Yes, it sounds horrible. That is why I did not come down.'

"Could I begin all over again? Go away from here without Piers or anybody? Forget about all of you?"

"Am I such a monster?"

Bess smiled. "No, you are passable, but you are one of the family, and I would have to leave everyone. Otherwise I'd be brought back. Do you think that I could do that?"

"No, I don't. You would just live miserably thinking about Piers. Much better to marry him and afterwards put him out of your mind."

"But if he was my husband I could never forget him."

"I am sure you will find that unexpectedly easy."

"This is what I have always longed for. Now it's mine. And you're trying to make me believe that I shall want to forget."

"Yes, that is just what I am saying."

"How exciting! I feel quite masterful." Bess paused, her face showed a sudden distress. "What will happen to Rachel? She can't stay here alone."

"Probably Adrian will live with her."

"Oh, but she does not really like him."

"Stop considering other people. Rachel has enough money to live comfortably, and she will soon find somebody to take your place. Besides, she must have some friends. What about the people next door?"

"No, Rachel hates them."

"Why?"

"Because they play tennis all the time. She thinks it frivolous, with the world in the state that it is."

Kate laughed. "Surely they don't play in this weather?"

"No, only in the summer. But Aunt Rachel can't forget the balls that come over into our garden. We can often hear them laughing. Their house hasn't been repainted for years. Aunt Rachel says that it will soon fall down, but they sound happy. One of the girls is beautiful. She is always out in the sun, and her skin is brown even now, in the winter. She is the worst of the lot, so Rachel says."

Kate sighed impatiently. Rachel says this and that, she thought. But what do you say and what do you think? Run, run, run and find out what you might say if you had a chance to speak for yourself.

"You had better go and pack."

"Suppose Piers won't come? And where shall we go?"

"There are plenty of hotels."

"But won't they be full up?"

"You'll find somewhere. If you really want to."

"I do. I do. But I am not capable. I have practical ideas, yet they come to nothing."

Kate walked over to the table in front of the window,

picked up her handbag and took from it a Yale key, which she handed to Bess, who accepted it doubtfully.

"If Piers is unable to find a hotel, here's the key to my flat. But don't make things too easy. But see that Piers is utterly exhausted before you produce it."

"That's awfully kind of you. I don't know why you should be so nice to me."

"How long have you lived with Rachel?"

"As long as I can remember. Nearly thirty years. Since I was about four."

"That is the answer. You must get away. Use Piers as a means to go. And don't come back."

"No, I won't ever come back. I shall feel guilty, though. Aunt Rachel has done so much for me."

"You must learn to do things for yourself. You have some money of your own, haven't you?"

"A little. Enough to buy my clothes. Perhaps sufficient to live on for a few months. I shouldn't starve."

"Keep it. Don't give any to Piers."

"I'll try not to."

"I shall stay here until Wednesday. That will give you four days in London—I mean if you go to the flat. That should be time enough to get married?"

"Yes, and then Piers and I will go to Reading, and find somewhere to live. He has only one room in some kind of University boarding-house."

"It's difficult to remember that Reading is a University."

"I am sure that I shall not be happy there. Sometimes I wish it could have been Thomas instead."

"Just as well it isn't. Marion would be formidable."

"Thomas is so kind. But of course he isn't clever."

"And do you expect cleverness from Piers?"

Bess did not answer.

"He knows a great many facts and he has passed several examinations, but it does not follow that he is clever. That is a different thing."

"I know all that. Even if I don't, it is too late now."

"Of course. Piers may turn out very well." Kate sounded dubious.

"When the war came," Bess said irrelevantly, "I thought that I should have to go. That was something to look forward to. The idea of being given a job, of being sent miles away, was stimulating. But Aunt Rachel saw to it that I did not get farther than the village canteen. I used to do washing up for three hours a day."

When Bess had gone away to her room to pack her small suitcase, Kate sat staring interestedly at the door. What had she precipitated? She did not wish to admit that she would encourage Bess, or anyone else, to walk inside a crocodile's mouth so that Kate should be able to witness what happened next.

Bess wandered about in her bedroom, touching the furniture lovingly. A chest of drawers that she had dusted and polished meant more to her, perhaps, than Aunt Rachel did? How absurd, she thought, to rush off like this. Piers will grumble and say that he is not well enough to travel today. There will be opposition from everyone: except from Kate, and even Kate I do not entirely trust. She is not much support, she is too negligent. Thomas will not help me to run off with Piers, whom he does not like. Marion will agree with Aunt Rachel that my conduct is monstrous and worse still, inconvenient. Then of course there is Adrian. I had almost forgotten him. Probably he is still drunk. He must have bottles of stuff hidden in his room. He might prove a diversion. Piers will be the chief obstacle. He does not want to marry me. Only just now and again when he has nothing better to do.

She paused, looking down at her bag: a few clothes neatly folded, pyjamas, dressing-gown, toothbrush, a box of face-powder and a jar of vanishing cream. She needed very little. Her other belongings could be sent on when she knew where she would be. Where else should she be but in Reading with Piers, with her husband? No. That did not sound feasible. She said the words aloud, and found that they would not do. Perhaps, after all, she ought to go away by herself? Go to Kate's flat and stay there. Stay there until she had made up her mind? How rash an undertaking that would be! She would ask Kate once more. Leaving her bag ready to hand just inside the doorway, Bess went to Kate's room. The door was open. There in full view on the dressing-table was a book. Bess's book. How had she failed to notice this before? Without hesitation she returned for her bag and began to descend the stairs.

Downstairs Rachel sat with her daughter and son-in-law. Piers had admitted that he could walk a few steps, and had wandered off to bathe his forehead. Rachel thought of

Piers—thought how much she would lose if she lost him. If he married Bess, Rachel would lose them both. Why this should be she did not know, but her instinct was unfailing. She would lose them both.

If Jonah had lived? That would have been a much better life for her; but, even so, Jonah would have been old by now, and she knew that she desired youth. Not, she told herself, not to interfere—just to be near those who are still young. Ah, Jonah! She blew her nose, turning her head away from an oval mirror that hung on the opposite wall, for in that mirror she would see that she did not match youth any longer.

Jonah had bought this mirror many years ago. Walking in London one late October afternoon, he had smelt the autumn with its faint mistiness of early evening. He had noticed the lights in the shop windows, heard the sound of voices left behind for a second to echo in the sharpening air by the women who laughed and talked as they hurried down Park Lane. This uncertain season had recalled a tenuous dissatisfaction that had been long absent. He was a man who liked to know where he was. The month was prankish. Midsummer in the mornings, December at night. And, he had thought, these betwixt and between afternoons are the very devil at my age. Now that it was term time, and the children old enough to be at boarding-schools, Rachel would, he supposed, be at it again. Why should he worry? For years he had not greatly cared. But he had been a young man then. Not that he was old, but he was no longer young and there was a distinctive difference. He had crossed the road, and looked back at the Marble Arch standing large and grey against the sky. A fine city. Good enough, he had thought, to come back to when one is not so young and when all the other cities of the world seem far away and difficult to reach. Journeying is a tiresome business, although once he had not thought so.

He had turned towards the north, leaving the centre of the city behind him.

He had hoped that Rachel would change a little. His thoughts kept in time with his steps. Why did not her beauty quieten with the years? He needed more than her loveliness now. He could, he admitted to himself, do with a great deal less of her charm, if only she would slow down, instead of pacing out her life. She was a continuous movement. Even when she sat still, the restlessness remained, an integral part of her spirit. Thinking, planning, falling in love—yes, still she fell in love. Oh, there was nothing in it. He knew that. A few kisses, flowers, a box at the theatre (for which he suspected that she paid), some letters shamelessly left about on her dressing-table, or used as shopping lists: a jet brooch, garnet ear-rings, a few tears. Within the law she was faithful, but within her amoral precepts she went, he thought, rather too far.

He resented the waste of hours. He regretted his mind's division: no matter where or with whom, he must remember Rachel with a futile undertone of distrust.

He needed to live slowly. He needed years to spend on ordinary things. This was the first time for many months that he had freed himself. Today he had noticed the park, but not until the grass was browned by frost; today he had seen the trees, but already the leaves were lying in golden-red mounds, studded by smooth horse-chestnuts. Would it always be the same? Would he never be able to look with a free heart at the first fall of snow, lying heavily white, untrodden? Never see the curling, light-edged clouds on summer's completest day without worrying about Rachel? And was Rachel worth all this? He left this question untouched. What Rachel was worth was not his concern: her existence was the best and worst of his life.

The farther he walked the darker the streets became. He left behind him the theatres, the eating-houses, the life of the evening, and came to the places to live in: cramped, grubby places. Gardens of a few feet of blackened earth walled in by grimy bricks; gardens of sooty grass and fig-trees on which no figs ever grew. Grim-fronted houses; long windows screened by lace curtains. The people who passed him were not on their way to music-halls, they were about the business of living. And they were not finding it easy. Jonah felt at home in these unfamiliar streets. Neither did he find life easy.

Soon the evening light had gone and night hid the squares of Mornington Crescent. Hid the once-prosperous houses clinging to their middle-class owners before the adjacent slums swamped them, taking away their wrought-iron gates (that were at one time opened in the day to let carriages pass, closed at night against the thief and the curious eyes of the people who did not live in squares), until, defenceless and neglected, the houses were let room by room. Although

Jonah could not see these houses, he felt that he was in a part of London that was resisting a weary, never-to-be-won encounter against time and a changing world. His personal daily defeat was unremarkable here. He passed the garish, steamy commotion of Camden Town, passed the grunting, shuffling figures around the coffee-stalls. These cosy street-boxes gave a promise of warmth; where one or two could band themselves against the terrors of the bleak side-streets.

That fellow in Copenhagen, Jonah thought, as he left the peopled cross-roads and climbed the hill towards the deserted dark. Miles. He was the first. Jonah saw that now. Perhaps he should have been firm? But he had thought it best to leave Rachel alone. He had pretended not to notice. Rachel's pale, discontented face had filled his days. When that was over—or had it never ended?—Rachel had smiled again. She had bought herself new clothes: frocks that rustled; hats hidden by sweeping feathers; long black gloves; a fur stole, and bronze kid dancing-shoes with ribbons to tie round her ankles, making her look like a schoolgirl. How could Jonah have known that a man whom Rachel had seen merely for a few weeks would push the rest of her life awry? Rachel had settled to her new unalterable way. First, Jonah thought, she had wanted Miles as an enchanted being within the orbit of her marriage. She had decided to keep Jonah as her right-hand security, and with her left hand to subdue Miles's undisciplined intelligence to a controlled adoration.

Miles had escaped, with a darting movement had wriggled himself free of the loving subjugation, leaving Jonah to withstand the heaviness of Rachel's loss.

At one time, although Jonah had taught himself to remain rigidly unperceptive, he knew that Rachel had been willing to leave him, to leave her new house, to leave her friends, to pursue a stranger living in a foreign country. An unresponsive stranger. She had never, he reminded himself, come to her senses. When he had seen the mirror in a shop window he had decided to buy it. It was beautiful enough for Rachel. She might even understand that he was asking her to see herself.

Rachel had never understood. She had kept the mirror because it was a present from Jonah. But she had never greatly liked it. She avoided whenever possible noticing that it was there.

To taunt herself, she looked sideways at the mirror, noting almost with pleasure that it needed re-silvering. Disquieted as always by the reflected face which seemed to have no link with her, she looked away again and sighed loudly. Neither Marion nor Thomas took any notice.

Rachel breathed deeply, then spoke in declamatory tones, "Life is not as simple as you think."

Thomas opened his mouth to deny any such misapprehension, but Rachel continued quickly: "Life does not burn or glow———"

"What is all this leading up to, Mother?" Marion asked briskly. How she longed for her everyday routine of typewriters and files, of appointments and conferences!

"That Thomas cannot behave like a barbarian whenever the mood takes him," Rachel said irritably.

"What a woman you are!"—Thomas's voice was

affectionate—"that you should dare to speak of life in such familiar terms."

"At your age you ought to know better," said Marion.

"Because of my age, as you so crudely put it"—Rachel was haughty—"I am qualified to speak of life."

"Then you have reversed the usual process. As for me, each day I am less certain than I was the day before. Not that I mind,"Thomas said sadly.

"You are both unpractical. All this talk in the clouds! I live by a time-table, apart from holidays like this, which do not count."

Thomas turned to his wife. "You have no fear because you have no imagination. But all the same you are a coward."

"Who is talking about fear? We were speaking of life!" Marion began impatiently to bite a finger-nail.

"Surely it is the same thing?" asked Thomas.

"You are both so clever," Rachel said sharply. "But it leads you nowhere. I brought Marion up in the right way. I am sure of that. I gave her a good education and taught her to read the Bible. And what does she turn into? Why, a dull-spirited creature who cares only for what she calls her office."

"Better than having ideas about life burning and blazing or whatever you said." Marion spoke angrily.

"If we are going to bring God in———"Thomas began.

Rachel disregarded him. "Well, you have chosen your own drab existence, and you have managed to find your-self a husband, and that is that. As for me, I can look back over the years and see a time when life was not colourless. Neither were people all of a piece, as they are nowadays."

"You should not judge from surface impressions. People have not changed, but your eyes are tired of seeing them." Thomas resigned himself to this conversation.

"That is not so, Thomas. For you know in your heart that I am capable of seeing more precisely, just because I have seen so much. The contrast is almost unbelievable. Why, when I was young there was something to live for. We had faith and hope and ideals. Life had a meaning then."

"And we only live because we must? Do you think that?" Thomas asked. His voice sounded thin and exhausted.

"Living! Keeping a roof over your heads, that is more like it. Yes, and both of you busy doing it. Just postponing death. There is no going forward today." Rachel's eyes misted with histrionic tears to think of what she had had and what she had missed.

"Thomas and I are nearly forty. We're middle-aged, Mother. Isn't it a bit late to lecture us about life, when our lives are more than half over?" Marion's voice was shrill with a wish to end this futility.

"I would have been ashamed to say such things. I had ambition. My ambitions were spiritual as well as mundane. I cannot live just for the present. I still think of life in good round terms, and so should you. And so should you!" Rachel gabbled excitedly.

"But suppose, Mother—suppose we do see it all, all that we can, and we do not care to look too closely? Things are not as easy or as pleasant as they were when you were young."

"Then I am sorry for you, Thomas—very sorry for you. What you tell me means that you are out of focus. You are looking at the world from the wrong angle. I have no patience with your limited intelligence."

Thomas laughed. "You win every time, Mother. If you can work yourself up over what you call life, then you possess something that we shall never have."

"Thomas is being the perfect little gentleman," Marion mocked. "I don't suppose he understands a word of this, any more than I do."

"Perhaps I don't. But I think that your Mother is trying to tell us something that I'd be glad to know. Not that it would make any difference to me now. I can't alter because I have lost the ability to accept new theories, and you can't, Marion, because you haven't enough brains. Apart from your interminable routine, you haven't a thought in your head."

"That's what I have to put up with!" Marion's voice rose to an exasperated scream. "A Mother who romanticises about life and a husband who insults me!"

"Oh Life, they said, was King of Kings," Thomas chanted irritatingly on a flat note.

"Love. Not Life," Marion corrected.

"Was that it?" Thomas asked innocently. "Well, well, fancy my forgetting. But, then, it was all so long ago."

Rachel looked suspiciously from one to the other. The King of Kings? Wasn't that blasphemy?

Is that being old, he wondered—not understanding sentences and references that have oblique meanings, that are intended to be small swords to pierce and disconcert; and yet to have an overwhelming belief in the importance of living? If that is being old, then age cannot come soon enough.

"Thomas, why do you go out of your way to be rude to me?" Marion asked abruptly.

"Do I? Yes, perhaps I do."

Marion glared at her Mother. "There! You see what he is like? How impossible he is?"

"Thomas is your husband." Rachel was detached. "You chose him. We all have our problems."

Thomas smiled. Now that he did not love Marion he felt more amiable towards her. There was no need for quarrels and retributions. "You shouldn't talk about life, Mother. That is what started all the trouble."

"Thomas is right, Mother. You should keep to facts."

"I should do this and not do that! All for what? To keep the peace between my daughter and her husband. You should be looking after me, instead of the other way about."

"I like facts. I am not interested in notions that cannot be proved." Marion was goaded almost beyond her endurance.

"Now, your father, my husband," Rachel explained carefully, "he was in some ways, indeed in most ways, a very difficult man. But he was content to be ruled by me. Ruled for his good. I did not dream of interfering in matters which were not in my sphere. Thomas would be just as considerate if you approached him properly."

"I'll leave you two to discuss me as much as you please," Thomas said good-humouredly. There was no longer any need for him to stand with his back to the window, nor to keep his wife's attention and his mother-in-law's vigilance centred on him, for he knew that Bess had made her escape and by this time would be in Seaford. Some minutes ago he had seen her, a dressing-case in her hand, walk quietly and quickly down the steps to the main road.

He wondered whether he would have screened her departure if Piers had been with her? Probably not. In any event, she was old enough to walk out on her own courage. Courage? Apart from Rachel, which of them possessed that quality? He had known, from the droop of Bess's back, that at one word from Rachel she would have returned. He would miss her. He was a happy martyr because he had let her go. He turned to his wife and mother-in-law.

"There's time for a stroll before lunch, isn't there?"

"If Mrs. Page has recovered sufficiently to prepare lunch," Rachel said gloomily.

"Bess and I will set to." Marion was efficient.

"Good Lord! Let Mrs. Page pull herself together!"

"We shall manage." Rachel was blandly superior. "You run along."

As an afterthought, Thomas called out, "Would you like to come, Marion?"

"Surely you do not want my company? An unintelligent, routine-ridden woman like me?" Marion was unforgiving.

"Forget all that," Thomas said wearily. There would be enough uproar when Bess could not be found, without the added burden of a feud between Marion and himself.

"You see, Mother! Thomas is miserable if I am angry with him. You needn't pretend otherwise."

Rachel nodded. No good trying to make me believe that, she thought. He doesn't care two pins for you—no, nor for any of us. You'll find that out one day. Not that I want you to be unhappy, but I have warned you often enough.

We ought to have spent Christmas at home, thought Marion. Thomas did not want to come here. How was I to know that this time he would be right, when before he has always been wrong? Every final decision is left to me. Why can't he insist occasionally? Being married to Thomas is like not having a husband. Worse than that, because I have to act for both of us.

Rachel shut her eyes to signify that she did not wish to be spoken to. She felt tired. Her malice had suddenly gone. She was an elderly woman sitting in a straight-backed chair. She would not allow herself soft-cushioned furniture, preferring to force herself into an upright position that gave her control over any situation. For the first time she pitied her self-chosen discomfort. Here she was, unrelaxed, and lacking the adventure of desire or the remembrance of accomplishment. For whatever picture of satisfaction she might present, she knew that she had fulfilled none of the promises she had made to herself. That was not all, for apart from what she had planned to do and to be, there had always remained a surprise that was yet to come. What it would be she had left to fate, but until lately she had still anticipated the wonderful present: the mysterious emotion that she had waited for from her youth. Until she had married she had thought that this rabbit from God's hat would be love. When love did not change the moon or the stars, then childbirth would be the magical transformation. After her children were born, Rachel became a little anxious. The glory was long in coming. Now she had a fearful thought. Could it be that this surprise would, after all, be death? Death common to all? And to think that she had lived away her years in anticipation of a cold, dark horror of nothingness. She could have beaten her knuckles against her forehead in some inherited gesture of despair. One after another of her friends had died within the last few years. They were all younger than she, and each had died unprepared, in a moment of astonishment. When and where had she lost her chance? There must have been one point in her life which had brought this adverse decision. When Jonah was alive she had felt more sure of herself. Not, she reminded herself, that he had been a perfect man: far from it. But for her he had possessed a quality of establishing her eternal rightness, her everlastingness. Without him she had become mortal.

Two women talked in penetrating voices, regardless of Bess's presence. The train noises made an effective background for their fierce tones. They had the added urgency of a time limit, conscious that they were being hurried towards London, to be pushed and jostled into the anonymity of the station crowds, whereas in this carriage they were supreme. They had obviously discounted Bess.

"What I say is, you can't change human nature. And you never will."

"Quite right."

"No matter what they say, you never will." The speaker stared at her companion.

"And, my dear, what do you think they asked me for?" The listener shook her head.

"Twice as much again. And only three years' lease."

"Tell them they know what they can do."

"I can't. Why, I've spent over a thousand on one room. Spanish style."

"Only the other day I went after a house———"

"Take it or leave it, they said. I'll take it for the present, but I'm off just as soon as I can. I shan't stay in this blasted country."

"Me neither. Not on your life. Better get out while there's still something left."

For the first time, they became aware of Bess, and they goggled accusingly at her. She closed her eyes, unwilling to meet the cat-like glances. She shivered slightly: a twinge of pain twitched her spine and darted towards her shoulder-blade, where it lodged as an intermittent jab. Miserably she envisaged the beginning of an illness, her collapse, and her forced return as a weakling, unable to support a few hours away from home.

Why was the book in Kate's room? Although Bess was easily provoked to jealousy, she could not seriously imagine that Kate and Piers . . . but anything was possible.

The cushions smelt of dust. The carriage windows were dirt-grimed: cigarette ends, brown and sodden, slithered about on the floor. She felt sick. The women's voices merged with the roaring tunnel, making a long moan of discontent.

"If you think you're better off without me . . . and you should have seen his face when I said that food is all I care about . . . it was a long time ago . . . ten years since he died . . . I must say that I like the river . . .we had a house in Bray . . . Twickenham for me . . . not at all rowdy . . . a different class from what I've been used to . . ."

Had they missed her yet? Piers would never forgive her. Would he write? Or would he insist on telling her what a fool she was? Would he threaten? She could hear his voice: "As we shall not see each other again, you will continue in my mind for ever and ever, in accordance with my last remembered impression." Words such as these he would use, meaningless to others, but sharply hurtful to her.

Piers could not forgive. He had no capacity for putting either words or actions quite out of mind. To him everything that was said or thought remained a part of one's immortal spirit now and for eternity.

One thing, she told herself, if I shall not see Piers again— what a comfortless idea—I must not go back. At least I shall not have those horrid days when Piers has just gone. I shall not have to go in his room when he has left, and smell the perfume that stays for weeks afterwards. Perhaps it is a bottle of cheaply potent brilliantine, or a tablet of over-scented soap. Even when the scent no longer hangs about the air of the room, still it remains in the cupboards and drawers.

Without the consciousness of the watchfulness of her surroundings, she could indulge in soft rememberings.

Already she was sure that Piers had decided not to marry her. She regretted leaving the mirror in her room, half believing that she and Piers were still reflected there. An unimportant momentary reflection on a day when life was simple and happy. She had not been prepared for the persistent inventory of trivialities that were waiting to take possession of her mind.

Perhaps he will beg me to marry him? The cold air coupled with the absurdity of this thought made her head throb. One vein on her left temple was swollen as if it was trying to break through the skin. She pushed her hat back from her forehead so that she could press her palm over the aching vein.

The women opposite were silent. They stared at Bess with hostile curiosity.

She could not go to an hotel. She felt too ill, too bleak, too insecure. Any place where she could be alone would be preferable to a large building full of self-important strangers.

Bess was thrust forward along the platform and out to the station yard, where several policemen endeavoured to clear the traffic-blocked roadway. She joined the taxi-cab queue, and when she said "Highgate" she found herself bundled into a cab in which two people already sat, leaning as far from each other as possible: a plump, middle-aged woman in a raincoat, and a pale young man wearing a Harris tweed overcoat and a bowler hat. On the floor of the cab a wad of newspapers gaped open to allow several fish-heads to slip out on to the floor. The young man looked sternly out of the window, dissociating himself from the slithering mass. The smell suggested that these heads had long since parted from their bodies. As the taxi-cab swung around corners, so did the fish-heads surge around the passengers' feet, and with each lurch the young man retreated. Either he had arrived at his destination or the journey was too great a strain, for suddenly he tapped on the dividing panel of glass, signalling the driver to stop at the Charing Cross Hotel. He stepped carefully down to the pavement, holding his head erect in consideration for the bowler's precariousness. After he had gone the woman chuckled as with a deft swooping movement she gathered the fish-heads back into the newspapers.

Bess looked out of the window, enjoying with deliberate self-pity the dreariness of Regent's Park. Late on a winter's afternoon, the people who were still in the park congregated around the bright lake, leaving the eastern grassland empty and cheerless.

The taxi stopped at Camden Town for the fish-woman to alight. From Camden Town onwards the taxi climbed higher and higher above London, along the flat Spaniards Road, where the sandy soil of the heath runs steeply away from the footpath; down the hill, around the narrow corner past the highwayman's inn; up a smooth incline, steepening near the summit, to Highgate Village. A sudden twist to the left and there in front of Bess was the block of flats. The building was large and squat, and in the darkening afternoon light the many windows looked grubby: the pieces of paper blowing about the small oblong lawn gave the place an unkempt, dilapidated air.

After paying the taxi-driver, Bess felt nervously in her pocket to reassure herself. The key was there, as she knew that it should be. Yet she was so affected by the strangeness of her surroundings that she could not be sure that she had actually received the key from Kate.

Bess opened the door timidly, wondering whether a porter would order her away. Once inside she felt relatively safe. What a dark, compact little box it was: minute strip of hall, sitting-room, bedroom, and one room without a window which was kitchen and bathroom combined.

In the sitting-room two china cats sat one on each side of the electric fire, as if daring the stranger to approach the hearth. Bess hesitated on the threshold. Her eyes could focus nothing except these peculiarly out-of-place cats whose malevolent gaze transfixed her. For a few seconds the cats triumphed. Their victory would have been assured if Bess had not forced herself to immediate action. One second longer and she would have picked up her dressing-case and rushed from the flat. Instead she ran towards them, and tucking one under each arm, she managed clumsily to open a cupboard by the side of the fireplace. A pile of books fell out, making room for the cats. Bess shut and locked the cupboard door. The books could remain on the floor.

She put her bag in the bedroom, and with some reluctance took off her hat and coat. Her outdoor clothes were symbols of a fleeting visit, and she was hardly ready to accept these rooms as even a temporary resting-place. Bess realised that she had had no lunch and that she was hungry. Kate had said that there were tins of milk and some food in the kitchen, and a packet of Ryvita. She fumbled in cupboards to discover a tin of milk and another of baked beans. On pulling out a canister marked "Coffee", which proved to be full of an indefinable substance—possibly ground rice that time had brought to a state of dust—a sheaf of small squares of paper fluttered on to the table. As Bess gathered these up she saw that they were short notes, most of them either dated or headed with the hour of the day. Some were in Kate's handwriting, the others in an unknown hand: *Back at eight, darling. See you later, and for God's sake give me something to eat. What, no salt?* Under these words was an imitation of the poster drawing of the half-man, half-bird face with a coyly astonished expression. *Back in an hour—I love you.* These were old ones; the cleaner, less creased papers expressed increasing irritability: *Shall we meet again? That is, if you're not too busy,* and another said briefly, *Off to the pub.* On one slip of paper Kate had listed furniture and clothes, presumably belonging to Alec, which she had instructed Carter Paterson's to deliver to an address in Cornwall. Then in Alec's handwriting, the strokes thicker and blacker than usual: *If you send any of the bloody stuff down to me I shall refuse to take it in. As for the clothes, burn them; that's all they are fit for.* One last one: *Good-bye, I'm off. Your bitchiness is memorable.* This note had been screwed up.

Bess stuffed the pieces of paper back and continued her search for the coffee which she found sealed with adhesive tape in a tin marked 'Spices.' Kate should know better than to leave such evidence lying about. Surely she realised that

these notes should either be destroyed or kept in sentimental remembrance locked away in a drawer? To throw
them one after another behind tins in the kitchen, not
even treating them with the respect that one would give
to a baker's bill! Besides, Bess wondered, what kind of a
life did these notes point to? Either they had lived openly
together—which seemed likely, if Alec kept his possessions
here—or they played an inexplicable game of return and
departure, otherwise these messages would not have been
necessary.

Bess looked around her. There was no telephone; she had
cut herself off from her particular world.

After she had eaten the baked beans and a few slices of
Ryvita, and had shuddered at the taste of coffee unpleasantly
diluted with evaporated milk, still the evening was only half
over. She washed her hands and face, and put on the grey
frock in an effort to restore her ebbing confidence.

The very name of London meant theatres, parties, well-
lit streets, the expensive informality of restaurants near
Shepherd Market.

One or two lights were switched on in the opposite
block, but immediately unseen hands pulled the curtains,
leaving darker blanks. Bess suddenly felt that she was being
spied upon, and drew the brown curtains over the window,
patting them into place so that not a sliver of light would
encourage the curious passer-by.

The quietness of the room pressed heavily, making her
physically unable to move. Her mind was unaccustomed
to thinking in a void; she had trained herself to consider

tomorrow's meals, Rachel's lumbago, Mrs. Page's unaccountably mischievous tricks, so that her thoughts were not adjusted to their release from the accepted pivot of a household, and floated around in a panic of freedom.

Irrelevant phrases of long-ago-dismissed conversation crowded upon her. Who had said that, if circumstances are favourable, one can remain for hours in a self-induced trance? Her body responded gratefully to this suggestion: she stretched herself in the chair, pushing her head against a cushion, willing herself to lie immobile, banishing sight, thought and feeling.

The crashing noise of a door being shut and of feet clumping towards the sitting-room appeared as the manifestations of a nightmare.

A heavily-built man precipitated himself into the doorway of the room and a loud voice said:

"What are you doing here? Thought you'd gone away. I've come for my passport. I persuaded the porter to let me in."

He saw Bess instead of the figure he had expected. "Sorry. Thought you were Kate." He was not disconcerted, whether Kate or an unknown woman was immaterial. With a habitual gesture he pulled an armchair nearer to the fire and sat down.

"Don't worry. I'm not a murderer nor a lunatic. I called out when I saw the light, in case Kate thought that I had returned to take up the struggle where we left off. My name——"

Bess had recovered sufficiently to ask, "Alec?"

"Yes. Have you heard how abominably I treated her?"

"No. She merely said that you and she"—Bess hesitated politely—"did not see much of each other now."

He laughed. A friendly roar. "What delicate understatement! Is she a reformed character?"

Bess smiled as she looked curiously at him. His face was broad, flat-featured, unremarkable except for a sad, bad-tempered mouth. His eyes looked about him with unresponsive acceptance. Only his mouth judged the world, and found it not to his liking.

"That remark," Bess reminded him, "was for family consumption."

"And what a family!"

"I am one of them." Bess was startled.

With an odd kindly attempt to make amends he said, "Don't take any notice of me. By the way, where is Kate?"

"She is not coming back until Wednesday. She said that I could stay here until then. I am Bess."

"Good Lord, yes. I thought you were the old lady's personal slave."

"I am. I wanted to think, to sort myself out; that is why I am here."

"And have you thought?"

"No." Bess was surprised to hear herself telling the truth to this inquisitive stranger. "I have forgotten how to. All I can think is how extraordinary it is to be alone."

"I know. It can be absolute hell."

She looked at his sullen mouth.

"As for this business of thinking—you are thinking the whole time, whether you like it or not. What you must do is to take an hour off, otherwise your mind will be a boiling cauldron."

"How can I decide what to do except by thinking?"

"That's an elementary method leading to further confusion. Look"—he leant forward—"say, for example, there are two alternatives." With one thick forefinger he drew two diverging lines upon the palm of his other hand. "That's before you start thinking. Then you take yourself off for a nice quiet worry. And what happens?"

Bess shook her head in bewilderment.

"After an hour or two there aren't just two alternatives, there are dozens." He sketched out the branching paths.

Bess sat silently, appalled by the complexities which this well-meaning man had conjured up while demonstrating the solution of every problem. She must speak, as he was obviously disappointed by her lack of enthusiasm.

"What do you do then?" she asked in a weak voice.

"I smell out my way." Alec was triumphant, snuffling at the air like a mastiff.

She looked doubtfully at him, wondering whether this was a joke.

Alec answered her unspoken question. "My dear child, I am not laughing at you. I mean it. It's an acquired sense which I have trained to perfection. Or near it. When I came into this room I knew straight away all that I needed to know. Not about you personally, but for my own purpose. For instance, that you would never concern me. There is no danger in you. Not for me. You'll never harm me; we have no fight, you and I. If I smell disaster, whether I retreat or advance depends on the state of the weather, whom I love, how right I am with myself, and so on. Do you understand?"

"Not properly. There is some meaning for you. Not for me. And yet I do understand." Bess smiled at her confusion.

"It's very simple. Follow your nose."

Bess nodded. She felt flatly disappointed.

"Besides," he said irrelevantly, "it will be warmer soon. Summer is an easy season."

"I can't wait as long as that." Bess was peevish.

"Can't you?" Alec had suddenly become indifferent. "You may have to."

"I am not going back."

"You are old enough to do as you please." A poor fish, he thought.

"But I can't decide what to do." Bess thought that her problem was immense, and therefore of general interest.

"Depends what you can do."

"Nothing." Bess realised the horror of this admission.

Alec offered the only panacea which he understood. "Never mind. There's a bottle of rye in that cupboard. I bought it myself."

To drink with a man who called whisky 'rye', that, she thought childishly, showed how she had progressed during the last few hours.

After a few gulps of whisky Bess's eyes glistened with sympathetic intensity. "Do forgive me, but I am sure that you miss Kate terribly. She isn't happy either. If I were you——"

Alec laughed with unnecessary boisterousness. "No good, my dear. You're out of your depth."

Bess's expression was petulant. She thought longingly of Thomas, who was always ready to listen or talk to her. "No wonder Kate left you!"

"Here, have some more." He poured a small amount of the spirit in her empty glass. "You are getting quite brave." Noticing Bess's speculative eyes, he added quickly, "Don't have any pretty notions about me. My heart isn't broken. My temper is not as whole as it used to be. Otherwise I'm fine."

Bess could not give up her illusions so readily. "But when I spoke about being alone . . . Well, you knew what I meant, so naturally——"

"Of course I knew what you meant. Being alone is preferable to being with some people. And Kate's one of them."

"Perhaps I ought not to say this"—the whisky gave her too much confidence—"but I have never understood Kate."

"Afraid I can't help you. Why do you want to understand her?"

"She is my cousin. Besides, something happened this morning that made me wonder whether Kate is what she appears."

"Don't be a fool. Kate's a hundred people. Depends which one you're talking about."

"Don't call me a fool!" Bess snapped. "I want to know if she is"—Bess faltered, conscious of Alec's questioning stare—"promiscuous. Would she sleep with anybody just for the fun of it?" Bess was proud of her daring which matched her new freedom.

"Kate doesn't go to bed professionally. So I suppose you might say that her choice depends on physical attraction. Is that what you mean by 'fun'?"

Bess recoiled slightly from this literal reply.

"Anyway," Alec said angrily, "what the hell does it matter to you? I'm the one who should care. But I don't."

Bess was distressed. If his brutality was not assumed, her romantic world dissolved. "You and Kate must have suited each other down to the ground. A thoroughly nasty couple." She was outraged to the point of truthfulness.

"What has Kate done to you? You haven't slept with her, by any chance?" He summed up Bess's attractions as she sat white-faced and speechless. "I wouldn't put it past Kate. You're not her type, though." He tried to soften the rejection.

Bess tried frantically to recall what Rachel would have said in such an emergency, but as she could not find fitting words, she jumped up, then, realising that there was little space for stamping about, weakly sat down again.

"Do keep still!" Alec shouted. Why, he wondered, do I bother about this ninny? Oh, God, she's going to cry in a minute. "Look here, you haven't had a proper meal. Let's go out and eat."

"So that you can have a better opportunity for insulting me?" Bess protested as vehemently as possible, but she was hungry.

"You are not all that important."

"I have been brought up to think that each one of us is important."

"That is the trouble. Kate has too. Do this. Don't do that. Expect me when you see me." He mimicked viciously.

"Although I don't altogether like Kate"—Bess was pleased that the conversation had come full circle—"she is very attractive. At least, sometimes."

"What has that to do with anything?"

"A great deal."

"A woman's behaviour should be according to the ratio of her beauty?"

"More or less."

"Don't try any charm-school talk with me." He spoke roughly as he hustled Bess into her coat, and opened her handbag to make sure that she had the key of the flat.

"Do you make a practice of looking in women's bags?" Bess asked primly.

"Don't be self-conscious. South-coat pruderies don't go with your precarious position."

He gripped her arm, propelling her into the courtyard, banging the front door behind them. Bess jumped. The cold air rushed at her, almost pushing her back into the warmth of the building. At the same time the crashing of the door precipitated her outwards. If these onslaughts, both human and inanimate, were customary, she did not like living in London. For some chilling seconds she did not like living. Oh, for a melancholy-minded companion who would translate her sorrows into words of the gentle pressure of fingers, instead of this food-seeking automaton who steered her with impersonal haste along dark streets.

"Where are we going?" she asked tremulously after ten minutes' relentless walking.

"Just round the corner. Anything wrong with your feet?" Alec knew only the reason why walking might be irksome.

"Certainly not." Bess was indignant.

They had walked for twenty minutes before they reached the restaurant, Inside the air was hot with a smell of fried potatoes.

Bess ate the thick steak which Alec has ordered for her. The meat was tender, the potatoes crisp.

"Good?" asked Alec when they had eaten and were drinking coffee.

She nodded. "I was awfully hungry."

"Horse." He barked this information helpfully, wanting Bess to know that such succulence was easily obtainable.

Bess pushed her coffee-cup away. "How beastly!"

"Why? You mopped it up."

"You should have told me before. Or not at all." Agitatedly she picked up a teaspoon and began to stir her coffee.

"Don't be so finicky." What a tedious woman! he thought.

"I can't change my ways. Things are not as bad as that. Not yet," Bess said wildly, thinking about the horsemeat.

"As bad as what? Let me get you some more coffee." He saw that in her agitation she had stirred most of the contents of her cup into the saucer and on to the table-cloth.

"No, thank you." Bess imagined that already she felt sick. "Yes, please." Perhaps coffee would do her good.

"That's better. Can't you change a few of your ideas now

that you're a free woman?" Alec's teasing was kind-hearted but unskilful.

"Why should I? I am used to myself as I am."

"Why should you indeed! Ever heard of progress?"

"Progress!" Bess hissed the word contemptuously. "Everything is getting worse. Nothing will improve."

"Not in your lifetime, perhaps. But there will be other people, you know—millions of them."

"What has that to do with me?"

"If you have children——"

"I shan't."

"Even so, there will still be people. Because you are alive now and because they will be alive at some future time, that is the link between you."

"Very fanciful," Bess's comment was one of desperation. She was utterly confused.

"You ought to go to America." Alec studied her critically. "Why?"

"Because you could get married there. Have children."

"You are obviously mad!"

"You want to get married, don't you?"

"Yes, I think so," Bess admitted miserably. To have come so far only to arrive at the same place.

"Well, there you are."

"Why America?"

"Because there are so many men in America." He snorted cigarette smoke, unaware of any offence in his suggestion. "They like English women. Even schoolteachers get married there." He spoke triumphantly.

"Thank you for your help." Her voice quavered. "I am going to be married. So I don't need to peddle my wares in the Colonies."

Alec roared delightedly. "The Colonies!"

"Oh, do be quiet." Bess screamed at him. "You know perfectly well what I mean. Everyone is staring at us."

"My dear child, you must toughen your hide a bit." Surely, he thought, she must accept the rebound of her asinine remarks.

"Toughen my hide!" Bess shuddered, remembering the horse.

"Look here, if you are going to get hysterical———"

Bess stiffened at the word, which was reserved for Rachel's tantrums. When Bess spoke again her voice was calm, although the effect was not effortless.

"I am never hysterical."

Success at last, he thought. But how long would it continue? "Shall we go now?"

Bess nodded, glad to escape from the eyes and ears around her. Only one sulky waitress listened and stared, in the intervals of biting her finger-nails. As her small, pointed teeth tore the protective horn from one quick after another she frowned at each new sharp pain.

As soon as they had stepped out of the swing doors on to the frosty pavement, Bess suffered a physical nausea at the realisation that she was miles from home; with a stranger who jeered at her; an unfamiliar flat to return to.

"I feel awfully ill," she whimpered, pulling the collar of per coat closer around her neck, burying her nose in the friendly-smelling fur.

"Stay there!" Alec bounded across the traffic-crowded road, and before Bess could be swamped by fearful fantasies, a taxi-cab drew up in front of her, out of which Alec jumped.

He had been very quick, she thought. Almost gallant. The idea pleased her. She had known so little gallantry. A quality that befitted life in London. She smiled carefully—a slow, coy widening of her lips, accompanied by an upward glance of feminine fragility and dependence.

"Go on, get in," Alec said impatiently. God help me, he thought. Must she stand there grimacing?

Bess sighed. She had hoped for too much.

"How do you feel now?"

"Better, thank you."

"A good night's rest, that's what you need."

Bess slumped disappointedly against the icy leather cushions. Although this man was unaccountable, she had hoped that he might take her to a club. Not exactly a night club. One of those clubs that people always talk about when they speak of London. Intimate and sophisticated.

Alec was worried by this sudden backward lurch. He wondered whether she really was ill. "Anything up?" he asked clumsily.

"Up? Up?" Bess was haughty.

"You all right? Not feeling worse?"

"No, I have quite recovered." She spoke emphatically. Of course, that was why he was taking her straight home.

"If you want to do anything—I mean go out anywhere—I am really quite well. And not at all tired." She was conscious of the futility of her hinted invitation.

"You aren't taking me far out of my way. I shall enjoy a walk. Besides, I must see you safely indoors."

Bess preened herself. They would sit and drink some more rye together. And after that? Why, anything might happen. Not that she would allow anything to happen. But to be in the position of refusing, that was what she longed for. She rehearsed the words of the anticipated climax. Her one big scene of renunciation. How romantic an ineffectual love affair could be! Suddenly she became horrified at the vulgarity of her make-believe. But she could not altogether relinquish her foolishness, and as the taxi-cab stopped she wondered whether Alec might prove intractable, refuse to play the rejected lover and insist upon the right true end of the story. His voice cut across her thoughts.

"Got your key?" His voice was business-like. "You're O.K. now?"

"Oh, yes, I feel marvellous."

"That's the stuff. I'll say good night, then." He thrust some silver at the taxi-driver, shook Bess's hand vigorously, turned with martial precision, calling over his shoulder, "Sleep well."

Bess heard the cab move off before she limped up the steps, tired and astounded. She could battle no longer.

Rachel sat by the fire. She was waiting eagerly for the moment when lunch would be ready. Not only for the aftermath of repletion, but because meal-times broke up the day, gave a meaning to the morning, a purpose to the afternoon, knowing that tea-time was near, and a certainty to the evening, which could be regarded in two parts: first there were the preparations for dinner, secondly the hours recovering from dinner, until one's body had adjusted itself to the demands of digestion. And, later, a cup of chocolate and a biscuit in bed to mitigate the first chill of the sheets. If the lustier appetites had left her, others took their places.

"Do you think, dear," she called out to her daughter, who was setting the luncheon table in the dining-room, "that we could play some round game this afternoon? Something jolly and Christmassy?"

"If you can think of a game that will be jolly." Marion's voice was not encouraging.

How uncooperative! Rachel thought. "Surely we could all pretend to be jolly. We must show a little Christmas spirit." Rachel was reproving.

Marion, who resented being shouted at from a distance, came to the doorway, so that she had the advantage of seeing her Mother's expression. All this commotion between Tommy and Piers, Marion thought, and all Mother cares about is a jolly game. Old people are extraordinarily self-centred and babyish.

"The trouble is," Marion explained, "that what would be jolly to you might be dull to me. And vice versa."

"Yes, I see," Rachel sniffed to show that she did not see.

As soon as Marion had gone back to her task, Rachel attacked tenaciously.

"There was a very nice game we used to play," she called

out stridently, "many years ago, when I was young." She sighed loudly to let Marion know how much one missed those happy, companionable days. "A very nice game."

"Well, Mother, what was it?" Marion abandoned the table napkins and the silver.

"We had a large bucket of water. Then we'd throw lots of apples in and take turns in bobbing for them." Rachel laughed merrily, refusing to look at her daughter. "Our heads and faces were dripping. The one who caught the most apples won a prize."

"Very messy. Besides, we haven't any apples. And surely that is Hallowe'en?"

"Is it?" Rachel plucked at her black silk skirt. How unkind people were!

"Then there was another game." Rachel was determined. "We pierced the apples and strung them up to a rope fixed on the ceiling. We jumped up and tried to bite one. Or were they toffee-apples? I can't remember."

"What's the use, Mother!" Marion was exasperated. "We haven't any apples. Fancy, at your age, thinking of prancing about or soaking your head in water. You'd have neuralgia for months afterwards."

"De Quincey"—Rachel used her special plaintive voice—"used to wash his hair every night and go to bed with his head wringing wet."

"Even if he did, that is no recommendation. An opium-smoking lunatic!"

"I haven't got as far as that yet. I'm only at page one hundred and thirteen," Rachel said discontentedly.

"Why can't you read sensible books—books you can understand?"

"I am quite capable of understanding. I may not have had your advantages, but I can read as intelligently as anyone. Besides, what can be better than the classics?" Rachel looked upwards, a mischievous glance which she still practised occasionally to keep her eyes ready for a pleasant emergency. "Do you mean that I should read silly love-stories?"

"Of course not. But what's the good of filling your head with rubbish? And unless you can interpret what you read, then it is rubbish."

"Don't you criticise me. My brain's as good as yours. I am working my way straight through all the classics. In the Everyman edition."

"All the classics!" Marion's voice rose almost to a scream.

"Yes. An ambitious programme." Rachel was smug. I can still surprise you, she thought.

Marion shrugged her shoulders with resignation to signify that she could not tolerate her Mother's vagaries. After that she marched into the dining-room to finish setting the table. She pushed the silver serving-spoons into symmetrical pairs and twitched the napkins before returning to her Mother.

"Perhaps you could remember another game—one that does not need apples," Marion suggested kindly, hoping to lead Rachel away from the classical arena.

"Even if I could, you would find some fault with it. Children and old people are always ordered about. So what's left of life to use as one likes?" Rachel asked accusingly. "A few middle years, and they go soon enough. The plans I have made! What has happened to everything?"

Marion patted her Mother's hand. "I can't conjure apples from nowhere. Anyway, all that water . . . really it would be very difficult to arrange."

"Perhaps we had better have something dull, like Birds, Beasts and Fishes. I'll get the paper and pencils ready." Rachel wandered upstairs, happy to have decided on a definite course of action.

It is very tiring, thought Marion, as she lit a cigarette inexpertly, puffing smoke into her eyes, to have Mother on my hands and the luncheon too. Mrs. Page is a slovenly woman. Surely they could find someone better. She walked briskly towards the kitchen to enquire when luncheon would be cooked and to leave Mrs. Page more determined to be disobliging than before. When Marion returned from the skirmish she found Thomas standing disconsolately by the window. "So you're back?" she asked meaninglessly.

Already Thomas was wondering whether his noble gesture of allowing Bess to escape might not lead to an overwhelmingly unpleasant climax.

"What have you been up to?" Marion was quick to notice Thomas's apologetic expression.

"Me?" He over-played his innocence. "Why, darling, what are you talking about? I've only come in this minute."

With dismay Thomas saw his practical, unemotional wife fumble for the handkerchief which she kept stuffed up the cuff of her jumper. She swung round on her heels and blew her nose. This was the nearest to tears that Marion had reached since she left school. For the first time she understood that crying might be unavoidable.

"My dear, what's the matter?"

"That's better. I am not your darling." She stressed the word.

What has happened? Does she imagine, thought Thomas, that I have had an assignation with Bess? He felt dashing, man-about-townish. As he had no personal experience, his mind held pictures of what would, in his father's day, have been a debonair, sophisticated fellow. He saw himself, well-dressed, sleek, moneyed, strolling—yes, that was the word—strolling through St. James's Park at about eleven o'clock on a sunny morning. The perfect moment when this rarefied version of himself would stop to look at the ducks as they moved with such soft swiftness that the water appeared to be carrying along stationary birds, that would be enough. To know that he was right in feeling, thoughts and environment for one exquisite moment.

"Oh, Thomas, do stop staring through me! I cannot stand any more. Adrian last night. Now this terrible morning. And Mother wants us to spend the afternoon dipping our head in buckets of water."

"You are overwrought," Thomas said soothingly, disturbed to see Marion so unlike herself, yet angry at the interruption. "You should have a nice lie down."

Marion laughed with a sobbing sound, as if she had forgotten how to cry. "They are all lying down. In each room there is somebody lying down." She polished the tip of her nose with her handkerchief.

"All of them?" Thomas asked carefully, wondering if Marion imagined that Bess was included.

"Yes, all. Except Mother. She has gone to get paper and pencils so that we can play Birds, Beasts and Fishes." Marion spoke excitedly. Her voice was strangely off key.

Thomas tried to follow these ramifications. "Why on earth are we going to play Birds, Beasts and Fishes?"

"Because there aren't any apples!" Marion shouted.

Thomas was distressed. Marion never lost her control. What ought he to do?

"Look here, old thing. I really do think that you should have a lie down. Do you the world of good."

Marion stared dully at him. Unreliable, she thought. He is forever telling me how unpliant, how unfeminine I am. When I want to depend upon him, he is about as much good as a spineless schoolboy. She shook herself as thoroughly as if she were a dog that had come out of the sea. Her eyes were rather smaller, more hidden than formerly, otherwise no traces of emotion remained.

Hearing the sound of footsteps, they glanced towards the stairs, where Piers was looking at himself in the mirror on the half-landing.

Not bad at all, thought Piers, as he saw his own dark eyes. The blackness of the pupils reassured him. On some days his eyes were dull, no-coloured, but today, even after his ordeal, they were young, shining eyes. Young. That was the core of the matter. Young in this house of old age. How wonderful to feel young as an animal, thoughtless as a plant! To feel oneself growing, pushing free. He side-stepped and swerved like a dancer. Those were the days when he wore neatly creased cream flannels as he played on the greenest grass he had ever seen, greener than any grass since. His waist was as slim, his body as supple, yet his wrist—he flicked experimentally in the air—was less strong, less sure. Noticing the watchers, he remembered his responsibilities both as a young professor and as Rachel's nephew. He decided to surprise them by presenting the sporting side of his nature. He strode towards Thomas, who, mistrusting the motive for the advance, backed away.

Piers smiled, a brilliant enchanting smile, as he leaned forward with his right hand outstretched. He knew how much more power he had to hurt than he was capable of feeling hurt himself. He knew that his insistent youthfulness, his arrogant false humility, flipped across Thomas's eyes.

"We both behaved frightfully badly," Piers said sweetly.

Thomas gave an unhappy nod.

Marion contrasted Piers's charming manners with her husband's boorish acceptance. Piers was quick to see that even Marion was a trifle dazzled by his bright performance.

"Sorry, Marion. Thomas and I had such a set-to!"

Affected young cub, thought Thomas. Surely she won't let him get away with that?

"Never mind, it is over now." Marion spoke agreeably, surprising herself by this meek concession.

Piers linked his arm in hers, drawing her away from Thomas towards the window, to show how easily women could be attracted by spurious bewitchments. Piers could not resist flickering his eyes at Thomas, as if to say, 'Neither of us cares. But you see how simple it is to take what some-body else values?'

"What's the big idea?" Foolishly Thomas sneered. "All this forgive and forget is not exactly in your line."

"Old Thomas is still a bit touchy." Piers enticed Marion to join the conspiracy against her husband.

After a few seconds Piers saw that the adjective had found its mark; suddenly he tired of the game and abruptly dropped Marion's arm.

"Before the others come down, I must ask you a question." Thomas felt protective towards Bess: he wanted to assure her future, dissolve her bewilderments, so that she would be grateful when she returned. Without looking at either his wife or Piers, Thomas gabbled the words before his courage failed: "Are you really going to marry Bess? Do you really want to?"

Piers's expression fell apart, leaving his eyes angry, his mouth uncertain, and his nose wavered between the two emotions.

"I don't know. Sometimes. What's it to do with you?"

Marion barked her opinion with customary lack of finesse. "Mother would never allow Bess to marry you. She wouldn't let you marry Bess either. So that's an end to that."

"Don't be silly, my dear. Bess isn't eighteen." Thomas wondered whether Marion would ever learn to keep quiet.

"Let me remind you, Marion, that in spite of your inter-ference, I shall do exactly as I please."

"My interference! You'll have to reckon with Mother.

And you'll have to climb down a bit. Your salary won't take you far."

The word echoed in Piers's mind. Far . . . far. Far was a word that they could translate into thousands of miles. Far meant that they could see for themselves that the Danube is not blue but a dirty greyish-green. Far might bring them memories of the featured prettiness of Mediterranean shores. Whereas to him it brought light-years. Illimitable space of planeted skies.

"I shall do what I like. Because it is of no importance at all."

Thomas turned away from the brutality of this statement. He is right, thought Thomas; we are splashing about in a children's bathing-pool. We shall never get out of it, and if we did we would be swept away by the first uncontrolled surge of water.

"Be quiet, Marion," he said irritably, begging his wife not to throw feathers of conventional arguments against Piers's implacable purpose.

Marion shrugged her shoulders. "The world is a poor place if we are all to be gagged and muzzled."

"What worries me," Piers said confidentially, disregarding Marion's remark, "is whether retrogression is ever for the best." Piers paused expectantly, although he realised that neither Marion nor Thomas could know what this meant. "There was a time when I thought that I needed Bess. Now that I can do without her, ought I to let myself need her again?"

Marion had no intention of taking a young man's

fripperies seriously. She turned to her husband, confident that everyone would benefit if the conversation could be pulled back to a factual sanity.

"Do you think that the electricity account will be very high? We had an immersion heater fixed some months ago. I am quite looking forward to seeing how it works out," she explained graciously to Piers.

"Are you?" Piers muttered, regarding her with glazed eyes. So that is what happens when one has a wife. Any wife. Every wife. He saw the entrance hall in the boarding-house, and the peg on which his dirty raincoat hung. He remembered the smell of frying that was part of the air of the house, because in each room there was a gas-ring in a cupboard. How chaotic and yet how comforting! He remembered, too, the mouth-organ that he loved and was ashamed of, hidden from his landlady's derision under a pile of shirts in the second drawer of the tallboy. Although his playing had often been heard, he liked to pretend it was a secret. He thought regretfully of the youth who used to live on the floor above and who had played the flute. What evenings they had had, flute and mouth-organ competing! Still, somebody just as amusing might arrive any day. A cello-player would be ideal. That would be a test of Piers's musical endurance. He would even buy himself a better mouth-organ. How, he wondered sadly, would Bess fit in to this existence of noisy pleasures? What about the cupboard in which he threw any of his belongings which he did not need at the moment? What about the marmalade jars, three or four different brands, sticky-rimmed, opened because he could not find yesterday's jar or because he fancied another flavour. What would happen to these, each with a teaspoon half-embedded in the jellied mass? What mattered if he had no teaspoons at tea-time? He knew where they were, and in an emergency one could be rescued from the nearest pot and either washed or, more often, licked moderately clean. What would Bess do to these dear familiar things? If she could be persuaded not to interfere except for her husband's greater comfort, she might be an asset. She could turn the mattress, ensuring that the bed did not prickle with the crumbs of last night's sandwiches and cake. She could dust the room and sweep the floor, as long as his books and papers were sacred immovables. Oh yes, by God, she could darn his socks. Perhaps re-knit them around the small pieces that remained intact. His shirts, too, needed every help and encouragement.

But would Bess begin by being satisfied to expend her devotion upon housewifely objects, and end by tearing and re-fashioning his life from morning to midnight? Would she stop there? Might she not hound him to bed just when his brain was alight with a way of working that he had lacked for many a dreary, wasted week? Would she insist on Sunday luncheons, no matter what or who beckoned? Piers's life was built and steadied around a sweet confusion which was the pivot of his existence.

"If I eat at regular hours I get sluggish and I cannot think." Piers made an incoherent attempt to present the essence of his uncertainty in one sentence.

"She can't force you to eat. Not if you are firm from the first." In spite of his dislike of Piers, Thomas saw the point.

"Who is forcing Piers to eat?" Men, thought Marion, are infinitely more scatter-brained than women.

Piers threw himself into a chair. All his boyishness had gone; he thought of himself as a disillusioned man.

Marion looked at Piers's sprawling legs. Lolling about, she thought—that shows a fundamental lack of discipline. "Work! Oh work! How glad I shall be to get back! To have something to do. Just imagine spending one's life sitting about like this."

"What does it matter where or how one lives? Anyway, there will soon be an end to all that." Piers spoke with relish.

"An end to what? To living? Or to us?" asked Thomas.

"Our end will come. All in good time." Piers grinned maliciously, pleased to brandish the inescapable skull at Marion's complacency. "An end to living where we choose."

"Why shouldn't I live where I please?" Marion asked in a prickly voice. "There's little else that we are permitted nowadays."

"We shall have to go where we are sent." That has startled her, thought Piers. "Probably underground. Perhaps Australia." He suggested wildly, anxious to impress impermanence and his special knowledge.

"Australia indeed!" Marion was more enraged at the idea of Australia than of subterranean living. After all, she reasoned, if we have to behave like moles, it will be a case of necessity. Australia was a mere whim. "I'd like to see them try to get me to Australia. I believe in work and in everyone doing his bit. But to be ordered out of the country, that would be beyond a joke. I really don't know what the Government is about!" She sounded very cross.

"Don't upset yourself yet," Thomas said mildly. "Nothing is settled. You haven't got to pack tomorrow." That will teach her, he thought, not to be carried away by a youthful bearing; or to be bemused by a veneer of scholarship.

Rachel trotted down the stairs, carrying a sheaf of papers and a bundle of pencils, from each of which dangled a coloured tassel.

"Look, Marion!" she said triumphantly, holding up the pencils. "I've found these. Left over from the last bridge-tea. Now, when was that? Why it must have been . . . let me see . . . over ten years ago." She noticed their mildly astonished faces and asked, "What are you all staring at?" Then she smiled at Piers to show that his ordeal had not passed unrecorded.

"Pencils! Bridge teas!" Marion snapped. "They won't be much good in Australia." It is not, she thought, as though I believe such nonsense, but today has been so vile that anything is possible. And why shouldn't Mother suffer the same sudden absurd fears that we have?

"Australia?" Placidly Rachel dismissed the unwanted continent. "You've made a mistake, Marion. That's what comes of not listening. I told you that I would like to go to the Bahamas."

"Piers says that we shall either have to live underground or go to Australia. The Government will make us. We shall have to go."

"Is that so, dear?" Rachel asked calmly. "Of course I should choose Australia. Western Australia, that is. I believe the climate is ideal, and there is plenty of gold about. I know that part very well. We did it at school." She spoke to Piers, but her eyes said 'not this time, my lad; you can't catch me'.

"Oh well," Piers mumbled, "it's not so impossible. A lot of people think it may happen. Evacuation on a grand scale."

"Hardly in my lifetime, dear boy," Rachel said smoothly. "Although I might enjoy a change of scene. As long as I could travel comfortably."

Piers made one last effort. "By then we shall be shot off in rockets. Very breath-taking."

"You may be. I shan't. I should never agree to that." Rachel was regally adamant.

Piers was completely subdued. He could have played the joke on his mouth-organ, but the words had fallen flat. This wretched household had taken him seriously. He whistled softly, out of tune, *En passant par Lorraine*, as he looked out of the window. "If it would snow properly we could toboggan on the downs."

Thomas thought that he might have said that. To hear childish trivial wishes expressed by another is disconcerting.

"I preferred skating," said Rachel. "That was very gay, and it gave me an excellent colour. I learnt with a chair. Most amusing. A friendly pastime."

"Go on, Mother. Tell us how you saw an ox roasted on the Thames." Marion was resigned.

"I know that things have changed and that simple pleasures no longer appeal. But as it happens I did see an ox roasted on the Thames."

"You know perfectly well that you did not see anything of the kind!" Marion was affectionately teasing.

"Didn't I? Well, I must have read about it. I can even see it now." She stared fixedly out of the window at the bleak lawn, where patches of grass showed faintly through a thin layer of watery snow. Why, there it is, she thought delightedly. Just where the bird-bath used to be. A whole ox speared through with two enormous skewers swinging over a roaring fire. "It is all the same thing. I could have seen it. I was born then. So whether or not I happened to be there at the exact moment is of no consequence."

"You look tired, Mother. You ought to have a change." Marion wondered uneasily whether Rachel's mind was wandering.

"Your mother is the lucky one. Why, she can see that ox now." Thomas saw the reconstruction in Rachel's eyes. Rachel wrinkled her nose at him. This small grimace made her face appear young and gay. Her dark eyes laughed at him, mocked him with their carelessness.

"That is just what I was saying to Bess. No, perhaps I didn't tell her. But I meant to. Bournemouth, perhaps. I'd like to look at the people, although of course that is the sea again."

"By the way, where is Bess?" asked Marion.

"Oh, somewhere about. She is always disappearing," Piers said vaguely. He was not eager to be confronted by Bess, who was no longer just Bess, but the symbol of a responsibility.

"What are we waiting for? Luncheon will be ready soon. Isn't it time we had our sherry?" Rachel turned towards

Piers, who fetched the decanter and glasses from a corner cupboard.

"This is good sherry. Much better than usual. Exceptionally dry. Men prefer dry wines." Rachel knew that her palate detected imperfections with greater certainty than either Piers or Thomas could, but she prided herself on tactful humility.

"You are rather shaky, Thomas." Marion noticed the unsteadiness of his hand as he poured out the wine. "You have spilt some. How clumsy!" She rubbed the small damp spot on her skirt.

"Here's to you, darling." Piers lifted his glass and glanced flirtatiously at Rachel. "I can always imagine you sitting here in this lovely room with your roses on the table behind you."

Rachel turned her head to look at the old-fashioned silver bowl full of dark-red flowers. "They are superb, aren't they? Especially in the wrong season. They are not nearly as attractive in the summer."

"Ridiculously extravagant. I don't know how you can do it, Mother. What with the income tax and everything," Marion reprimanded.

"I am extravagant. And why shouldn't I be? You must remember, my dear, that I have no one to buy me beautiful things nowadays. Jonah always gave me roses at Christmas. He would want me still to have them."

I must not forget, thought Piers; red roses next Christmas. Bundles of them. Oh God, and a wife to keep! He sighed.

"What a sad sound!" Rachel looked enquiringly at him. "Is anything the matter?"

"No. Well, yes, in a way."

"What is it, dear boy? We mustn't have you worried."

"I can't explain. Not now." He glanced swiftly at Marion and Thomas, who felt embarrassed.

"If you want us to go———" began Marion.

"Of course not," Piers said sulkily.

"If it is very private, then we had better wait until you can tell me at length." That proves, thought Rachel, how Piers relies on my judgment. "We mustn't have you troubled, dear, must we? You're the brains of the family."

Piers blushed angrily. For once he suspected Rachel's fulsome praise of having a contemptuous undertone. "Where is Bess?" he asked desperately, hoping to divert attention from himself.

"Bess! Bess!" Rachel called out loudly. "Where are you? Piers cannot support your absence." She winked with splendid vulgarity at Thomas, inviting him to join in the mockery.

"Now, Rachel darling"—Piers spoke miserably—"I didn't say that."

"If you are going to marry Bess, you should not be able to let her out of your sight." Rachel did not for one second believe in this marriage. It was, she thought, merely a harlequinade before the pantomime began. A dancing, fighting harlequinade, quite in the old tradition. Piers lying on the floor, felled by the villain. Thomas was not sufficiently virile for his role, but he would have to do. Her own graceful arrival. Her lace handkerchief. Nobody was hurt because nothing was meant. A party charade. "Beatrice!" Rachel called again. The use of the unfamiliar name denoted increasing displeasure.

"I'll go up and see where she is," Piers said quickly.

He returned in a few minutes. "She is not in her room."

"How very odd," Rachel said disinterestedly. Bess is being sullen somewhere, she thought. That is what comes of kindness to one's husband's relatives. Jonah was a good man, but there is undoubtedly bad blood in his family. "And why aren't Kate and Adrian down here? Luncheon is almost ready."

"They are busy," Piers grinned. "Kate says will you please call them at the last minute?"

"Busy! On Boxing Day! And what are they busy at?" Rachel was jealous. She would dearly love to be busy. How dare her house be filled by contented busyness in which she had no part?

"Playing gin rummy. Adrian seems to have won."

"Are they gambling for money?" Marion was shocked at this unprincipled waste of hours.

"You must try to move with the times, Marion. What-else would they play for? What other reason for playing anything?" Rachel felt very modern.

Thomas laughed. "You are an old pet," he said affectionately.

"Yes, darling, you are absolutely sweet." Piers was annoyed with himself for missing his opportunities.

"This morning Marion mislaid her husband. You've lost Bess even before you are married. Very careless."

Someone might ask me to have another glass of sherry, Rachel thought. I never touch any wine except at Christmas or Easter or some out-of-season celebration. Such as the end of the war. Although there was really more excitement at the beginning. Of course it was all extremely terrible and very frightening. But the end was not exactly satisfactory. Most indefinite. First one bit ended and then another. She remembered how she and Bess had taken the train to London to join in one day of rejoicing, but London was not as gay as Rachel had expected. There had been a lot of people, of course. Holding arms, nine or ten in a row. All of them shouting. Some wore paper hats. But no one was behaving quite as joyously as she had hoped. In Trafalgar Square the crowds swayed aimlessly to and fro. There had been one girl standing by herself, crying. That had spoilt Rachel's day. For if one person could stand miserably apart, that had showed all was not well in the world. On such a day the whole of England should have been filled with such exuberance that everyone would have been forced to laugh because of the general joy. Suddenly she had become tired, and all because of that girl. Bess had had to stop a private car to beg the driver to take them to Victoria. A very rude man, too, who said that old people ought not to over-tax themselves and should know before they were on the point of collapse. That only showed, thought Rachel, that one should never go out unless escorted by a man. Otherwise one was humiliated left and right.

"I saw Bess go out," Thomas said. "An hour or so ago."

"Gone out at lunch-time! I don't know what has come

over all of you." Rachel was peevish. "Now my rheumatism has begun again. That is because I have had such an upsetting morning."

"More likely sherry," said Marion. "You know that it doesn't agree with you."

"Don't preach, dear." Then Rachel rounded upon Piers. "Do something. Go and find Bess and bring her back at once. Tell her that luncheon has been ready for over an hour."

"But it hasn't."

"Never mind. Tell her it has. Otherwise she will not realise the inconvenience she has caused."

"Did she say where she was going?" Piers asked Thomas.

"I didn't speak to her." Thomas waited until Piers had struggled into his overcoat and wound a long woollen scarf untidily around his neck. "I don't think you'll find her," he said with enjoyment. "She did not look as though she would be back for lunch."

"Tommy, what do you mean! What has happened to Bess? Where has she gone?" Marion asked her husband sharply.

"She had a dressing-case or some kind of bag. She was walking very quickly." Thomas could not resist this extraneous information.

"Why didn't you stop her?" Marion was bewildered.

"Why should I? She must be nearly forty" (Piers swallowed with a gulping noise) "and naturally I imagined she could do what she pleased."

"Nobody can. Don't trot out that old waffle," snapped Marion.

Rachel was silent. She could not believe that Bess was

capable of behaving in such an uncontrolled and eccentric manner. To walk out just when the house was full of people. No, it was not possible.

"Well, Mother, what's to be done?" Marion asked. She was convinced that some action should be taken. Not that Bess was a prisoner, but whatever happened outside the routine, action must be taken either for or against. To sit passively was a sign of moral decadence.

"That is a question for you and Thomas to answer. You should look after your husband, Marion. Allowing him to connive with Bess. I cannot speak about it, I am too distraught." Rachel was playing for time, knowing perfectly well that little could be done, yet to admit this was not in her nature.

"Distraught! What good will come of your being distraught?"

"Why don't you say something, Thomas?" Rachel pretended that he was the culprit. "Did you help Bess to plan this fantastic exit?"

"Certainly not." Thomas felt that he had unwittingly become a principal in one of the silliest mock dramas imaginable. Because a woman happens to decide that she prefers to have a few hours, or a few days, away from her relations and omits the usual farewells, everyone behaves as if it were a tragedy.

"I am shocked by your complete lack of family obligations." Rachel accused them all.

"What do you want us to do?" asked Marion.

"As Piers is the most directly concerned—after

myself—perhaps you should ask him." Rachel cleverly transferred the initiative.

"Why can't we have lunch?" Piers spoke with conscious bravado.

Rachel refused to meet his eyes. She wanted to agree, yet realised that a protest was expected. "How can you consider food!" Rachel desired not only consent, but persuasion. "Although perhaps we should . . .?"

"There appears to be no harm in our eating," Marion admitted grudgingly. The day might even now be broken up by the need of planned movement.

"And afterwards," Rachel took control again, "you must all go different ways. One of you is sure to pick up the trail."

"That would be useless." Thomas's voice was amused. The effort of not smiling deepened the small lines around his eyes.

Noticing this, Rachel thought about herself. 'Age shall not wither her.' Who had told her that? And how many years ago? It was true, too. Age had plumped her out, pushed away the deep creases running from her nose towards her chin. She put up one hand to stroke her cheek with gentle, explorative fingers, patting the soft cushion of flesh over her cheekbone that had once showed a hard outline. She wished that she could remember who had spoken those prophetic words to her. For indeed she had been a thin-bodied, pointed-faced girl who would be likely to wrinkle and wither. Which is better, she wondered, to shrink towards the bones, for the flesh to lose its goodness and to become a creased wrapping-paper for the skeleton, or for the flesh to puff and swell until the original outline is distorted and finally forgotten? Thomas, she thought, as she scrutinised her son-in-law, is already beginning to wither. She looked again, and saw that his long, tired face was also in the process of acquiring knowledge. What is he on the point of knowing? No, she corrected herself, it will take a long while: perhaps years. Thomas was looking at her with kindly questioning.

"What did you say, dear?" Rachel's voice was low, intimate with a particularly feminine inflection—a voice that singled out Thomas, chose him for its own, seemed to tweak his ear affectionately, telling him that Rachel had been thinking about him.

"I was saying, Rachel dear"—(Rachel blinked with a delighted confusion that warmed her cheeks. Why should Thomas call her 'Rachel' instead of 'Mother' unless he knew her mind? She bent her head so that she could glance up at him to acknowledge their small secret)—Thomas grinned at her. "You haven't heard a word," he said in mock reproof.

Marion fidgeted impatiently. What has come over everyone? she wondered. "Thomas has been trying to explain that this is not a paper-chase. What clues are we supposed to find?"

"You could ask people." Rachel's mouth suggested a pout.

"Oh no, we couldn't, Mother. Certainly not."

"Very well, Marion. You can stay here while your cousin struggles in the sea. A terrible thought. How could you ever forgive yourself?"

"You do not really believe that Bess would do such a thing." Thomas spoke soothingly, although he knew that Rachel was quite capable of believing whatever would cause the greatest inconvenience.

"I've studied Bess. She isn't a suicidal type." Piers spoke with lordly conviction.

"Then your studies should have warned you that Bess was likely to rush off," Rachel snubbed him.

Thomas said that he would fetch Kate and Adrian. He would tell them about Bess, he thought, and so prevent Rachel from re-enacting the drama.

They were seated at a small table in Kate's room, playing cards with intensity, stopping only to mark the scores on sheets of squared paper. Adrian's thinning hair appeared to have receded farther, his forehead glistened large and flat. His soft, plump hands shuffled the cards expertly. Occasionally with tender gestures his fingers patted the silver coins piled in front of him. He had the gambler's ecstatic remoteness. He sighed as Thomas came into the room.

"We are only just finishing this game," Adrian said pettishly.

Disregarding him, Thomas spoke directly to Kate, telling her briefly that Bess had gone and that Rachel was tottering between high tragedy and hunger.

"I know." Kate sounded omniscient. "Anyway, she has Piers with her."

"Oh no, she hasn't." Thomas could not keep an exultancy out of his voice.

Adrian looked curiously at his brother-in-law. So that was it. Well, isn't that interesting? He noted the information in his mind. He would need these scraps of knowledge one day. He would cherish them, smooth them out, fit them in their rightful places, until suddenly the whole would be in his hand, ready to be used in any way at all.

"Bess came in here to talk to me earlier this morning. I persuaded her to go away with Piers, and not to wait until tomorrow." Kate frowned worriedly, conscious that she would be held responsible.

"She has taken the part of your advice that suited her." Thomas tried to sound impersonal.

"As she is set on marrying Piers, I thought that she'd better make sure of him," Kate said unhappily, excusing herself for this unexpected breaking-up of her schemes.

Adrian's small eyes moved from Kate's face back to Thomas's. Intent little eyes that gathered material for conclusions. Eyes that lived by the grace of their own percipiency.

"If you do not come down soon, Rachel will make us fast as a penance," Thomas said.

"You both go down. I shall not be a minute." The excitement is stimulating, she thought, as she brushed her hair. What I need is for things to happen. Not necessarily to me, but at least within sight and hearing. She smiled at herself in the mirror as she painted her lips before she ran downstairs.

Adrian was very hungry. Nothing like winning to give one an appetite, he thought as he bounced towards his chair. Except, perhaps, losing.

"No doubt Thomas has told you about Bess?" Rachel asked her son.

Adrian nodded. "Well, what d'jer know!" He spoke with evident admiration of Bess's agility and courage.

"I know nothing whatever. I am kept absolutely in the dark." Rachel chose to misinterpret her son's idiom.

Kate scurried in, saying as she sat down: "Yes, Aunt Rachel, Thomas has told us everything." She hoped to prevent an impassioned recital.

"So Thomas has told you everything!" Rachel repeated. "That is very clever of him. Why hasn't he told me? If Thomas knows why and where Bess has gone, he might be civil enough to share this essential information with all of us." Rachel had been cheated of her story, and this provoked her to turn against her favourite of five minutes ago.

Thomas remained purposefully obtuse, offering rolls, butter and salt with detached consideration. Rachel ate with good appetite, as if her hands fed her mouth absent-mindedly against her will.

Now that I am old, she thought, whipping herself to a fury, people go away from me. Go off without a word of love or explanation. My own family, too. They know that I need them. I used to have such pleasant friends, but they are not near me. She tried to forget that most of them had died. But the knife-point of knowledge found and pricked her, just there, on her left side, between the ribs. Should she move about or remain inactive, waiting for what was to come? For at her age every gap in the bulwark of her family walls was a portent of death. Suppose she shouted, 'Bess must come back or death will take her place'? What would they say? Would they hold her hands and speak soothingly to her? Or would they telephone for the doctor? Would they give her brandy or Sedobrol? How could she explain that of late years she had felt that death was waiting for a chance to get in? That death was ready to seat himself in an empty chair, ready to eat at her table? She shivered: her voice was almost tremulous.

"Put that chair back, Thomas. Bess can't expect us to keep luncheon for her."

Thomas rose obediently. As he passed, he touched Rachel lightly yet comfortingly on the shoulder. "Bess will come back. Everyone canters off at one time or another."

Marion kept herself from speaking. The effort puckered her forehead. She longed to relate the end of the tale. How the jaunty wanderer returned, limping and tired, having achieved nothing except that he was in a worse position than when he started out.

"I cannot think where she can be. She catches cold so easily, too." Rachel sounded almost self-reproachful.

"Don't worry. She may have gone to my flat. I told her she could if she wanted to." Kate hoped to quieten Rachel's fears.

"You did, did you? Extraordinary the way you young people make arrangements without any consideration for the feelings of others," Rachel grumbled, trying to hide her relief.

"Just as well that I'm here." Adrian's voice was startling. He had sat so quietly, watching, awaiting his moment, that he had been forgotten. "Even if she doesn't come back, you won't be alone." He looked from one face to another, assessing his position. But the faces conveyed only varying degrees of surprise. Uneasy thoughts brought a sensation of physical discomfort behind his eyes. Even his blood felt heated by a fire of spitefulness. That he should have to fight for his rights, for his inheritance, was unpleasant, but not unnatural. The realisation that he had been passed over, forgotten, that neither his presence nor his absence was noticeable, that was a blacker pit than he had anticipated.

He picked up a knife and with deliberate sawing movements cut his roll first into halves, then into quarters, and lastly into segments of eight. He looked up to see Piers regarding the mutilated roll with disgust. Adrian smiled. That will teach you a lesson, my popinjay, he thought. You are so damn sure of yourself that even when your girl runs off you sit there stuffing. But you're not made of stone. You can still shudder when your common uncle cuts his roll, instead of breaking it with his fingers, as gentlemen do. Piers looked away.

"So you won't be alone, Mother," Adrian persisted.

Rachel knew that Adrian would be worse than nobody, then immediately tried to retract. Oh, how wicked I am! she thought. And not so long ago I spoke of God. Some power has snatched Bess from me. I must be careful. I must be humble. If I am unkind to Adrian, what may not happen next?

"That is a great blessing. I shall have my son."

Adrian drooped with disappointment. He was prepared to defend his position; ready to hate them all. Suddenly he was

239

trapped by this reversal. What would become of his tricks of ingratiation? What must he do now that he was a welcome guest? He could not recall what was expected of him. His preparations were for enmity. Vaguely he realised—although the thought was as yet a mere tadpole of feeling that swam in his head—that he could not stay for long in this house where he was wanted. There was little point in his rotting away on this dull coast.

Piers pushed his chair away from the table and stood up. "I shall go after Bess. I'll see that she comes back."

"But you haven't finished your lunch." Marion would have preferred to be the master of ceremonies.

"Naturally Piers feels that he must go. It is his place to look after Bess," Rachel said approvingly. "I'll see that she comes back"; there is safety in that.

Piers smiled his loving thanks and banged out of the room before he could be hindered by further comments or counter-suggestions. Rachel, he thought, was the one joy: she was herself. Kate had possibilities, yet apart from her argumentativeness she did not actually amount to much. As for the others, Marion and Thomas were pretty grim. Adrian was too, too ghastly. Piers told himself that he had had more than he could stand.

He clattered noisily about in his bedroom, opening and shutting drawers. He had no intention of returning this Christmas. Perhaps never, he thought with romantic abandon.

His possessions were few, and he had proudly schooled himself to be able to leave everything and to walk away without many regrets for what was behind him, whether people, clothes or personal belongings. Other people clutter their lives, he alone remained free. Rachel would, of course, forward all his things, but this he put out of mind because the certainty marred his grand gesture of relinquishment.

From a tumbler on the glass shelf above the wash-basin he took three toothbrushes, which he wrapped in a torn envelope and put carefully into his pocket. One brush for morning, another for evening, and a third for his gums. He was proud of his teeth. Into a dispatch-case already stuffed with papers and odds and ends of chewing-gum, visiting-cards, a thermometer, hair-oil and shaving-soap, he pushed two pairs of socks; neither pair was clean. He threw his overcoat over his shoulders, then changed his mind and put his arms into the sleeves.

Swinging his dispatch-case, he strode on to the landing. The case was rather fuller than he had planned, but in spite of this he contrived to feel free as the air. Suddenly he galloped back into the bedroom to retrieve from the bottom of the wardrobe where they rested among two or three pairs of unmendable shoes, his most secret possessions. Four exercise-books in which were pages of technicalities about igneous rocks and the potholes found in Limestone Regions, interspersed with schoolboy essays. Here were facts about the moon, each detail annotated by footnotes in cramped handwriting, and bracketed among these notes were quotations from Henley and Kipling. There were pages of pretentious remarks about himself, heavily written in black-leaded pencil which interrupted lengthy passages about the Great Chalk Sea. Odd geometric designs, algebraic equations, some excitedly scrawled sentences (crossed out) about a new planet, followed by an immature working out of sums showing his overdraft at the bank. Here was all that he determined to accomplish, his desires and regrets.

He sighed happily. Soon he would be away from this house. A wanderer who had left behind his clothes, even his shoes (apart from the only wearable pair which he had on his feet).

He had only to spend a short space of time sorting matters out with Bess. He was sure that everything would be resolved by the inspiration of the moment.

When Piers arrived at the flat it was after midnight. He had stopped on the way to eat a heavy dinner. He had persuaded a head waiter to cash Rachel's cheque. He felt tired, and wondered whether he would go to an hotel for the night, putting off until tomorrow the tricky interview with Bess. But hotels were damned expensive; he resented wasting money on ephemeral comforts. Nothing to show for it afterwards. Better to see Bess and get it over. He could sleep on a settee. Mustn't start anything again, he told himself firmly.

He rang the bell, which sounded over-insistent in the quietness of the corridor. Bess opened the door. She had obviously gone to bed: she was half-asleep and rather cross. She looked gloomily at Piers. She was sure that he had come at this unearthly hour to tell her something that she did not wish to hear. His arrival could not be for her good.

242

Why did he have to present himself now, just when she had endeavoured to concentrate upon the familiar tyranny of Rachel's domination and the settled background of a house that one has lived in for years?

"Aren't you going to ask me to come in?" Piers said irritably. "They are worried to death. What possessed you to go off like that?"

Bess stood aside to let him enter. "You needn't have come to fetch me. I am going home tomorrow anyway."

Piers looked uneasily at her. What did she mean by that? Was she returning to him? How had their relationship been left? He could hardly remember. There were always so many ups and downs. A catch-as-catch-can game to relieve the tedium of hours when he was away from his own surroundings: a game which had mistakenly become serious. Why, he had even considered marriage.

"I suppose you'll let me stay here tonight? I could sleep on that."

Bess looked doubtfully towards the settee at which he pointed. The springs sagged. She nodded. "Just as you like. As long as you don't ask questions."

"What questions?" Piers asked numbly. He had prepared vague half-composed phrases that would take them carefully back to a time before marriage had been mentioned.

"Any questions. I chose to come here. I am going home tomorrow. That's my choice, too. Although you happen to have come after me, I have made up my own mind."

"That's fine," Piers said snappishly. She was, he thought, being a damned sight too off-hand. He had made this long journey in the bitter cold, to use his persuasiveness on a truant, and had found a woman who was meekly going back tomorrow.

"I like people to be themselves. I want them complete. You have become different. Perhaps"—her voice lost its false surety, became the light-toned asking voice that Piers recognised—"you have tried to be different for me. But it doesn't suit you." A tumult of self-pity humiliated her. She looked steadfastly at the carpet, hoping that her pleading had not been apparent.

"Good God, no!" The idea that he might be influenced was ludicrous. "We both made a mistake." The 'both' was, he thought, very magnanimous. "But still, we discovered it in time." The conclusion had, he thought happily, been unexpectedly easy.

Bess wondered why she did not hate him. To dismiss her with a careless sentence coupling her with his own destructiveness.

She muttered a few trivialities about blankets to which Piers listened stolidly. She left him without another word.

"Sleep tight," Piers called after her amiably. He yawned luxuriously. He had an infinite capacity for putting people aside. Bess had receded to her proper place: well out of sight. He unlaced his shoes, switched off the table-lamp, swung his legs on to the settee, groaned as he found it too short for comfort. He draped his overcoat like a quilt over himself, and then got up again to switch on the electric fire. In his head he wrote to Rachel: *Rachel darling, I didn't come back because the atmosphere is a bit sticky. Tu comprends? I packed*

Bess home, but only after a struggle. Then at the last minute she pretended that she was going to return anyway: I hated not saying good-bye to you, darling: but I think things had better calm down. What a fool I've been: But you are an angel, I can always rely on you to dig me out, can't I? Forgive me—your errant (but most loving) Piers. 'Errant': an excellent word. He congratulated himself and fell asleep well satisfied.

CHAPTER FOUR

The Return

TOGETHER they walked to the station. The morning air was cold, the sky bright with the clarity of early light.

Piers was a healthy young man striding through pine-forests. His coat flapped open, his scarf hung loosely from his shoulders. He felt extremely cold. If he had realised that the temperature was nearly at freezing point he would have chosen another role. But he had adapted himself to the character of nonchalant youth, and now he could not change it until Bess had gone. He glanced at her abstracted expression. He might just as well not have bothered: however, his honour would not allow him to relax until his audience had left.

"What will you do afterwards?" Bess asked, adding quickly: "Not that it concerns me. I don't really want to know." With some effort she dissociated herself from Piers's present and from his future. Soon she would succeed in partially dissociating herself from their joint past: that she had promised herself during the night when she had sipped orange squash out of a tooth-glass. The drink was thick and sweet, yet it left an acid taste in her mouth.

"You are very edgy this morning."

"I am cold." Bess thought of the fire at home. Kate would be sitting on the low stool nearly inside the fireplace. Her hair would be red in the reflected glow. Sitting there crouched and warm, she might stretch out her hands preparatory to moving: or she might sleep for half an hour. That is the way to live, thought Bess. To sit warmed and waiting. Not to run out into the biting afternoon only to return in the even colder morning.

The road to the station led them by a small backwater of a disused canal. The water, dark and cloudy, flattened itself against the muddy banks. Victorian houses stood high along one side of the water. These houses, neglected and for years unpainted, still retained a tired reticence. Ugly and remote, they held themselves away from the stagnant pond.

Bess hesitated, then stood still. This unlooked-for canal, the gaunt houses, the stillness of the place, transformed personal despair into a distant prospect.

With a peremptory, unfamiliar gesture, she lifted her hand, asking Piers not to speak. He stamped his feet like a horse that senses fear.

Is this the place? he wondered. Must we stand looking down on that horrible water while we try to explain our thoughts and actions from the first moment until we reach the negation of the present?

"This," he said vaguely, "should have happened in the summer."

Bess tried to imagine what the summer might be by this canal. She could not bring the sun to mind, neither could she see herself and Piers here in the early hours of any morning that might be the prelude to a hot day. This place was right for her, and for this interval between trains. A curious contentment relaxed her body. She could think here, and she might even be able to speak some of her thoughts. For once she was a figure which belonged to the background. Whereas Piers, pulling at his scarf-ends, was an afterthought, painted in when the picture was complete.

Piers blew miserably upon his fingers. Why was Bess pretending to bewilder him? He reminded himself that he had her taped. But what was she doing mooning around in this damp hole? What was she doing?

"You'll miss your train," he said gloomily.

Slowly Bess walked away from the water. She did not look back. For a few minutes all that she saw had been hers.

"When you spoke about the summer"—her voice faltered slightly with the endeavour to compress into one sentence the numberless nearly formulated thoughts that were illusive points of light in her mind. "We have expected summer. So we were wrong even from the beginning. Lately it has become worse." How hopeless! she thought. Those words mean nothing. Her face expressed the urgency of one who, after all has been said, demands not love, but a recognisable comprehension.

Even Piers realised that something was expected, and braced himself to give the impression that he understood perfectly.

"Yes, I believe I see what you mean." He frowned to show that he was a young man who could be trusted with grave pronouncements. Some women, he told himself, cry; some women are angry; others become philosophers. He was pleased with this addition to his worldly knowledge. He smiled affectionately as he took her arm, and with a quick movement pulled her towards him.

"Darling, it's been absolute hell for both of us." His voice had the charm of boyish confession, of repentance, almost the tones of his earlier years, when he had been lonely, balanced between the many differing lives from which, he was convinced, he could have chosen.

"It doesn't matter. I know now that we could not be together. We needed each other only when neither of us knew what we really wanted." Her impassivity gave the commonplace words the dignity of discovered truth.

What she could not tell him was that she desired above all not to be charming: not to care. Men must be charmed. That was so in her world. To be able to dismiss charm she must dismiss future voices and knowledge of eyes; she would forget the swift joy of fingers resting on her shoulder, claiming her in a crowded room, making herself remember, only to put aside. She thought of people in houses, in blocks of flats, in taxis, in restaurants: all of them meeting and parting, all of them planning to meet again or to search for other new encounters. She thought of herself when Rachel had died: even this solitude did not appal her. Already she saw herself as an incident in the lives of others. This review of the future brought her some measure of contentment.

"Perhaps we might see each other once again. I'll probably be leaving England soon." Piers spoke fretfully. He wanted to ensure that Bess would remember him for ever and ever. He had renounced all securities except this: that Bess should occasionally wake in the night to feel herself the most wretched of women. That she should always have by her side an insistent thought of him: that she should never cease to miss him. Without the security of a home in her mind, he was lost: worse than that, he would become what he had pretended to be—a wanderer with nothing of his own, a scholar who has renounced the world of hands and hastily scrawled letters. He would be forced to live the bleakly logical conclusion of his mental masquerade.

But supposing, thought Bess, this sternness of purpose should leave me as suddenly as it came? Panic rested heavily on her throat. The physical sensation was so real that she put her hand against her neck. Such desperate fear might surely solidify? Her throat was the same as ever, thin, lacking strength.

She walked more quickly, determined to get away from Piers while she could still keep her face moulded into a blank denial of the present.

Piers, panting a little, caught hold of her sleeve to pull her back. The roughness of the gesture quieted her.

"Whatever happens," Piers coaxed, "you and I have meant something special to each other. You'll never forget that, will you?"

She had only to promise and immediately Piers would speak those sweet phrases that she would recall as well next year as tomorrow: words which Piers himself would be incapable of remembering this afternoon.

"You are the most completely selfish person I have ever known." She had inflicted her own wound: she stiffened herself for the great axe to fall.

Piers wavered between admiration and mockery. "Now you are a real Beatrice. Bess was getting to be a bit of a bore, dear." He hoped that she had understood. "But seriously, my sweet, why couldn't you have been like this yesterday?"

Bess turned venomously upon him. "You never like me as I am. Always yesterday or tomorrow. Never now! Never now!"

"Temper, temper!" Piers said ineffectually, hoping that she would calm down by the time they reached the station. He could imagine the curious ears and inquisitive eyes of early morning travellers, not yet accustomed to taking up the day's experience, yet sufficiently awake to be sniggering spectators.

"There is no one about." She sensed his dread of appearing ridiculous.

"You are being bloody awkward." Piers was petulant.

"I understand perfectly what a horrible position you're in. You don't know what to say next, do you? That is how I have lived for three—or is it four?—years. Never knowing what I should say or do either to please or to pacify you. Five minutes is unpleasant. Four years is intolerable. Because you think you are wonderful, and because you have made me think so too, just because of that I have wasted four years."

Piers licked his lips. This is most unfair, he thought. I have been too kind, too loving. That is my handicap, my nice nature.

"Whose fault is it?"

"Mine entirely. I have run after you." Bess's sharpness

was directed at herself. "But haven't you enjoyed yourself! Going away, coming back, sometimes loving me a little, sometimes not at all. Sidestepping and pirouetting, looking at yourself in mirrors: listening to your own pretty speeches, clapping your own play-acting. I saw it all, but I didn't care. In spite of all your knowledge, you are still a posturing fool to have about the house. But I wanted you about the house. More than anything else I wanted you to be there, no matter how disgracefully you behaved. You have been the greatest worry of my life. Now I am sick of being worried, and I am going home to live quietly. I have no more capacity for worrying about you."

Her joints felt loose, as if jolted from their sockets. She wished she was already in the train. She was angry at having mistimed her words, and wondered why she had not kept silent until the last few minutes. Then she could have cracked her little whip as the train took her away. Why couldn't she have saved this effort at a grand gesture for a final unanswerable sentence?

A boy on a bicycle turned his head to grin impudently at the two tensed figures who had halted in the middle of the deserted street.

The boy's grin added to Piers's furious confusion. His gentle Bess, his meek worshipper, had become mad for love of him. But his conceit had momentarily lost the power to people his world with adoring subjects.

"You might have waited. You should either have said this much earlier, or much later." He watched his breath take form in the cold air.

"I couldn't choose. Besides, what difference does it make? You have seldom noticed what I have said or what I did not say."

With distasteful clarity scenes and figures and the remembrance of what he had felt at such a time or in such a place crowded upon him. Everywhere, whether at a party, or shuffling down a snow-thick street, or riding in buses when the mid-day sun burned through the windows—everywhere he could see Bess's eyes, trying to imprison his bad temper, trying to forward his cause, trying, above all, to explain. Her eyes had been always too following, too deeply curious. The ingratitude of women! He had almost loved her—at least, he had cared sufficiently to accept her affection—and now she turned upon him, endeavouring to destroy him. Gradually his innermost conviction was restored: he was Piers, the handsome, the beloved, the discoverer.

"You won't do anything awful, will you?" he asked with inconsistent concern, recalling Kate's words. "I mean throw yourself out of the train . . .?"

"Why should I?"

"Some women do."

"Not women like me."

"Darling, why are you like this today? You have made everything quite unbearable."

Bess did not reply. She told herself, not entirely truthfully, that she had reached the peak of her achievement—she was not listening.

They had come to the station. Before they had time even to look at each other, the train arrived, whistling and screeching, breaking the air, leaving a high echo of a scream that sounded even when there was silence.

Piers dived towards her, held her shoulders, kissed her clumsily, missing her mouth. Then he pushed her into the train. The carriage window crashed down, leaving her unprotected, as if in an empty three-sided room.

"Look after yourself, darling," he said casually, with an insolent disregard of the need of the moment.

"Good-bye," Bess could not resist the word. She stood uncomfortably at the window, waiting for Piers to speak.

The train began to move. She clutched at the dusty window-frame to stop herself from falling. She could not believe that Piers had nothing more to say. Only when she had been taken some distance from him, when already he had become shorter and smaller to her eyes, she realised that he had said nothing, nothing at all.

"Piers! Piers!" Her voice was a high, desperate cry.

She could not see his face clearly. He raised his arm to wave to her: not the gesture that anticipates a return. An unmistakable finality.

Before the train was out of sight, Piers turned away. He knotted his scarf around his neck, and stuffed his hands in his pockets. He walked towards the buffet. He thought about the coffee that he would drink. Filthy muck. What else could you expect in this country? But apart from his forebodings about the coffee, he was satisfied. He carried in his ears the sound of Bess's voice; her cry was as lightly insistent as mountain bells.

She had had to give in at the very end.

Marion looked at her wrist-watch for the third time in ten minutes.

"Half-past nine," she said emphatically. "I said it's half-past nine, Mother."

"Yes, dear, I know. Five minutes ago you were kind enough to tell me that it was twenty-five minutes past."

"They have had all night. Not a word. Piers could surely have telephoned? I can't think how you can sit still."

"I have not finished my breakfast." Rachel turned towards Thomas. "Is Marion such a chatterbox at home? Men like to be quiet at breakfast—at least, they did in my day."

"They still do." Thomas lit a cigarette, and as an after-thought offered one to his wife, which she accepted with an air of fatality, grimacing as she tasted the first mouthful of smoke.

"In the usual way I smoke hardly at all, and never before the evening." Marion regarded her cigarette with an expression of abhorrence. "I never allow my department to smoke during office hours. The very smell of smoke in a room gives the impression of laxness." She looked accusingly at Thomas, who disregarded the challenge.

"You must remember, Marion, that we are not your department." Rachel's eyes accepted the silent applause, while Kate ostentatiously lit another cigarette from the stub of her last one.

"In my opinion you are treating this business of Bess and Piers far too lightly." Adrian was peevish. He had taken the trouble to get up at a ridiculously early hour, although nobody had remarked on this sacrifice, nor had he been asked whether he would like a kipper; he had been forced to help himself from the dish on the sideboard just as if he had never gone away. He had come down to breakfast because he did not want to miss the crisis, and now they were pretending that the crisis did not exist.

"What are you making a fuss about?" Rachel picked up her plate, on which were the greasy remains of skin and bones, and held it helplessly in the air as a sign that it should be removed. Thomas took it away from her. Bess, she thought irritably, would have realised long ago that, having eaten the kipper, Rachel could not bear to be reminded of it. "Is no one going to pass me the butter?" Rachel regarded the remains of the toast, made half an hour before, with distaste.

Immediately the room fluttered with movement. Kate ran into the kitchen to make fresh toast, while Thomas, Marion and Adrian hastily pushed butter, marmalade, honey and black cherry jam in front of Rachel, who smiled welcomingly at the newly filled toast-rack which Kate placed on the table.

"I do enjoy eating," Rachel said happily, engrossed in the pleasures of the moment, forgetting that she had graver matters to consider.

"Can you spare me one piece of that toast?" Thomas asked. "I am quite hungry again."

"Splendid, dear boy, splendid!" Not good-looking, she

thought, but neat and presentable, certainly second-best now that Piers is not here. She glanced towards Adrian, then looked hastily away. Almost nasty, she thought guiltily. His eyes seem to be dropping on to his face.

"Don't worry, darling." Kate believed, mistakenly, that Rachel was over-eating to keep her courage up. "They will come back."

"That is not the point. People nearly always do come back. But I want Bess as she was."

"Surely you don't want Piers as he was?" Marion demanded. "There's a great deal of room for improvement in that young man."

Rachel brushed crumbs, and Marion's remark, off the table-cloth. "Piers is Piers. He is fundamentally unalterable." Rachel dismissed Marion and Adrian and spoke only to Kate and Thomas. "Bess is ready to become anything at all. You do see that, don't you?"

Adrian sighed. The complexities of life in England had tired him out. He longed for sharp contrasts, not these nebulous undertones.

"Some people can go away for years and still remain the same." Rachel asked for reassurance.

"I think we can put it right," said Thomas gently. He had no idea what he meant, but he could not refuse to give Rachel the comfort she required.

"If I may say so, Mother, this is entirely your doing." Marion lectured. "If you had encouraged Bess to lead a more normal life she would not have lost her head over a mere boy. It is all very unpleasant and unsuitable."

"And if I may say so, Marion, the trouble is that you are incapable of losing your head, and that makes you a very tedious woman," Rachel snapped.

Adrian giggled. Thomas looked reproachfully at Rachel. Had he not supported her? Now his reward was to be impaled between the loyalty that he should give to his wife and the sympathy he felt for his mother-in-law.

Kate fidgeted with a teaspoon. She thought that they were all being very tiresome this morning. If only she had not encouraged Bess to go off. . . .

Marion was unperturbed. She was accustomed to her Mother's verbal attacks. She promised herself the pleasure of giving Thomas a good talking-to later. The restraint was irksome, but Thomas was not himself here; she must wait until he was isolated, away from her family. Besides, in his weak-willed way he was a little too fond of Bess, which made him prejudiced and unpredictable. What a fine couple Bess and Thomas would make! Talk about the blind leading the blind . . . Contempt and affection confused Marion's clear-cut purpose.

"Isn't this all rather futile?" Kate spoke carelessly. "Bess can surely do as she likes for once. If she succeeds in marrying Piers, good luck to her. Perhaps she would prefer to be unhappy than to feel nothing at all. I would."

"What you would prefer doesn't apply to Bess." Thomas was surprised by his own conviction. For a few seconds he understood Bess, knew what she could bear and what would destroy her. "You are stimulated by your emotions. You think that you have a great capacity for feeling, but in reality you are not greatly affected. You are merely there, and you feel what is blown towards you. That is not the same as holding an emotion and having to carry it around for hours, perhaps for years."

"Tommy, Tommy, what are you chattering about? Why don't you write it down? It's far too clever for me." Marion's voice was a reminder that he was her husband, her property, and that she had had enough of his nonsense.

"Thomas is right. That is what I mean. Bess must be protected from herself." Rachel stuck out her lower lip and folded her hands, so that she was unmistakably a protector.

Kate stared broodingly at Thomas. I forgive you, her eyes said, although these skirmishes are tiring especially so early in the day.

"All this yapping about Bess! Poor Bess, dear Bess, deluded Bess! She is just a little silly. Perhaps she is not responsible. But what about Piers? He ought to know better. What are his plans? I'll tell you—to marry Bess, get enough money from you"—Marion wagged her head at Rachel—"to live on for the rest of his life and—" Rachel began to speak, but Marion shouted furiously, "You just listen to me for a change! And he'll leave Bess high and dry, and she'll come back to live on you. It's plain enough to me. God knows why you can't see it." Marion's face was flushed and her forehead shone.

Rachel breathed deeply. Not from the chest, she told herself. Breathe low down in the stomach. That is how opera-singers breathe. It is not only calming, but it gives greater power and resonance to the voice. She noticed with satisfaction that when she spoke her tone was rounded and full.

"Don't excite yourself, Marion. For one thing, it is unbecoming." Rachel stared fixedly at her daughter's gleaming forehead. "There is no reason for Piers to go to the elaborate lengths that you suggest. I may as well tell you—and Adrian, too, if he is interested—that I do not consider myself fortunate in my children. A terrible admission, but there it is. Although the relationship is not such a close one, I have greater obligations towards Bess and Piers. As for you, Kate, within your limitations you are amiable, although obtuse."

"Really, Mother, I can assure you that Marion insists upon working. I am able and willing to keep her in moderate comfort." Thomas was unsure whether or not he had suffered an indirect thrust.

"I am aware of that, Thomas." Rachel smiled condescendingly. "Although I do consider that you should put your foot down more often." Thomas shut his eyes: the oft-repeated platitude had almost overcome him.

"Now perhaps I may be permitted to continue? Why should Piers behave in such a complicated way to get what he would in any case be given? He has always had as much as I could spare. I have a weakness for people who have affectionate natures. And now"—she smiled victoriously—"we all know where we stand, and we shall say no more."

Adrian looked pale and shaken. He fumbled in his pocket to find a flat tin of indigestion tablets. He put two into his mouth, sucking at them miserably. Occasionally he uttered a practically inaudible squeak, which was his cry of distress. Procrastination, he thought, had brought him to this plight. Why hadn't he tackled his Mother yesterday? She would have agreed to pay his fare back, and given him enough for a year or two. When life ran at its normal speed she accepted some maternal responsibility. Supposing he told her that he had been offered a job in America? Desperately he tried to work out the difference between the fare to America and what it would cost him to get to Naples, to see how much he would have left.

"Just look at Adrian," Marion said cruelly. "You have nearly knocked him out."

Rachel panted slightly.

"Aunt Rachel, do please relax, there's a dear. It is bad for you to get too excited." Kate spoke soothingly, although she felt that Rachel probably had more stamina than anyone.

"You are a good girl." Rachel patted Kate's hand. "But before Bess and Piers return, I do want you to know that I blame all of you for what has happened." Rachel looked gravely at their astonished faces. "You have brought the most disturbing influences with you. There's Marion and Thomas, squabbling and bickering. Thomas mooning after Bess—oh, yes, I have noticed—provoking Piers to a vulgar brawl. Marion tied up with her ridiculous office, neglecting her husband, and no doubt neglecting her home, too. I see faults on both sides, but I also see the consequences." Rachel pointed a plump forefinger at her son. "And then you, Adrian, arriving in a disgraceful state of intoxication, having to be treated like a child. Your behaviour does not bear thinking of. As for you, Kate, you are intelligent, but too lazy to use your brains. You do not know the harm you do. I can just imagine what you've told Bess. Making her believe that you lead a gay, unhampered life in a flat of your own." Rachel raised a silencing hand: "No, don't tell me. It's your life. I don't want to hear about it. No doubt you set yourself some standards of morality, but they are not high enough for me. And in one particular your conduct here has been, to say the least, unbelievably indiscreet. That, however, will remain a private matter known only to three people." Rachel looked mysterious as she paused for a second to give Kate's guilty flush time to deepen in hue. "I shall never refer to this again." Rachel paused a second to take breath for the greater effectiveness of her remarks. "As for your suggesting that Bess should stay at your flat—no doubt that was well meant, but a little impulsive."

Kate mumbled a few inaudible words. She had not yet collected her wits.

"So I'm the black sheep, am I? I have polluted your spotless household by my filthy drunkenness? After that I'll tell you why your sweet little Bess ran off. Because she knew damned well what had been going on between Kate and Piers. They've slept together under your roof. How d'you like that? I am surprised at your loose-living ways, really I am." Adrian's Cockney whine gave an added flavour to the words.

The silence was thick, as if it had grown into the walls.

Rachel rose to the occasion: "When I said that you were intoxicated when you arrived, I was wrong. You are intoxicated still."

"Ho! Am I, am I?" Adrian stood up, a short, trembling figure. He steadied himself by placing his hands on the edge of the table. "I had a long talk with Missus wots-er-name"— he jerked his head towards the kitchen—"and we put two and two together, and then we added the noises and the goings-on, and there's no mistake about it." He sat down again.

"Can't I say anything—" Kate began anxiously.

"Not yet!" Rachel snapped, then, turning to her son, "Tittle-tattling with charwomen! I didn't think that you would be so coarsened!"

"Aunt Rachel, do stop protecting me! Piers was in my room the night before last. And you can all make what you like of that." Kate spoke with obstinate sullenness.

Rachel looked reproachfully at her. What a mulish child! she thought. If she goes through life like that she won't get anywhere.

"There's no need to be huffy, Kate. I am not asking for an explanation." Rachel managed to imply a great disappointment at Kate's lack of perception.

"This is in very bad taste. I would prefer not to listen to matters that do not concern me." Thomas half rose from his chair, but Marion's firm restraining hand pushed him back.

"This is something that concerns us as a family." Marion was determined not to miss further revelations.

Adrian's face had a look of enquiry. Surely he had for once succeeded in setting them by the ears? "I just thought you'd like to know." His voice lacked its former conclusiveness.

"Very kind of you, Adrian. Most thoughtful." Rachel was ominous. "However, it's no news to me. I am perfectly aware that Piers spent the night in Kate's room. That is unimportant. I think nothing of it."

Kate looked gratefully towards her aunt, but Rachel turned her head away. She would take Kate's part because justice must be done. Kate must understand, however, that justice is not condonation.

Thomas and Marion were drawn together by their common distrust of the moment. Together they could face the shocking unpredictability of others. If this is what goes on, thought Thomas, I want no part of it. Why should I be forced to listen to the crude betrayals of youth? Each sentence shows me that I have no knowledge of these people. They deceived me into believing that I was one of them, and all the time, behind my back, they have lived different lives.

"How do you know so much?" Adrian spoke to his Mother, pleased that he had discovered the flaw. "I hope you haven't been hob-nobbing with the staff." He pulled smirking faces.

Kate laughed. She met Rachel's eyes, shrewdly affectionate, although still shadowed by reproof. "How are you going to account for that, darling?" It is impossible, she thought, not to love Rachel, in spite of her deliberate manœuvring for position.

"Because," Rachel said in her best manner of disdainful achievement, "I make it my business to know what goes on in my own house. I do not rely on second-hand information.

I heard voices, so naturally I got up to listen. Then again early in the morning——" She broke off to say irritably to Kate: "You didn't even lock the door!"

Kate remembered the footsteps and the sound of a latch. Admiration won over annoyance. "If you know so much, then you know that my behaviour was most proper. Piers came in to talk to me and we fell asleep." Kate spoke urgently. Whatever Marion, Adrian or even Thomas might think was neither here nor there, but Rachel must believe the truth. For Rachel was capable of putting aside all trivial complications and fixing on the bone of the matter.

"Yes, I know that, too." Rachel's face crinkled into forgiveness. "But it was not wise. You must not forget that the truth cannot be understood by fools." Adrian blew his nose as if to dissociate himself from this suggestion. "Nor"—Rachel was determined to play her scene to the end—"by limited minds."

Thomas looked at the carpet. He had failed Kate. Although she did not need his support, the failure was apparent. He had allied himself to the philistines. He was back again. There had been, after all, no progression.

"And now we will bring this unpleasant and unnecessary interlude to an end. We don't want any more misinterpretations. Bess must know nothing of this. You understand. Nothing." The finality of Rachel's words needed no answering promises.

"We had better go. There has been so much . . ." Thomas tried to formulate his confused thoughts, then abandoned the effort. "Anyhow, we had better go. I'll get our things together." Without looking about him, Thomas rose as he spoke and walked quickly from the room.

Marion stood up. She could not imagine why Thomas had arranged this peremptory departure, but it suited her very well. Tommy was more like his old self. They would have lunch on the train, and while they sat warmed and comfortable they could talk over these amazements.

"That's right, dear." Rachel was pleased to see that Marion had the good sense to abide by her husband's decision. "That would be for the best. So that everything is the same when Bess comes back. The normal routine."

"As soon as Bess arrives, I shall go, too," Kate said hastily.

"You don't mind, do you?" Rachel asked hopefully. "You and Piers . . . Often it's not easy to know how or when things start . . . And I do want her to be happy, even if it is not in the way I would choose for her. I do want her to be happy."

"Yes, of course you do." Kate thought of the ceaseless yearning for happiness. A word which because of its infinite meanings is meaningless: a trick of light making an afternoon memorable; the healing tissue growing over the inflamed nerve; footsteps in the street; drab curtains in a familiar room; an occasional second when death does not exist.

"I'm off upstairs." Adrian was chilled by his Mother's obvious expectancy. "I have no home to go to. But I'll get away just as soon as I can."

"We shall see, we shall see." Rachel dismissed every other consideration. The rest of the day she would consecrate to willing Bess to return, and afterwards to having her back.

Rachel was alone. She had been so near to sleep that she did not know whether she had waited minutes or hours before she heard a faint sound, as if someone hesitated, put a key against the lock, then drew away uncertainly. It was essential that Bess should open the door and return as one of the family. If she rang the bell, she would enter as a stranger.

As Bess came quietly into the room, Rachel moved with unexpected swiftness towards her. Bess halted, dreading the too-powerful embrace, the kiss that claimed allegiance. Controlling her joy, Rachel assumed a diffident air. She held her hands towards Bess's cold fingers. There they stood for several seconds, hands clasped. By the lightness of hand resting on hand, Rachel said that she had learnt her lesson. She would not snatch again: she would never again tighten her fingers until flight was the only alternative.

Bess shivered a little, but her eyes were steady as they looked with wary comprehension at Rachel.

"The train was cold." Her voice was tiredly non-committal.

"Of course, of course." Rachel was matter-of-fact, urging Bess towards the fire. "That's better. You'll soon warm up."

Bess sat on her usual chair: she still wore her hat and coat, although she had evidently come to stay.

Rachel wondered whether the question could safely be asked, and decided to take the risk.

"You are alone?" Her voice was soft, muted by the necessity for keeping a delicate balance between carelessness and concern.

Bess nodded.

"And Piers?" Rachel became bolder.

"He isn't here." Bess protected herself by the flat statement.

Rachel said nothing, disturbed by the realisation of distress. She was unaccustomed to finding herself so deeply involved that she had to support another's grief. "What can I do?" Rachel asked at last.

Bess shook her head.

"What happened?" Rachel felt life returning, and with it came her boundless curiosity.

"Nothing at all. He just isn't here. He won't come back. That is definite. It is no use your asking how or why. I haven't anything to tell you." Bess spoke firmly: her weak mouth thinned to an obstinate line.

Rachel tried to keep the humiliating pity from her voice: "I'll get him back for you, my darling. I'll get him back."

"How?" Even now Bess found Rachel irresistibly preposterous.

"Piers always has need of something. Not only money," Rachel added quickly. "But he must have someone to turn to. He'll come back to you. We'll work it out together. You will forget all this, and when you are married"—Rachel's voice soared to a triumphant song proclaiming her wholehearted conviction that whatever she determined would come to pass—"you shall live here with me. Just the three of us." I may have been wrong, Rachel scolded herself mildly, but I will more than make up for it.

"Perhaps," Bess said gently. She did not believe one word. "Perhaps."

"Very inconvenient your going off like that. There has been nobody to think of things. They haven't even remembered to get the fuse mended, and it is getting dark already."

"Never mind. I'll see to it." Bess moved towards the telephone. She was irretrievably defeated, which in some curious indefinable way was a great comfort.

Afterword
by Robert Cochrane

Mistletoe Malice entered my life just after Kathleen Farrell left it in November 1999. Although Kathleen had gifted me two of her books during our friendship – which endured for the final two years of her life – I was never able to locate copies of the others. At her request, after her funeral, our mutual friend the novelist Sebastian Beaumont handed me Kathleen's sole copy of her 1951 debut novel, along with her edition of *Cider with Rosie* by Laurie Lee. It was one of her favourite books, and mine, although sadly we'd never discussed it, but she wished me to have it as a memento mori. She had also left precise instructions that her mourners should be amply fed with smoked salmon, washed down with copious amounts of champagne. It rather echoed the sunny afternoon, two years previously, when we had first met through Sebastian, who remembers her as follows:

I first met Kathleen Farrell in 1996 when my publisher, Peter Burton – her close friend – suggested that I might take some part-time work looking after her affairs. She was in her early eighties at that time, with advanced arthritis and 'windswept' fingers that made it almost impossible for her to write. It was by far the best part-time job I have ever had and lasted four years until her death in 1999. I would meet with her twice a week from two until five in the afternoon, and we would go through her mail. I would answer anything that needed to be answered. This would take about an hour of the three hours that I was paid for. Once we had 'quite exhausted' ourselves with this simple task, she would suggest a suitable reward. This would always be a good-quality vodka with tonic. It was lovely to be paid to drink in the afternoon, but the real pleasure was Kathleen herself, who was a quite brilliant raconteur and had met and become friends with many writers and celebrities of her day. Five o'clock would come, and often it would go, and we would talk well into the evening.

That day, Peter, Sebastian and I had been suitably refreshed with generous drinks as we undertook the duty of witnessing her will. When we took our leave of Kathleen – who waved us off from the doorway of her apartment, as the Brighton early evening sea air entered our lungs – I leant across and kissed her lightly on the cheek: a genuine gesture of beguilement by her wistful yet grounded company. A few weeks later I received the following words on a postcard written with spidery determination:

Thursday, I think.

Your delicious and heart-warming kiss was one of the nicest things that has happened to me in many years. I was too stunned to tell you so . . . Kathleen.

From then on we corresponded regularly, swapping books and ideas. That November, when Sebastian visited me for my birthday, she sent with him a bottle of champagne. On his return, Kathleen wondered if I'd enjoyed it. When informed that we both had, she airily replied: 'Well, if we can't seduce him with one bottle, then next year I shall have to send two!'

I first read *Mistletoe Malice* in Ireland after Kathleen's death in Christmas 1999. It proved an experience I had no desire to end but one that I would often repeat. Enchanted by the civilised tone, yet occasionally shocked by the directness of the finely crafted sentences, I knew this was a book that deserved to be rediscovered and celebrated.

Mistletoe Malice employs a classic country house setting but in a coastal location – reminiscent of an Agatha Christie novel – in which a group of perfectly disagreeable souls assemble. All could murder each other, but don't; instead, they merely scratch, bicker and add to the overall misery of their daily lives, supposedly in the business of celebrating Christ's birthday. The heart of the novel focuses on Rachel, the alert but totally self-centred matriarch, slavishly attended with scant thanks by Bess, an ineffectual goose of a woman, hopelessly in love with the handsome Piers – who is only really in love with himself. Add to this melting pot of tensions the arrival of Rachel's daughter, Marion, an inflexible buttress of conformity and routine; her ineffectual but kindly husband, Thomas; and Adrian, her alcoholic, financially embarrassed and embarrassing sibling. Finally, there is Kate, an onlooker and a bad-tempered cook who harbours many richly servile resentments. Such groupings usually occur at weddings or funerals but here Farrell throws them together in a heavy seasonal potpourri. Tinsel and talons bared, she details their vendettas, tarnished needs and thwarted expectations; all except Adrian, who remains sloshed, a comedic giggler at their machinations. While stating nothing of his emotional life, the implication from the colour of his suit and the absence of a significant other is that he is homosexual. All this creates a Christmas that is aridly amusing for readers but deeply unhappy for all involved. It could all happen at any time and still does – but with Farrell it was concealed in deceptively inviting gift wrap. The knowingness she reveals of human nature is unflinching and – although comical – doesn't elicit guffaws, but rather draws nervous outbursts from the unwanted recognition of unsavoury truths. If you tend to suspect that all families are by nature dysfunctional, then Farrell is a novelist who will speak for you.

It was a brave gambit by Kathleen to position her debut novel over those few portent-laden days known as the Festive Season. Such a particular staging does not bode well for a long life upon the shelves, being the literary equivalent of marooning a catchy melody within a Christmas record (indeed, *Mistletoe Malice* wasn't her original title, but one imposed upon her by the publisher Rupert Hart-Davis). Beyond yet of her time, Kathleen was never a bestseller, more a benchmark of excellence. Written over a period of twelve years, none of her five novels – which all betray a profound economy of style coupled with mischievous and withering insights – made it into paperback. Despite a critically enthusiastic reception, her work slid out of fashion and print, trampled into a perceived irrelevance under the heavier heels of 'angry young men' of the later fifties. And her almost surgical observations certainly ruffled the feathers of post-war conformity; the truth is sometimes too bitter a pill for mass consumption, especially for an audience seeking reassurance instead of revelation. When a publisher wrote expressing a desire to reprint her books in the 1980s, Kathleen neglected to open the letter; it only came to light when Sebastian opened it years later. By then the publisher had long since ceased to exist, and she expressed a mere flickering of regret at this squandered opportunity.

In her late thirties by the time *Mistletoe Malice* was written, Kathleen was no innocent abroad on the edge of a literary adventure. She had worked during the Second World War as assistant to Hastings Lees-Smith MP, Secretary General of the Labour Party, whom she accompanied to transcribe late-night conferences with Churchill in his bunker. After the war she formed the successful literary agency Gilbert Wright, the novelist Olivia Manning being one of her many authors – but having private means, earning a living was never a major priority for her, and she focused on writing. Peter Burton remarked astutely in his obituary for Kathleen in the *Guardian* that: 'All her books were published during the two decades she shared with the novelist, critic and sometime publisher Kay Dick. Close contact with intense creativity can be a spur to a talent that might otherwise lie dormant.' When Kay – her lifetime friend and sometime lover – and Kathleen split in 1962, Kathleen never published another novel, while Kay fell silent for more than a decade.

Burton often surmised to me that Kay's best work was *They*, and it proved to be a worthy assessment, as that strange dystopian novel was recently rediscovered to tremendous acclaim. In fact, it was after seeing Faber's announcement about republishing *They* that I posted first editions of Kathleen's novels to the publisher's offices to champion republication. For years, I'd tried to resurrect interest and even elicited enthusiasm from her old friend Barry Humphries – who said: 'She was a marvellous woman who was very kind to me, and her books are a delight' – but despite his overtures, Kathleen remained marooned in the shadows. Then in January 2022, Faber's Heritage Editor, Ella Griffiths, recalls encountering 'a mysterious parcel' in her pigeonhole, describing how:

As soon as I read the front flap of the gorgeous 1951 edition of the novel – 'Do you really enjoy spending Christmas with your family? Or do they talk too much? Ask too many questions? Push your life away?' – I knew we had to republish it. Faber are so proud to be bringing this subversive tragicomedy of manners back into print for the first time in seventy years – a lost gem ranking with classics by Barbara Pym, Sylvia Townsend Warner, Muriel Spark, Stella Gibbons and Jean Rhys.

On her death in 1999, nearly forty years after the appearance of her final novel in 1962, Kathleen was the subject of fondly appreciative obituaries, remembered as much as a friend of writers Muriel Spark, Francis King, Stevie Smith, C. P. Snow, Pamela Hansford Johnson, Ivy Compton-Burnett and Angus Wilson as for her own sparkling literary creations, a fact that would have delighted her nature.

She was a petite, charming presence whose politeness concealed a steeliness of soul. Discussing *The Shelf* – a 1977 novel by Kay Dick – she observed with caustic delicacy that it had been 'excellently edited' by Francis King, since it contained 'sentences with verbs in them and proper punctuation'. Her delicate wit could often be applied to herself with delicious irony. She once told Sebastian in a moment of reflective candour over her late morning tipple that: 'I often found it was a good idea when a relationship came to an end, to move house' – adding with a naughty twinkle in her mischievous eyes: 'And I did move house rather a lot, you know.' While awaiting her initial vodka of the day, she remarked to Sebastian that although her medication stated: 'Not to Be Taken With Alcohol', 'I find they go rather well together!' Kathleen has been described as being exactly like 'a nice homely squirrel intent on the efficient harvesting of the moment', with a curiosity and passion which she assiduously maintained to the end. She once confided to me in a letter about her friend Quentin Crisp that he was: 'A nice man. Many years ago he used to come and see me for coffee and a sandwich or a game of chess – he was much better than I was – and he would take me to the local pub. I went to a show he had in Brighton – the theatre I think. I slid out at the interval – far too large and a terrible audience, rowdy and noisy and barging and shouting, all laughing at him and not with him. I found it quite distressing.' It was a perfect insight into her refined but astute nature that so elegantly imbues her novels. These sentiments are echoed by Sebastian, who became her literary executor:

Kathleen had said to me: 'I don't know why I have left my work to anyone. No one would be at all interested in it these days.' How wrong she was! Her friend Rob Cochrane never lost his enthusiasm for the quality of her oeuvre and used every opportunity he could to publicise her work. And so, when I heard that his tireless efforts on Kathleen's behalf had led to Faber reprinting Mistletoe Malice, *I was delighted: not just because it deserves to be back in print, but also because Farrell herself deserves to be rediscovered as a sublimely talented writer and a keen observer of human nature. This is what makes her work so timeless: that she understood what makes people tick. Her work gets beneath the skin of the characters she writes about and under my skin as a reader. What she saw then, I experience now, as it timelessly unfolds. Her wit and her unsentimental insight belie an underlying kindness she felt towards people who behaved well. It was by this barometer that she measured both her characters and herself. Unstintingly generous of spirit, she saw the best in people, and it was perhaps through this lens that she* could write so amusingly and with such heart-rending pathos about people for whom circumstances are less than kind.

Kathleen Farrell has now been reanimated, lingering like the traces of a fine perfume. Recently, she revisited me via an old letter, in which she gifted me the following poem:

FOR AND BY KATHLEEN
3 February 2023

A forgotten letter from you,
appropriately slipped between books,
was laced with a scattering
of scutter-by thoughts.
One towards the end
made me smile
and miss you afresh.
'It is a lovely evening.
A sky of cotton wool clouds
and women in summer dresses,
waving goodbye.'

Robert Cochrane
Manchester
2 May 2023